SHADOWS ON THE RIDGE

Jenna Maeson

Prologue

The wind clawed at Emily's thin jacket, sharper than it should have on a summer evening. She stood at the Ridge, staring out over the dark expanse below, the usual comfort of the view now swallowed by an unsettling chill. The air held a weight that made her stomach twist, her pulse quickening without reason.

Her phone glowed in her hand, an empty message thread open, waiting for something that never came. Emily couldn't shake the strange, off feeling that had settled over her. She felt unsteady, as if the ground beneath her was shifting, but she couldn't pinpoint why. Her thoughts were a little foggy and her balance was just slightly off, as though her body was betraying her. She didn't know why she felt this way, but it was hard to ignore. She wasn't sure why she had agreed to meet here so late, but the urgency of the request had gnawed at her until she relented. Now, as she waited in the quiet night, something felt wrong.

The quiet stretched, broken only by the occasional rustle of leaves and the distant hoot of an owl. She glanced around, feeling a sense of unease creeping over her. Something wasn't right.

A noise, sharp and deliberate, sliced through the silence. Footsteps, slow and heavy, crunched on the gravel behind her. Emily's breath caught, her fingers tensing around her phone as she turned, heart thudding in her chest.

A figure approached, half-shrouded in the thinning light, their face obscured by the deep shadows cast by the trees. No greeting came, just the soft shuffling of feet, stopping just short of the light.

"Hello?" Emily called out, the uncertainty in her voice slicing through the quiet. Her attempt at a smile faltered as the figure remained still, unmoving.

Seconds dragged like hours. "I wasn't sure you'd show," she added, trying to steady her breath. "If you needed to talk we could have just met at the office..." The silence that followed gnawed at her nerves, cold and foreboding.

The figure shifted, just enough for the faint light to catch the edge of their profile. The glint in their eyes was like ice—cold and unreadable. The hair on the back of Emily's neck stood up. Emily's familiarity with them had been twisted, warped into something unrecognizable.

"You like to talk, don't you?" The voice was low, nearly lost to the wind. It dripped with something she couldn't quite place.

Emily swallowed, stepping back instinctively as her heel met the rocky edge. "I don't understand. What's this about?"

The figure stepped closer, and Emily's breath caught in her throat. "Talking's never been a problem for you, has it? Always talking, telling people what you think they want to hear. Spouting off your opinions."

Emily's mind raced, flipping through memories, trying to latch onto anything that would explain this confrontation. "Look, I don't know what you think I've done, but—"

"You never do, do you?" The figure cut her off, stepping fully into the light. There was a flicker of conflicting emotions in their eyes—fear, anger, and something else that Emily couldn't quite place—but ultimately, they settled into a steely determination that sent a chill down her spine.

Emily's pulse thundered in her ears as the figure lunged forward, and the world tilted. She gasped, reaching for anything, but the emptiness around her offered no purchase. The wind screamed past her as she fell, the ground racing up to meet her, and then—nothing.

From the cover of the trees, a figure paused mid-step, eyes wide as the scene played out before them. An evening walk, meant to clear a restless mind, had led them near the Ridge. The usually tranquil night, accompanied by the chirping of crickets, now felt suffocating and charged with tension.

Their quickening heartbeat thudded loudly in their chest, instincts kicking in. They squinted, trying to make sense of the shadows moving in the dim light. The lone figure at the edge leaned forward briefly as if confirming the fall. The stance was chilling—deliberate and detached.

Though the face remained obscured by darkness, a familiar silhouette emerged from the shadows, and in that moment, the spectator recognized who it was. The shadowy figure moved quickly, slipping away down a side trail and vanishing from sight.

The hidden observer felt rooted in place, shock, and disbelief anchoring them to the spot. Their mind raced, torn between the urge to follow and the instinct to remain unseen.

Taking a measured step back into the cover of the trees, the observer assessed the scene with a keen eye. A chill crept through them, not from fear, but from the realization that they were the only one who had witnessed what had just unfolded. Whatever had transpired was no accident.

CHAPTER 1

The summer sun kissed Olivia Morgan's arm as the breeze played with her fingers, dangling out the open window of her blue Jeep. The winding mountain roads leading back to Emerald Ridge stretched out before her, leading her home. She had to admit, despite everything, she'd missed this—clean air, endless trees, the feeling of being far from the city's constant rush. Back in the city, the only trees were the ones struggling to survive between skyscrapers.

As she took a sharp left, the familiar worn sign greeted her: *Welcome to Emerald Ridge, Home of the Emerald Ridge Ravens!*

She shook her head, smirking. The Ravens? Really? The football team hadn't been noteworthy since...ever, as far as she knew. Maybe they'd won a championship in the '70s, and the town just clung to that victory like a badge of honor. Nowadays, Emerald Ridge High was more about focused on conservation and preservation than winning on the gridiron.

Olivia's thoughts scattered as a sudden blur of fur shot into the road. Her heart leapt, and she slammed on the brakes just in time to avoid a squirrel that had stopped, wide-eyed and paralyzed, halfway across the street. The squirrel scurried to the other side of the road, then turned to give her the most indignant look. *Watch where you're going, huh?!*

Olivia rolled her eyes, shouting out the window, "Maybe you should watch where you're going, buddy!"

With a flick of its tail, the squirrel disappeared between two shops. Olivia sighed, shaking her head. "Why do squirrels always have such bad attitudes?" she muttered to herself.

A few pedestrians, including the ever-nosy women from the Doozie beauty shop, were staring. She could feel their eyes on her, their eyebrows raised at her seemingly one-sided conversation. "Right. Not everyone talks to squirrels, Liv," she reminded herself as she fought the urge to bang her head against the steering wheel.

Olivia had grown used to hearing animals' thoughts, and while she often forgot that most people didn't share that ability, she saw it as a unique part of who she was. It was a gift that set her apart, something she had come to embrace, even if it was sometimes a bit annoying.

It had all started when she was ten while riding a trail horse that kept complaining about how bored it was of the same old path. Olivia could still vividly recall the horse's thoughts, a stream of chatter that made her giggle as she imagined its rolling eyes. She had mentioned it to the guide, expecting a laugh, but instead, he brushed it off like a whimsical child's tale. Later, when she shared the experience with her mom, she hadn't been surprised at all. "You're special, Liv," her mother had said with a knowing smile. "Just embrace it." Her mother, Cassandra Morgan, the town's resident psychic, always said everyone had intuitive gifts. It was just a matter of paying attention to them.

And embrace it she did. Over the years, Olivia learned to find joy in the thoughts of the animals around her, the silent conversations becoming a comforting backdrop to her daily life. It felt good to connect with creatures who didn't hide their feelings behind complex human emotions. However, she occasionally wished for someone who could understand her world, someone who could join in her unique experiences.

As she sat in her car, gripping the steering wheel, Olivia felt a wave of affection wash over her for the animals she could communicate with, even when they had bad attitudes. Yes, it could be distracting at times—like when a particularly chatty squirrel insisted on sharing its thoughts during a quiet moment—but even those moments brought a smile to her face.

She had grown accustomed to this quirky aspect of her life, recognizing that while it sometimes made her feel different, it was also a source of joy and connection. Olivia appreciated the uniqueness of her ability. It was a delightful quirk that colored her world in ways most people could only imagine, despite its occasional annoyance.

She shook off the squirrel's complaints and the lingering stares of the tourists, rolling her shoulders as she drove further into town. Emerald Ridge was still exactly as she'd left it—weathered storefronts, the faint scent of fried food from the diner, and the ever-present chatter of small-town life. A sense of familiarity tugged at her as she passed the places she'd once known like the back of her hand.

Just as she slowed to a stop at the intersection, a voice pulled her out of her thoughts.

"Liv! Good to see you back in town!"

Olivia glanced out the window and spotted Samuel Carter, the retired sheriff and current head of the Emerald Ridge Neighborhood Watch, standing on the sidewalk and waving cheerfully. He hadn't changed much over the years. Even in his seventies, he remained an imposing figure—tall with broad shoulders—though time had begun to take its toll, and he was starting to develop a slight hunch from years of working the beat. Despite that, he still wore that same knowing grin, as if he had the whole town figured out.

"Hi, Mr. Carter!" she called, waving back.

He squinted at her Jeep, oblivious to the fact that she was blocking traffic. "Your mom didn't mention you were coming home."

"Yeah, I thought I'd surprise her. I'm just here for the weekend to watch Emily's new dog while she's at a conference," Olivia explained, trying to ignore the impatient honk of a car behind her. Definitely a tourist—locals would never honk.

"Emily's pup, huh? I see them walking by my house every day. That dog's gonna be huge when he's finished growing," Sam said with a grin.

"Yeah, he's a handful, I hear," Olivia replied, glancing nervously at the car behind her. "Well, I should—"

Beep!

She winced. *Okay, okay, I get it.* "Nice seeing you, Mr. Carter! Gotta go!" Olivia called, giving him a wave as she finally drove off.

As she continued down the familiar road, a wave of nostalgia hit her. She could almost picture herself and Emily, arms linked and laughter echoing, walking to the old ice cream shop after school. Emily's hair had always been wild, refusing to stay tamed even in the neatest ponytail. "We're like the wind, Liv," Emily used to say, shaking out her curls with a grin. *Nothing can hold us back.* She always had been a free spirit.

Olivia's chest tightened at the thought, a bittersweet ache. It had been months since their last real conversation. Life had gotten busy, and distance had crept in, even though they promised it wouldn't. Emily's passion for her work had consumed her time, and Olivia ... well, she had been lost in her world, trying to make sense of her next steps.

As Olivia made her way further into town, a familiar scene unfolded that made her heart skip with excitement: the Emerald Ridge summer farmers market. In the summer, this market was the town's pride, drawing everyone from locals to tourists with its rustic charm and fresh finds. Some weeks it popped up once, but during the peak of summer, it could be found buzzing with activity two or even three times a week. Today, it seemed she'd lucked out.

The market was set up just as she remembered, sprawling across the town square with stalls brimming with bright produce, handmade crafts, and colorful blooms. It was the perfect snapshot of small-town life—a place where neighbors exchanged gossip over fresh peaches and kids ran around clutching paper cones of kettle corn. Olivia smiled to herself, the sight tugging at a memory of her and Emily once trying to haggle with the berry vendor for extra starling berry preserves. They hadn't succeeded, but they did walk away with berry-stained smiles and a scolding for "being too cute to bargain seriously."

She parked her Jeep and stepped out, taking in the symphony of market sounds: the hum of friendly chatter, the cheerful bark of a dog waiting at its owner's feet, and the occasional squeal of a toddler seeing their balloon float away. Olivia wondered if any of the usual summer delicacies were here yet, like the coveted starling berry preserves. She made a mental note to grab a jar for her mom—maybe it would make breaking the news about dropping out of school a little easier. *Hey Mom, I quit business school. But look, preserves!*

Olivia chuckled at herself as she started weaving through the stalls. "Starling berry preserve!" called out a woman from a nearby stall, her voice rich and inviting. Olivia turned, spotting the vendor with sun-kissed skin and a wide-brimmed hat holding up a jar filled with dark, glossy preserves. "Limited batch, straight from the old Grover's Orchard. Get your jars before they're gone!" Starling berries were legendary in Emerald Ridge, known for their almost black hue and rumored restorative properties.

"Olivia Morgan! Back from the city, I see!" the vendor exclaimed, her eyes brightening with recognition. "It's been ages, hasn't it? Your mom was just asking about these a few weeks ago, but the berries weren't quite ready yet." She tapped the side of the jar in her hand with a playful grin. "You better pick some of these up for her while you're here. I can already hear her if she finds out I had starling berry preserves and you didn't bring any home. You know how she gets—she'll think you've betrayed her!"

Olivia chuckled, warmth spreading in her chest. "That sounds like her, all right."

The vendor leaned in, her voice dropping to a conspiratorial whisper. "Did you know the starling berry has a reputation that goes back generations around here? Your mom must have shared the stories about that doctor who claimed to have discovered the berry's healing properties. Turns out, his knowledge was *borrowed*. All the information he had came from some generous indigenous people living in the area at the time." She shook her head, *tsking* in disapproval. "Such a shame."

Olivia nodded slowly, memories stirring. The tale had been woven into the fabric of the town, always a source of quiet intrigue and whispered judgment. She glanced at the jars of preserves lined up in the vendor's stall. There was something enchanting about the starling berries, a whisper of stories untold and secrets buried beneath their vibrant color. Memories flooded back of her mother's tales—of the doctor's claims, the whispered warnings from the locals, and the ancient lore surrounding the berry's healing powers. It was as if the jar held not just preserves, but the echoes of history.

As Olivia continued to gaze at the jar, the vendor's eyes sparkled with enthusiasm. "These preserves aren't just delicious; they're steeped in history. You're getting a taste of something truly special," she said, gesturing to the jars. "And this is the first batch of the season, too."

With a smile, Olivia nodded, feeling a sense of excitement. "I'll take a jar," she said, her voice firm with resolve. "I can't miss out on the first batch of the year."

The vendor beamed as she carefully handed Olivia the jar. "You won't regret it! Be sure to tell your mom that this is the first batch of the season. Just wait until you see her face when she opens it—that'll be the real magic."

Olivia took the jar, feeling the cool glass against her palm. "Thank you," she said, tucking the jar securely under her arm.

As she stepped away from the stall, Olivia glanced back at the vendor, who was already busy serving the next customer. A sense of satisfaction washed over her, knowing she had not only purchased a jar of preserves but also a piece of her connection to the community. The simple act felt like a step toward embracing her roots, and she couldn't help but smile at the thought of sharing it with her mom.

The scent of fresh produce and wildflowers mingled in the air as Olivia continued to wander through the bustling market. The sun cast golden patches of light over the cobblestone path, and the familiar chatter of townsfolk surrounded her. It was as if the market itself had frozen in time, unchanged since her teenage years.

A soft breeze rustled the striped awnings of the stalls, carrying with it the tantalizing aroma of fresh-baked bread and honeyed pastries. Olivia let the sounds and scents wash over her, grounding herself in the familiarity of home.

A familiar voice cut through her thoughts, low and warm, tinged with surprise. "Olivia?"

She turned, heart jolting. Noah Wilkins, her high school boyfriend, stood a few feet away, a paper bag of apples cradled in one arm. He looked much the same as he had in high school, but more settled, the angles of his face a touch more defined. His dark eyes held a spark of curiosity, mixed with something else—memories, maybe.

"Noah," Olivia said, her voice catching slightly before she cleared her throat. "I didn't expect to run into you here."

A grin broke across his face, effortlessly charming. "It's not every day you get a blast from the past at the town farmer's market. Thought the city had claimed you for good."

Olivia shrugged, the playful banter easing the sudden tightness in her chest. "Guess the mountains have a way of calling you back."

They stood for a moment, the busy chatter of the market fading around them. It was as though the years that had stretched between them condensed into a heartbeat, leaving them standing on the same ground they once shared.

"You here for long?" Noah asked, shifting the bag in his arm.

"Just a visit," Olivia replied, but even as she said it, she wondered how temporary her return would be. The market, with its vibrant chaos and familiar faces, felt more like home than she wanted to admit.

As Olivia finished her chat with Noah, a sense of warmth filled her. Their easy banter had rekindled a connection she had almost forgotten. With a final wave, Noah disappeared into the bustle of the market, leaving her with a smile stretched across her face.

With the jar of starling berry preserves tucked safely under her arm, she made her way through the market, the vibrant colors and lively chatter surrounding her. Each step felt lighter, the worries of the day melting away. She relished the simple joy of the moment, the familiar faces, and the scents of fresh produce filling the air. The sun filtered through the overhead bunting, casting playful shadows across the cobblestone square. She exchanged a few nods and smiles with familiar faces, a warmth settling in her chest. This was home, in all its chaotic, charming glory.

As Olivia returned to her Jeep after her stroll through the farmers market, she started the engine and pulled out of the market square, driving through the winding streets lined with old brick buildings and hanging flower baskets. The closer she got to her mom's house, the quieter the town became, the vibrant energy of the market giving way to the serene hum of cicadas and the gentle whisper of wind in the trees.

CHAPTER 2

Emerald Ridge had always been more than just a picturesque town nestled in the mountains; it was a place where history and nature intertwined in a delicate dance. Conservation wasn't just a buzzword here but a way of life. The townspeople took pride in their efforts to protect the native plants and animals that called the surrounding forests and hills home. Every spring, schoolchildren learned about the region's unique ecosystems, taking field trips to the Ridge to spot wildflowers and learn to identify the chirps and calls of local birds.

This dedication to preservation was woven into the very fabric of the town. Strolling down Main Street, one could see posters announcing seasonal clean-ups, lectures on sustainable gardening, and the occasional town hall meeting focused on protecting local trails. The Ridge itself, with its winding paths and hidden groves, was more than just a hiking spot—it was a symbol of the town's identity, a piece of history that residents fiercely guarded.

Even the shops reflected the town's values; the florist showcased native blooms grown without pesticides, the diner served produce from local farmers, and the apothecary stocked tinctures and teas made from the surrounding herbs. Olivia noticed that even the hardware store had gotten into the spirit, with a display of eco-friendly products proudly showcased by the entrance. The community's commitment to conservation was more than a shared value—it was a legacy passed down through generations as if protecting the land was as inherent as breathing.

Olivia felt a sense of pride as she drove through town. Her eyes caught the banners strung up along the street, advertising the upcoming *Heritage and Conservation Festival*, a beloved event where locals shared stories of the town's early days, celebrated traditional crafts, and reaffirmed their connection to the land.

Growing up, she'd spent countless afternoons with Emily poring over old books in the library, listening to Mr. Lyle, the town historian, recount tales of the settlers and the land's earliest caretakers. They would trace their fingers over faded maps and imagine the world as it had been, wild and untamed. And now, returning to Emerald Ridge, Olivia could feel those stories bubbling up to the surface, pulling her back into a world where every tree, every stone, and every wildflower had a story.

Emerald Ridge wasn't just her hometown; it was a place where history and conservation lived side by side, a constant reminder that the past was never truly gone—it echoed in the rustle of leaves, the call of a bird, and the whispers of the townsfolk who cherished it.

The sun blazed high in the sky as Olivia's Jeep rolled down the winding road into Emerald Ridge, casting dappled patterns of light and shadow across the dashboard. The familiar scent of pine and wildflowers seeped in through the open windows, mixing with the nostalgic undertones of fresh mountain air. Summer had always been the most vibrant season in Emerald Ridge, not just for its picturesque views but for the energy that thrummed through the small town. This was the peak of conservation awareness season—a time when residents and visitors alike turned their attention to the town's legacy of preserving its unique environment.

Summer wasn't just a season for lazy afternoons and outdoor festivals—it was a time when Emerald Ridge's leaders began to lay the groundwork for their upcoming election platforms. Conservation and environmental sustainability were at the heart of every campaign, with candidates vying to prove their dedication to protecting the region's natural beauty. It was a badge of honor to champion a policy that promised to secure the town's ecological legacy for future generations.

As she turned down Stoneleigh Drive, her mom's property came into view. The gravel crunched beneath her tires as the gate came into view. The path wound upward through the trees until it leveled out in front of the barn-style house she had called home for so many years. Parked next to her mom's SUV and her brother Jake's beat-up Ford Bronco, her Jeep fit right in.

Olivia grabbed her canvas bag, slung it over her shoulder, and paused, taking a deep breath of the fresh mountain air. The house stood proudly in the clearing, its reclaimed wood exterior blending into the natural surroundings. Off to the right was her mom's cottage, where she did her psychic readings and sold her herbs and tinctures.

Pushing open the front door, she was immediately hit by the familiar scents of vanilla and sandalwood. Her mom was clearly burning her usual calming candles. The house hadn't changed one bit: an open floor plan with cozy corners, a giant rock fireplace as the centerpiece, and stairs leading up to the lofts she and her brother had called bedrooms. Privacy? Optional.

Before she could take another step, a voice interrupted her thoughts.

You're home. Why?

Olivia glanced over to see the family's black cat, Aster, perched on the arm of the sofa, eyeing her with her usual disdain.

"I live here too, you know," Olivia muttered.

Aster gave her a slow blink, clearly unimpressed. *You were gone long enough that I forgot.*

She rolled her eyes. "Where's Mom and Jake?"

Out back, playing in the dirt. Payment for this information: belly rubs and ear scratches. Aster replied lazily, rolling onto her back in full expectation of petting.

Olivia laughed, giving her the obligatory scratches before heading outside to investigate. Sure enough, there were her mom and Jake, knee-deep in what looked like giant wooden planter boxes, shoveling dirt like their lives depended on it.

"Hi, guys!" Olivia called, making her way over.

Her mom straightened up, pushing her sun hat back to see Olivia better. "Livy! What are you doing home?"

Olivia shrugged. "I figured I'd surprise you. Emily needed someone to watch her dog while she's out of town and I agreed to do it."

Her mom hurried over, wrapping Olivia in a warm hug. "You should have told me you were coming. I would've made your favorite dinner!"

"Don't you have psychic powers for that?" Olivia teased, earning an exaggerated eye roll from her mom.

"Not how it works," Cassandra replied with a chuckle.

Jake sauntered over, shovel in hand. "Well, since you're here, feel free to grab a shovel and help with Mom's new 'go big or go home' garden project."

Olivia raised an eyebrow. "I'll pass, thanks."

Her mom laughed. "Come inside, let's get something to drink. I have that passion berry lemonade you love."

Once inside, Olivia settled at the old wooden table with a glass of lemonade, letting the familiar sweetness wash over her. For a moment, it felt like nothing had changed. But she knew better.

"So," her mom began, setting her glass down and eyeing Olivia carefully, "what's really going on, Livy? You never just drop by without calling."

Olivia's stomach twisted like a knot being pulled tighter with each passing second. She glanced down at her glass, the condensation dripping onto her fingers, and she wished she could disappear. The afternoon sunlight shining through the window felt unbearably bright, spotlighting her as if the whole world was watching the confession she was about to make unfold. She swirled her lemonade, the ice clinking softly, a distraction that couldn't drown out the rush of her heartbeat pounding in her ears.

Her mom's gaze softened with concern, while Jake's eyebrows inched upward, a hint of confusion in his eyes. Their expectant silence wrapped around her like a vise.

Olivia swallowed, her mouth dry despite the cool drink in her hand. The truth felt heavy, suffocating, pressing against her lungs and making it hard to breathe. She had replayed this moment countless times in her mind, picturing their reactions, bracing herself for the disappointment, the questions, the why didn't you tell us sooner.

"Well…about that," she started, her voice barely above a whisper. She placed her glass on the table and looked up, catching the hint of worry in her mom's eyes.

The silence stretched on, growing unbearable.

"I dropped out of business school," Olivia blurted, the words tumbling out in a rush. The weight lifted off her chest only to come crashing back down, heavier this time, as if daring her to face the consequences.

Olivia's voice trembled as she spoke, each word clawing its way out of the tangled mess of guilt and fear that had built up over the past months. Nights spent hunched over textbooks that made her eyes blur, the constant thrum of anxiety that left her wide awake at three a.m., staring at the ceiling while her mind replayed every mistake, every missed assignment, every botched exam. The endless cycle of waking up exhausted and feeling the weight of another day filled with things she didn't love and didn't understand.

She hadn't wanted to disappoint anyone—especially not her mom. Failure had become an uninvited shadow that seemed to follow her, lurking behind every decision she made. Quitting, starting over, and quitting again; it had become a rhythm she couldn't break. When she'd started business school, she'd told herself it would be different. *This* would be the thing that clicked, the thing that made everyone proud, the thing to prove she wasn't just aimlessly drifting from one failed plan to another.

But as the weeks turned into months, that hope had crumbled under the weight of her growing dread. The pressure was suffocating, a constant knot in her chest that wouldn't untangle no matter how many hours she poured into studying or how many times she told herself to push through. Every time she opened another thick, jargon-filled book or sat through a lecture that felt like it was spoken in a foreign language, the doubts grew louder. The whisper of *not again, not another thing you'll fail at.* The harder she pushed the more everything began to feel like quicksand around her feet.

For a moment, everything was still. The soft rustle of the trees, the distant hum of a lawnmower, all muted as she waited for the first response. The air seemed too thick, pressing down on her shoulders, making her feel smaller.

Her mom's eyes widened, shock flickering across her face before giving way to a mix of confusion and concern. Olivia forced herself not to look away, bracing for the questions that were sure to follow, each one a reminder of how hard it was to admit that her path had veered off course. Again.

"I tried, Mom. I really did. But it wasn't for me. The classes, the pressure—it was just too much."

The words spilled out, raw and heavy, but there was an odd, hollow sense of relief in finally speaking them aloud.

Her mom's face softened, her tone gentle. "Oh, Livy…"

Jake, ever the charmer, leaned back in his chair with a grin. "Guess that means more time for you to help Mom with the garden, huh?"

Olivia shot him a look, but his teasing broke the tension, and she managed a small smile. Her mom reached across the table, squeezing her hand. "You'll figure it out, sweetie. You always do. Dropping out doesn't mean you've failed; it just means you're finding your own path."

A pause settled between them, the silence thick with unspoken understanding. Olivia's gaze drifted to a small vial of dark-hued liquid sitting innocently on the counter, glimmering in the light like a potion straight out of a fairy tale. She was accustomed to her mom's herbal concoctions—some of which could probably revive the dead or at least put a good dent in a bad headache—but this one was a mystery.

"What's that?" Olivia asked, pointing to the mysterious jar with the kind of curiosity typically reserved for strange artifacts in a museum.

Cassandra turned her head, following Olivia's finger. "Ah, that's the new tincture Emily has been working on. I believe it's what she's planning to present at that conference."

"Really?" Olivia blinked, a mix of surprise and guilt washing over her. She hadn't realized how out of the loop she was with Emily's latest projects. Maybe if she'd checked in more often, she wouldn't feel like she was two steps behind on the gossip train.

Her mom nodded, a soft smile breaking through. "She's been absolutely thrilled about it! Said it was different from anything else she's worked on before. She didn't go into too much detail, but I remember her mentioning that she hoped it would really help her therapy clients. You know, like some sort of magic elixir for the soul."

"Sounds a bit like a witch's brew," Olivia joked, raising an eyebrow. "Did she promise it would turn them into toads if it didn't work?"

Cassandra chuckled, shaking her head. "Frankly, it is a pretty volatile compound," she said, lowering her voice conspiratorially, "but she seemed confident. I suppose that's all that really matters—right?"

Just then, Olivia's phone buzzed on the counter, jolting her from her thoughts. It was a text from Ashley, another longtime friend from Emerald Ridge.

Ashley: *Rumor has it you're in town.*

Olivia: *Rumor is true.*

Ashley: *You better get down here and say hi before I hunt you down.*

Olivia: *On my way.*

Olivia smiled, shoving her phone into her pocket as she stood. "I'm heading into town to see Ash. I'll be back for dinner," she said, already feeling the anticipation of reconnecting with her friend.

As she hopped into her Jeep and started the engine, Olivia's mind wandered back to her mom's earlier words about Emily's tincture. It sounded like something Emily was genuinely passionate about, and Olivia made a mental note to ask her more about it that evening while they discussed the ins and outs of pet sitting.

CHAPTER 3

The drive to Perks and Peaks was short, but it gave Olivia just enough time to collect her thoughts—or at least try.

Pulling up to the familiar, quaint storefront of Perks and Peaks, she couldn't help but smile. The place hadn't changed a bit—its weathered sign still hanging slightly crooked, the same way it had throughout high school. The cozy shop had been her second home back then, where she could hide from the world with a latte and the company of friends. Ashley was one of Olivia's closest friends and her family had owned Perks and Peaks for as long as she could remember.

As Olivia walked in, the bell above the door jingled, and the rich aroma of freshly brewed coffee enveloped her like a warm hug. It was the kind of smell that made you feel like everything was going to be okay, even when it felt like it wasn't.

Ashley, standing behind the counter, looked up and immediately broke into a wide grin. "Well, if it isn't the prodigal daughter!" she called out, her voice full of playful teasing.

Olivia laughed, feeling a bit of the weight on her shoulders lift. "Hey, Ash. Got a coffee for a dropout?"

Ashley rolled her eyes dramatically. "You mean for my favorite dropout? Always." She didn't even have to ask for the order, already moving to make Olivia's usual—a vanilla latte with a hint of cinnamon.

The shop was bustling with its usual crowd: locals catching up on the latest town gossip, tourists taking a breather from their scenic hikes, and the regulars, who seemed to have permanent residency at the café's corner tables. It was a small bubble of normalcy in the chaos of Olivia's life lately.

As Ashley slid the steaming cup across the counter, she leaned in, her eyes twinkling with curiosity. "So...what happened this time?"

Olivia took a sip, savoring the warmth, the familiarity of it all. "Long story short? Turns out business school and I weren't exactly soulmates."

Ashley shook her head, giving her a knowing smile. "Well, at least you're home now. We'll figure it out." She leaned on the counter, her grin widening. "Hey, if you need a job to keep you afloat, you know we can always use another set of hands around here. You could revive your barista career."

Olivia snorted, nearly choking on her coffee. "Yeah, we both know how that went last time. I'm pretty sure I almost poisoned half the town with my attempts at latte art."

Ashley burst out laughing. "True. We'll just make sure you're nowhere near the coffee. Maybe you can hand out muffins? You can't screw up muffins, right?"

Olivia grinned. "I'll keep that in mind if things get desperate."

Olivia settled into her favorite corner booth by the window, the perfect spot for indulging her love of people-watching. It felt comforting to be back, surrounded by familiar faces in a place that truly felt like home. There was a time when she had longed to escape Emerald Ridge, dreaming of far-off places and new beginnings. But now, in this moment, a wave of welcome comfort enveloped her. Here, she could set aside her uncertainties about the future and simply breathe.

The afternoon drifted by in a blur of tourists meandering past the shop, locals popping in for their late-day pick-me-ups, and Olivia letting herself sink into the warmth of the coffee shop.

But just as the sun began to dip low in the western sky, flooding the town in shades of pale oranges and pinks, Olivia started gathering her things to head home.

Just then, the door jingled, and in strolled Noah, completely unaware of Olivia's presence.

Ashley's eyebrows shot up, and her gaze darted between Noah and Olivia with a mix of excitement and mischief. Olivia hadn't had the chance to tell Ashley about her earlier encounter with Noah at the farmers market, and now Ashley's expression was a whirlwind of anticipation.

"Hey, Noah! The usual?" Ashley called out, her tone bright.

"That'd be great, Ash, thanks," Noah replied, leaning casually against the counter, exuding that effortless charm that always made Olivia's heart skip a beat.

Olivia held her breath, hoping he wouldn't notice her. After all, they had already had a friendly chat at the farmers market. Why was she so nervous? Maybe if she remained perfectly still, she'd magically become invisible.

"So, what's the latest town gossip?" Noah asked, as Ashley began making his drink.

Ashley shot a glance at Olivia and couldn't help but smirk.

"Well," Ashley said, dragging out the word for dramatic effect, "I did hear one interesting thing today."

"Oh yeah? What's that?" Noah asked, genuinely intrigued.

"Looks like Olivia's back in town," Ashley said, her eyes twinkling with mischief.

Noah nodded, and for a moment, silence enveloped them. "Yeah, I saw her earlier at the farmers market. She looked...good," he said, a hint of warmth in his voice.

Olivia felt her cheeks heat up, wishing she could sink into the floor. How could she be this flustered?

Ashley slid a cup across the counter, snapping the lid on it. "All set."

"Thanks, Ash," Noah said, grabbing the drink. As he turned to leave, his eyes finally landed on Olivia.

They both froze—again. His expression mirrored hers: wide-eyed and uncertain, like two deer caught in headlights.

In a desperate attempt to appear nonchalant, Olivia leaned back against the booth, though she felt more like a rabbit ready to bolt. But as she leaned, her elbow slipped off the table, and she stumbled awkwardly to the side. *Smooth move, Liv.*

"Oh, hi, Noah! Funny seeing you twice in one day!" she blurted, her voice a bit too bright and chipper. "I totally didn't see you walk in!"

Noah raised an eyebrow, his lips curling into a teasing smirk. "Is that so?"

"Yep! I was just so, uh, caught up in my book. Didn't even notice," she stammered, feeling her face warm even more.

Noah's smirk deepened. "Oh yeah? What are you reading?"

"Uh...it's, um, a book on...how to...train dragons," she said, wincing at her own words. "*How to Train Your Dragon.* You know, the, uh, manual."

Noah chuckled, crossing his arms. "Sounds useful."

Olivia nodded, trying to keep a straight face. "Yep, very practical. You know, with my mom being into all that mystical stuff and all, you just never know when you might need some dragon training tips."

What is happening, Olivia thought, as she suddenly found a random spot on the floor incredibly interesting.

Noah's gaze drifted to the door, clearly just as eager to escape this conversation as she was. "Well, good to see you—again, Liv."

With that, he turned and pushed through the door, casting one last unreadable glance her way before disappearing into the evening.

The second the door shut behind him, Olivia collapsed back into the booth, groaning. "Ughhh!" she muttered, covering her face with her hands. She could hear Ashley chuckling from behind the counter.

"That was..."

"Awful!" Olivia interrupted, peeking out from behind her fingers. "Beyond cringy! I'm never showing my face here again!"

Ashley smirked, wiping down the counter. "I was going to say *entertaining*, but train wreck works too."

Olivia groaned louder, sinking deeper into her booth. "He's probably mortified."

"Mortified? Nah," Ashley said, grinning. "He's still got it bad for you."

Olivia peeked over her hands, frowning. "What? It's been like, eight years! How can you tell anything from that disaster of a conversation?"

Ashley shrugged, her smile mischievous. "Just can."

Before Olivia could argue, her phone buzzed, interrupting the conversation. It was a text from her mom.

Mom: *Coming home for dinner?*

Olivia glanced at the time and shot off a quick reply.

Olivia: *Yeah, heading home now.*

She sighed and stood up, gathering her things. "I gotta go, Ash. Mom's expecting me for dinner."

Ashley waved her off, still smirking. "No worries. See you soon. We've got the best coffee in town, and if I don't see you, I know where to find you."

Olivia rolled her eyes but smiled as she slipped out the door.

As Olivia slid into the driver's seat of her Jeep, her phone buzzed again. This time, it was Emily.

Emily: *Did you make it into town?*

Olivia: *Yep, got here earlier today.*

Emily: *Great! Are you still up for coming by tonight to meet Elmer?*

Olivia: *I can swing by after dinner if that works.*

Emily: *Perfect. I have one last client at 6:00, so how about 7:30?*

Olivia: *Sounds good. Can't wait to meet Elmer!*

With a smile, Olivia tossed her phone into the passenger seat and started the Jeep, the engine rumbling to life. She backed out of the lot and merged onto Market Street, heading home. As she drove, her mind wandered back to Noah. Of course, it did.

Her thoughts drifted to high school, to that fateful chemistry class when their worlds had first collided. The memory of Noah leaning over a shared lab table, his eyes meeting hers with a mischievous glint as he whispered a joke only she could hear, tugged at her, pulling her back into a time when life felt simpler. They'd spent hours elbow to elbow, carefully mixing chemicals and comparing notes, their laughter bubbling up whenever one of their experiments went awry. Noah would nudge her with his shoulder, feigning shock when she'd correctly answer the professor's tricky questions, and she'd roll her eyes with a grin, feeling a warm rush of pride and camaraderie.

Noah had been that guy—the one everyone pined after but never thought they'd actually get. Olivia enjoyed his company, and sure she thought he was cute—like every other girl in the school—but she had no intention of being anything more than friends. It wasn't like a guy like that would date her anyway, so she didn't think much of it, just enjoyed having a partner in crime in the chemistry lab.

With his easy smile and laid-back charm, he'd seemed untouchable. And then, suddenly, he wasn't.

It happened one warm evening at the park, after a grueling afternoon of studying for a chemistry test. They had ended up in the park after a casual dinner that had somehow turned into a spontaneous adventure. They were supposed to be just walking off dessert—chocolate cake, which Olivia could still taste on her lips—but instead, they found themselves sprawled on a picnic blanket under a sky sprinkled with stars.

"Look at that one!" Noah had exclaimed, pointing dramatically. "That's definitely a shooting star. Or a meteor. I'm pretty sure I read somewhere that they're made of leftover pizza from space."

Olivia burst into laughter, shaking her head. "I think you've been watching too many sci-fi movies, Noah."

"Hey, I only watch the classics," he said with a mock-seriousness that made her laugh even harder. "Anyway, what do you wish for when you see a shooting star?"

Olivia paused, her heart racing. "I don't know, maybe...for someone to kiss me?" She hadn't meant to say it out loud, but the words hung in the air like a challenge.

Noah's eyes widened for a moment, and then he leaned in, the teasing smile on his face transforming into something softer. "Well, in that case..."

And just like that, the world around them faded away as their lips met. It was a sweet, clumsy kiss, filled with laughter and the taste of chocolate cake, and somehow felt like everything they had been waiting for. She could almost hear a chorus of angels singing—or maybe it was just the crickets in the park.

When they finally pulled apart, Olivia couldn't help but tease, "Not quite what I had in mind when I said I wanted a shooting-star moment."

Noah chuckled, a playful glint in his eyes. "Oh really? What were you expecting? A grand, cinematic kiss in the rain? I mean, I can make it rain if you want."

"Let's not," she laughed, her heart still fluttering. "I'd prefer to keep the evening from turning into a soggy disaster."

From that moment on, their relationship blossomed. They went from being chemistry partners to friends to something deeper, navigating the ups and downs of dating with a mix of humor and sincerity. Noah had a way of making her feel safe and understood, even as they bumbled through the awkwardness of first dates and shared secrets.

Olivia often found herself wondering how she had ever thought she could leave Emerald Ridge behind. With Noah by her side, she felt like she had finally found her place—not just in the town, but in his heart as well.

Those days had a spark—before the relentless weight of expectations dimmed it. Before the path she'd been so sure of started to fracture, leaving her grasping for the pieces.

For a while, everything felt perfect. But life had other plans, as it often does. They hadn't talked about the future—*not really*—until it was too late. Graduation had been looming, and Olivia had been dreaming of escape. Europe, adventure, anything but staying in their small town.

Noah, though…He'd always been a part of the town. He loved it, loved his job at the auto shop, loved the rhythm of life in Emerald Ridge. They both had dreams, just in opposite directions. And when Olivia had sprung the Europe trip on him, their world had cracked.

That moment at the graduation bonfire was seared into her memory—him with that small box in his hand, her blurting out her plans before he could say a word. She hadn't wanted to see what was in that box. Not really. It was too much, too final. So she'd run off to Europe and left Noah, the what-ifs trailing behind her.

Now, years later, here she was. Back in town, and back to bumping into Noah at the most inopportune moments. *Great job, Liv,* she thought, mentally kicking herself for the awkward encounter at Perks and Peaks.

As the Jeep rumbled to a stop in front of her house, Olivia shook off the nostalgia. She had more important things to focus on right now, like catching up with Emily later that evening.

Olivia barely made it through the front door before the wail of police sirens shattered the quiet of the evening. She turned back, eyes narrowing as two patrol cars sped down the road, their lights flashing urgently as they veered toward the Ridge—the local hiking trail that meandered through the scenic hills just outside town.

"What on earth is going on?" she muttered, closing the door with a thud. The sirens lingered in her ears, making her heart pound as she set her bag on the kitchen counter.

The Ridge. That was right near Emily's house. A shiver crawled up her spine, the unease sticking to her like a shadow. Her mom had always told her that intuition was never wrong. And right now hers was saying something wasn't right.

Meanwhile, just a few streets over, Samuel Carter settled into his old recliner, a mug of tea in one hand and his police scanner crackling softly on the side table. Years off the force hadn't dulled his habit of listening in on the town's happenings. Old habits died hard, especially when you were once the chief.

The static cut out, replaced by the dispatcher's tense voice: "All available Summit County units, report to the Ridge hiking trail, Emerald Ridge."

Samuel's brow furrowed. The Ridge? That was only a short walk up the hill from his place. He set down his mug, leaning forward, the leather of his chair creaking. What could have happened there? Maybe someone had a bad fall, or it was just a false alarm.

"Report from hikers: the body of a twenty-something female found on the lower trail," the dispatcher continued, the weight of the words filling the room.

Samuel's eyes widened. A body? In Emerald Ridge? This wasn't a place where bodies turned up like something out of a true-crime podcast; this was a town where the biggest scandal involved Mrs. Greer forgetting to pay her tab at the diner. A sense of unease settled over him as memories of his earlier walk replayed in his mind. He had hoped he was just imagining things, but did he really see what he thought he saw?

He sat for a moment, the news hanging in the air, then reached for his phone. If anyone knew what was happening, it would be Millie Partridge, queen of the town's grapevine and unofficial keeper of all secrets. Samuel thumbed through his contacts, smirking to himself. Word would be out faster than a cat on a hot tin roof, and Millie would already be on it.

Just as he dialed her number, the phone rang once in his hand, Millie's name lighting up on the screen. "Sam!" she squawked before he could even say hello. "Did you hear about the Ridge? They found a body!"

Samuel sighed, glancing out his window at the flashing lights in the distance. Emerald Ridge wasn't going to sleep easy

CHAPTER 4

The evening air was thick as Olivia approached Emily's house. It stood eerily silent, and the unease she'd felt earlier that evening came rushing back. Seeing the police cars earlier had been strange, but now, standing there with no sign of Emily, it seemed ominous. The lights were on, the house looked normal, but something about it felt *off*. She knocked, each thud echoing in the stillness, her pulse quickening when no one answered. Elmer, Emily's dog, barked, followed by the sound of snuffling and whining on the other side of the door. Olivia was about to try Emily's phone again when the sound of tires crunching gravel made her turn.

From the porch, Olivia's eyes locked on the distant, flashing lights at the Ridge, their rhythmic glow slicing through the night like an alarm. Her stomach clenched as a police car, marked with the Summit County Sheriff's Department logo, rolled to a stop behind her Jeep. An officer stepped out, his expression grave, each step he took toward her amplifying the thudding in her chest.

"Are you Olivia? A friend of Emily Harris?" he asked, his voice thick with the weight of unspoken words.

"Yes, I'm Olivia. Emily's my best friend," she said, her voice trembling as dread coiled tight in her gut.

The officer's eyes softened, his hat clutched to his chest as he took a step closer. "I'm sorry to have to tell you this," he began, pausing as if the words themselves were too heavy. "There's been an incident involving Ms. Harris. When we recovered her phone, we saw you were the last person she contacted."

The world seemed to blur around Olivia, his words slamming into her like a physical blow. The officer's gaze met hers, steady but full of sympathy.

"Wait," Olivia said, shaking her head as she struggled to process what he had just revealed. "How did you recover Emily's phone? I thought she always kept it with her. Why didn't she have it when..." Her voice trailed off, the implications of the question hanging heavy in the air.

The officer hesitated, glancing down for a brief moment before meeting her eyes again. "There was an accident at the Ridge involving Ms. Harris," he said quietly. "She...she didn't make it."

"We found her phone, but it was damaged. It looks like it may have slipped from her hand during the...incident. We're still trying to piece together the timeline of what happened."

The silence that followed was deafening, a roar of disbelief filling the space where her heartbeat had been moments before.

"You must be mistaken," Olivia said, trying to keep her voice steady. "I'm supposed to meet Emily here this evening. I'm dog-sitting for her."

Officer Bennett's eyes softened with pity, and Olivia's stomach dropped. "I'm afraid that won't be happening. Olivia, Emily is gone."

Disbelief surged through her. "No! I need to see her! There's no way she's gone! I talked to her two hours ago." Ignoring his attempts to stop her, she marched down the road toward the Ridge, heart pounding in her chest.

Gravel crunched behind her, and she turned to see the sheriff's deputy pulling up. "Get in," he said, holding the door open. Olivia slid into the front seat, and they sped toward the flashing lights.

The normally serene mountaintop, with its cliffs overlooking the valley, was now a chaotic scene. Blue and red lights flickered, police cruisers and ambulances were parked haphazardly, and law enforcement officers swarmed the area. A small group of onlookers stood at the edge of the scene, murmuring amongst themselves.

The deputy led Olivia to the edge of the crime scene but stopped her before she could get too close. "I'm sorry, but you can't go any further."

Olivia's heart ached as her eyes landed on a covered figure in the distance. Medical personnel worked quickly, securing the body to a stretcher, preparing to lift it to the mountaintop. A lock of wavy auburn hair fell from under the sheet, and the reality of Emily's death sank in like a punch to the gut.

Officer Bennett approached again, his voice gentle. "I know this is hard, Olivia. We're doing everything we can to figure out what happened."

She nodded, tears blurring her vision as the deputy guided her away from the scene. The weight of the loss pressed down on her, suffocating her in its intensity. Emily was gone, and nothing would ever be the same.

Her legs gave out, and she collapsed to her knees, tears streaming down her face as she whispered a final, shaky goodbye to her friend. Finding Officer Bennett again, she asked, "What details do you have about what happened?"

The officer hesitated, glancing around as if checking that no one would reprimand him for sharing too much. "We're still piecing it together, but it looks like she had a fall from the top of the Ridge."

Olivia's brow furrowed, confusion and concern swirling in her mind. Emily was athletic, in great shape, and an avid hiker who frequented these trails. She knew every nook and cranny, every hidden rock and precarious ledge. Emily would have instinctively known where to step, what was stable, and what posed a danger.

The more Olivia contemplated it, the more unsettling it became. How could someone so knowledgeable about the terrain find themselves in such a precarious situation?

A wave of unease washed over her, accompanied by a creeping sense of dread. *But accidents happen, right?* she reasoned, trying to convince herself that it was possible.

Yet, deep down, Olivia felt a gnawing doubt. This didn't sit right. Was it really an accident, or was there something more at play? Her heart raced as she grappled with the implications of Emily's fall. What if there had been some kind of unexpected factor? She shook her head, trying to dispel the dark thoughts.

No, she told herself firmly. *I can't think like that.* But the nagging feeling wouldn't let up, and as she glanced around at the familiar landscape, it suddenly felt foreign and threatening.

Her gaze drifted back to the ambulance, where they were about to close the doors. A glint caught her eye—Emily's shoe sticking out from under the sheet. Olivia blinked, her heart dropping. *Black flats?* Emily would have never worn those for a hike. Those were her work shoes, her favorite black flats, the ones she always chose for client meetings.

But...she had a client this evening, Olivia thought, a wave of confusion crashing over her. Why would Emily be out on the trail now, right after an appointment? It didn't make sense. Emily was always so meticulous about her schedule, carefully balancing her work and her love for the outdoors. She wouldn't risk ruining her favorite shoes—or worse, putting herself in a situation where she could get hurt, right?

Olivia felt a knot tightening in her stomach. What had happened that led Emily to leave her meeting and venture into the woods? Had she been distracted or rushed? Or was there something about that meeting that had driven her to take a walk in the first place? A flicker of concern danced through Olivia's mind. *Was something wrong?*

The thought nagged at her, unsettling her more than the sight of Emily's shoe. There had to be more to the story.

"Officer Bennett," Olivia said, turning back to him, "who reported the incident?

He nodded toward a young couple speaking with another deputy. "Those two. Tourists. They were hiking the Miner's Trail and found her in some brush past the last switchback."

Olivia nodded, trying to process everything.

"Thank you," she said, her voice flat as she walked away, her mind still circling around those black flats. *Emily wouldn't have worn them hiking. If she had actually intended to go hiking at all. She wouldn't.*

She wandered away from the chaos of the scene, unable to bear the sight of the flashing lights and police tape any longer. Instead, she made her way up the hillside toward a clearing she and Emily had always called their own. It was a small oasis tucked into the trees, offering a stunning view of the mountains and valley.

As Olivia sat down on a large, mossy rock in the heart of their familiar clearing, memories rushed back like the cool breeze whispering through the trees. This was their spot—a serene oasis tucked away in the woods, where sunlight filtered through the leaves, casting playful patterns on the forest floor. Here, they had escaped everything, sharing secrets, laughter, and the occasional tear. They had talked about their hopes and dreams, envisioning a future that stretched before them like an open road.

But now, the clearing felt different—empty and hollow. The vibrant colors of the forest appeared muted, overshadowed by the weight of Emily's absence. The laughter that once echoed between them was replaced by a profound silence that pressed in around her. Olivia pressed her hand against the cool earth, a deep ache settling in her chest, as if the very ground beneath her mourned the loss of her friend.

The gentle evening breeze, once comforting, felt harsh against her skin, and she wished she could curl up and disappear among the roots of the trees. The void left by Emily's absence was palpable, filling the air with a heavy sadness that lingered like a thick fog. Closing her eyes, Olivia took a deep breath, trying to summon the strength to face the harsh reality of the situation, but all she could feel was the profound loss—the irreplaceable space where Emily should have been.

Tears flowed freely as Olivia pulled her knees to her chest. The forest around her seeming to echo with the conversations they'd once had. For a fleeting moment, she could almost feel Emily there beside her, as though her presence lingered in the wind, in the rustle of the leaves. But there was something else, something more—an unsettling tug at her consciousness, as if Emily were trying to reach out to her. Trying to tell her something.

Suddenly, a realization struck her like a bolt of lightning. "Elmer," she whispered aloud, the name echoing in the quiet clearing. She hadn't even met him yet, but the thought of the dog left alone without Emily was a crushing weight on her heart. Images of Elmer, confused and searching for his owner, filled her mind. The very idea of him feeling lost and abandoned sent fresh tears rushing to her eyes.

The emotional turmoil swirled within her, a mix of grief and urgency. She stood up abruptly, wiping the dirt from her pants with shaky hands. *I can't let him be alone,* she thought, a fierce determination igniting inside her. The chaos surrounding her felt overwhelming, a tide of helplessness threatening to pull her under. So much had happened that was beyond her control, so many unanswered questions and heart-wrenching moments. But taking care of Elmer was one thing she could do—one tangible action amidst the confusion.

In that moment, the idea of nurturing and protecting Emily's dog became a lifeline, a way to channel her grief into something meaningful. She envisioned Elmer's wagging tail, the way he would look up at her with those trusting eyes. If she could just get to him and provide the comfort he needed, it would be a small victory in a

situation that felt so bleak. She owed it to Emily too make sure he was okay.

This sense of purpose anchored her, allowing her to focus amidst the storm of emotions swirling in her heart. She squared her shoulders and took a deep breath, reminding herself that while she couldn't change what had happened to Emily, she could make sure Elmer didn't feel the sting of loss alone. With renewed determination, Olivia set off in the direction of Emily's house, feeling the weight of responsibility mixed with the flicker of hope.

The air was heavy with unspoken grief as Olivia trudged back toward the Ridge. The initial chaos of police sirens and hurried voices had subsided, leaving a quiet that felt even louder than the noise that had preceded it. Time had passed since the emergency crews had departed, and in their wake, a vigil had formed. Townsfolk gathered with candles, their soft, flickering light casting a warm glow that danced across tear-streaked cheeks and illuminated eyes filled with shock, disbelief, and deep, collective sorrow.

Olivia paused to take in the sight, the reality settling in her chest like a heavy weight. The news had swept through Emerald Ridge with its usual, uncanny speed—passed from neighbor to neighbor, whispered through phone calls, relayed in hurried messages. It hadn't been long since the tragic news broke, yet already, the entire town stood together at the edge of the place that had once brought Emily so much peace. The somber assembly felt like a tribute to her spirit, a testament to the profound impact she had made in their lives.

Emily had become a cornerstone of the Emerald Ridge community, not only as the main therapist but also as a tireless advocate for mental health. She devoted countless hours to volunteering at the local high school, where she shared her expertise to help teens navigate the challenges of adolescence. With her larger-than-life personality and unapologetic opinions, she spoke her mind freely, often igniting lively discussions that left others both inspired and entertained—occasionally ruffling a few feathers along the way.

But beneath her vibrant exterior was a heart as big as the mountains surrounding the town. Emily was always the first to roll up her sleeves when someone was in need, whether it was organizing a charity drive or simply lending a compassionate ear to a friend in distress. Her ability to connect with people made her not just a therapist but a confidante, a mentor, and a beloved figure in the lives of many. Her absence would leave a void not only in the hearts of those she had helped but throughout the entire community she cherished.

Olivia wove her way through the gathered crowd, faces she knew nodding silently at her, their expressions a blend of recognition and shared sadness. The soft hum of whispers rose and fell like the rustling of leaves, a background to the vigil's solemnity. Lydia Fletcher, the town librarian, stepped forward and handed Olivia a small candle. No words were needed. Everyone knew how close she and Emily had been.

Olivia placed her candle near the center, where the largest flame burned steadily, surrounded by offerings of flowers, handwritten notes, and photos of Emily. The warmth of the flames flickered against the cheap gold-plated bracelet on her wrist, the half-heart engraved with "Best." The other half, marked "Friends," had always been with Emily. The ache in Olivia's chest tightened, a painful reminder that part of her was missing now, gone with the one person who had shared so much of her history.

As she straightened, a familiar voice broke the hush, low and insistent. Millie Partridge, the town's unofficial keeper of whispers, was standing just behind Olivia, speaking to a group of women who hung on her every word.

"Emily was such a free spirit, wasn't she?" Millie's voice carried, despite her attempt at hushed tones. "Always so passionate, always pushing. I bet there are a few folks in town who won't miss the fuss she stirred up. But to speak ill so soon after such a tragic accident…well, it's just talk, of course."

Olivia's jaw tightened, a mixture of irritation and disbelief simmering beneath her grief. Millie's words, though vague, felt cold, a stark contrast to the warmth of the vigil. It was just like her to add a note of drama where none was needed. Olivia turned slightly, catching Millie's eye for just a moment. The older woman shifted, her gaze flitting away, as though she knew she'd been caught overstepping.

The crowd began to shift, murmurs rippling as more candles were added and silent prayers were offered. Olivia's heart ached with the rawness of it all. She had half a mind to say something to Millie but decided against it. It was neither the time nor the place, and besides, it was only Millie, with her endless appetite for speculation.

As she gazed into the flame, willing herself to believe that none of this was real, she heard a soft whisper. as vivid in her mind as if it were echoing around her. *"Find out."*

She glanced around, startled. The words hadn't come from anyone nearby.

"Find out," came the whisper again, this time fainter, almost like an echo in her mind. Olivia's heart raced. She knew that voice—it was Emily's. And she knew she couldn't ignore it. She took a deep breath, holding onto the moment, even as her mind flitted to the thought that would leave her: nothing about this felt right. But she pushed it away for now, letting the shared grief wash over her. The questions could wait. Tonight was for Emily.

CHAPTER 5

As the summer night settled around her, Olivia made her way from the Ridge back to Emily's house, where her Jeep was parked in the driveway. The sky had deepened to a bruised shade of purple, rapidly succumbing to the encroaching darkness of night, and the cool breeze carried the lingering scent of pine and earth. Emily had always kept a spare key under one of the flowerpots on the front porch—a testament to the small-town trust that defined Emerald Ridge.

As Olivia reached the porch, the muffled whines and sniffles of Elmer drifted through the door. His urgency pulled at her heartstrings, and she wondered when he had last been outside or had a proper meal. One by one, she began lifting the pots, each one heavy with soil and memory. Beneath a bright pink pot filled with white daisies—Emily's favorite—she found the key taped to the bottom. The sight of the cheerful flowers contrasted sharply with the grief that weighed on her chest.

Her hands trembled as she peeled the key away and attempted to fit it into the lock. After a few shaky tries, it slid into place, and she pushed the door open. Before she could brace herself, two giant paws landed squarely on her chest, nearly knocking her off the porch.

"Oof!" Olivia gasped, stumbling back a few steps. A bundle of golden fur spun around her legs. *So this is Elmer,* she thought, looking down at the excited dog as he circled her, snuffling at her shoes and gazing up with expectant eyes. Even without her unique ability to understand animals, his message was loud and clear: *Potty! Potty! Potty!*

"Do you need to go outside, bud?" she asked. Without further prompting, Elmer bolted toward the back door, his enthusiasm reminiscent of a child at recess. Olivia opened it, and Elmer bounded out into the yard like a furry tornado, a blur of excitement and pent-up energy.

While Elmer explored, Olivia took a moment to survey the space, scanning for any clues that might help her "find out" what had happened. Emily's kitchen was as pristine as ever—everything meticulously in its place. Olivia's eyes fell on a piece of paper on the counter, Emily's neat handwriting outlining instructions for Elmer's care. Seeing Emily's familiar script made Olivia's heart tighten, a tangible reminder of her absence.

Elmer pawed at the back door, signaling that he was ready to come back inside. She opened it, and he trotted in, wagging his tail and sitting at her feet, eyes wide and full of expectation. *Thank you!* Olivia heard, clear as a bell in her mind.

"You're welcome, buddy," she responded absentmindedly before freezing.

You can hear me? Elmer's voice echoed in her mind, uncertain but hopeful.

Olivia often forgot that her ability to telepathically communicate with animals caught them as off-guard as it did people. She knelt down to Elmer's level, stroking his head. "Hey, Elmer. My name's Olivia. Your owner, Emily, was my best friend. I'm going to be taking care of you for a while."

Elmer's ears drooped slightly, his gaze drifting toward Emily's room upstairs. *I know she's leaving. Her bag's still upstairs.* His thoughts carried a note of sadness.

Olivia's heart sank. This was uncharted territory—breaking this kind of news to a pet. She continued to stroke Elmer's fur, her voice trembling. "I'm so sorry, buddy, but Emily isn't coming back. There was an accident. She died. She's gone...forever."

Elmer lowered his head onto his paws, his eyes dull with confusion and sorrow. *No more snuggles? No more treats?* he asked his voice barely a whisper in her mind.

Olivia's tears blurred her vision as she sat down beside him. "I know it's hard, Elmer. But I'm here now, and I promise you'll still get snuggles, and pets, and treats. We'll figure this out together."

Elmer looked up at her, his deep brown eyes searching hers as if trying to make sense of her words. Slowly, he scooted closer, resting his head in her lap. *We're both sad. Sad about Emily,* he thought.

"Yeah, we are," Olivia whispered, her fingers brushing through his fur, offering comfort. Her phone buzzed, snapping her back to the present. She glanced at the screen, seeing a string of worried messages from her mom and a few others.

Mom: *Olivia, where are you? What happened to Emily?*

Mom: *Please let me know you're okay.*

Mom: *Olivia? Please respond to me.*

She quickly typed a reply.

Olivia: *Mom, I'm okay. I'm at Emily's house. Just wanted to let you know I'll be bringing her dog home with me.*

Mom: *Thank God you're okay. That's all I needed to know. And of course, bring the poor guy home with you.*

Olivia: *Thanks, Mom. I'll be home in a little while. Just need to pack up a few things.*

Olivia set her phone aside and looked down at Elmer, who was watching her intently. "Let's get your stuff packed up, big guy," she said, standing.

Elmer followed her around the house, his tail wagging softly as she collected his toys, bed, and a few other belongings. Each item she picked up reminded her of

Emily's presence, and with every memory came a fresh wave of loss. By the time they were ready to leave, Olivia felt both physically and emotionally drained.

As she led Elmer to the door, she glanced at the pile of his things stacked nearby. "Okay, this should last you for the night. We'll figure the rest of this mess out tomorrow."

At the word "mess," Elmer's head perked up. Without warning, he bolted toward the staircase, racing up with surprising speed for such a large dog.

Olivia blinked. "What's gotten into him?" she muttered, following him to the bottom of the stairs.

Elmer stood at the top, his tail wagging as he glanced back at her, barking softly. *Mess!* he repeated, trotting down the hall toward Emily's office.

Curious, Olivia followed. When she reached the top of the stairs, she noticed something odd—all the lights in the upstairs hallway were on. That wasn't like Emily. She never left a light on unnecessarily.

Elmer nudged Emily's office door open with his nose, revealing a scene that stopped Olivia in her tracks. Papers were scattered across the floor, the chairs were askew, and a teacup lay shattered on the carpet. Her desk drawers were half-open, as if someone had rummaged through them hastily. Only one drawer remained shut, held firmly in place by a sturdy lock.

"What happened here?" Olivia murmured, stepping further into the room. Elmer sniffed around, his nose pressed against the floorboards.

Scary lady. She was mad. Olivia heard Elmer think.

Olivia's blood ran cold. "Scary lady? Who?" she asked, her voice tight with urgency. But Elmer offered nothing more. His ears drooped, and he turned his head away, shifting his gaze to a spot on the floor as if studying an invisible crack. The silence between them grew heavy, pressing down on Olivia like a weight she couldn't shrug off.

She reached out and gently touched Elmer's fur, hoping the contact might coax him back. But he didn't budge, only let out a quiet, shuddering sigh that felt more like a surrender than an answer. It wasn't just the silence that unnerved her; it was the way his eyes had gone dull, like shutters closed against the world. Elmer had just been full of life, bounding around the backyard. She didn't know him well but she could read animals and she knew what his body language was telling her. he looked deflated, almost haunted, as if the memory of the "scary lady" had stolen a piece of him.

Olivia's heart twisted. The silence wasn't just a pause; it was an absence, a void where his usual warmth and trust should have been. It was as if he'd drawn a line, unwilling to revisit whatever memory had flashed in his mind.

"Elmer," she whispered, her throat tight, "it's okay. You're safe now." But even as she said it, she wasn't sure if she believed it herself. If Elmer, with his boundless spirit, could be silenced by a memory, then whatever—or whoever—he had seen was more terrifying than she wanted to imagine.

Her heart pounded as she took out her phone and snapped a few pictures of the scene. "Come on, Elmer. Let's get out of here," she whispered, backing out of the office and closing the door behind her.

Back downstairs, Olivia gathered the last of Elmer's things, the quiet of Emily's house pressing in around her. The silence felt heavier than it should have, tinged with the absence of Emily's familiar laughter. She took a last, long look at the living room, trying to hold back the swell of emotion in her chest. Shaking it off, she locked the door behind her and walked with Elmer toward the Jeep.

As they reached the car, Elmer paused at the passenger side, sitting down with an air of expectation. Olivia raised an eyebrow. "You want to ride up front?" He barked once, the sound breaking the silence that had wrapped around them. "Okay, buddy," she said, a faint smile breaking through her somber expression as she opened the door for him.

Elmer hopped in, his tail thumping against the seat as he stuck his head out of the window, ears flapping in the cool breeze. Olivia started the engine, the familiar rumble somehow grounding her. She was about to pull away when a flicker of movement caught her eye.

Across the street, half-shrouded in shadow, stood Samuel Carter. The former sheriff and current head of the neighborhood watch was a fixture in Emerald Ridge, known for his meticulous patrolling and unyielding gaze. Even now, he watched Olivia with that same intensity, his eyes following her every move as if trying to read her thoughts.

A shiver ran down her spine, not exactly from fear, but from the unsettling awareness of being observed so closely. Samuel's presence was hard to ignore; his reputation for knowing the town's secrets was as solid as the mountains that surrounded them. What struck Olivia as odd, however, was the fact that he was here—she knew he didn't live around this area. His usual haunts were further away, and his unexpected appearance felt like a dark cloud looming over her.

Maybe he's just being vigilant, she thought. In light of Emily's recent incident, it wouldn't be surprising for him to keep an eye on the place, ensuring nothing else went awry.

Olivia forced herself to meet his gaze, offering a polite nod before looking away. He raised one hand in a silent gesture of acknowledgment, his expression unreadable, before shifting his attention to the rest of the street. *What brought him here, of all places?* she wondered, a mix of curiosity and unease swirling within her.

The engine hummed beneath her, Elmer's tail still thumping in a steady rhythm, oblivious to the tension in the air. Olivia took a deep breath, gripping the steering wheel tighter as she eased the Jeep into gear.

As they pulled away, she cast one last glance in the rearview mirror. Samuel was still there, eyes locked on her Jeep as it disappeared down the road. A prickle of unease settled in her chest. Samuel Carter was known for being thorough, sometimes too thorough. And the way he had watched her just now felt like more than a casual glance.

Road trip! Elmer's cheerful bark brought her back to the moment, his excitement a welcome distraction from the gnawing thoughts beginning to take shape. *At least one of us found something to be happy about,* she thought as the dark mountain road stretched ahead, winding into the unknown.

CHAPTER 6

Olivia arrived home with Elmer about fifteen minutes later, guiding the big dog into her house. As soon as the door opened, his nose twitched and flared, taking in the new symphony of scents—vanilla, lavender, and, no doubt, the unmistakable scent of Aster, the cat. Elmer bounded into the living room, his golden tail wagging furiously, ears perked in curiosity as he moved from one spot to the next, sniffing at every corner like a detective on a mission.

Olivia leaned against the kitchen counter, watching the unfolding scene between Elmer and Aster. With her unique ability to catch the whispers of their thoughts, she had a front-row seat to the intricate exchange between the enthusiastic dog and the regal cat. The room buzzed with a silent energy, a kind of wordless negotiation playing out before her.

Aster, perched on the armchair like a queen presiding over her realm, narrowed her yellow eyes at Elmer, who had skidded to a stop, paws splayed wide on the hardwood. The cat's expression was pure, unfiltered disdain, punctuated by the rhythmic flick of her tail. *Who dares disturb my sanctuary?* she asked, with a silent elegance that only a cat could pull off.

Elmer, ever the optimist, wagged his tail with unbridled enthusiasm. *Hey there, I'm Elmer! Wanna play?* The thought buzzed through Olivia's mind, infused with innocence and excitement. He was a whirlwind of boundless energy, blissfully ignorant of Aster's simmering annoyance.

Play? With you? Aster's thoughts oozed condescension. She lifted a paw, claws extending in a delicate warning. The air around her practically crackled with haughty authority.

Elmer's ears perked up, his tail thumping like a metronome on overdrive. *We could chase stuff! Or sniff things! Or, oh, we could roll in the dirt!* The last thought practically vibrated out of him, his excitement nearly contagious.

Aster's whiskers twitched in visible irritation. *Roll in the dirt? How uncouth.* She shifted, her tail flicking lazily as she regarded him with narrowed eyes. *This creature has the sophistication of a garden gnome.*

For a moment, Elmer's cheer faltered. His head drooped, and Olivia felt a pang of sympathy wash over her. But then, Aster's expression softened, just enough for Olivia to notice. *Perhaps...there could be a compromise.*

Fetch my feather toy, Aster's thought was laced with reluctant acceptance, and she nodded toward the corner where it lay as if bestowing a royal favor.

Elmer's joy reignited instantly. He trotted to the corner and retrieved the feather toy with the care one might use to carry a priceless artifact. He laid it at Aster's feet, tail wagging furiously, eyes bright with pride. *See? We can be friends!* he said.

Aster regarded the toy, giving it a gentle nudge with her paw. The corners of her mouth lifted in what Olivia swore was the tiniest, most reluctant smile. *Perhaps. But remember, this is my domain, and you are merely tolerated.*

Elmer barked happily, completely missing the nuance of Aster's thought, but it didn't matter. He was overjoyed, and Olivia couldn't help but laugh, the sound ringing through the room and breaking the tension.

The silent, delicate truce between them was a testament to the unspoken bonds that could form even between the most unlikely companions. And for Olivia, witnessing their little agreement felt like a warm reminder that harmony could exist, even in the smallest of places.

As Olivia prepared to take Elmer upstairs to settle in, her mom emerged from the kitchen, her warm smile radiating relief. "Is this the famous Elmer we've heard so much about?" she asked, crouching down to meet him at eye level.

Elmer tilted his head, his big brown eyes sparkling with curiosity, sensing the affection emanating from her. "Well, aren't you just the cutest thing!" Olivia's mom exclaimed, reaching out to scratch behind his ears. Elmer leaned into her touch, letting out a contented sigh that filled the room with warmth.

Just then, Jake ambled into the room, his expression shifting from casual indifference to surprise. "Whoa, you weren't kidding! He's a big guy!" He crouched beside their mom, a grin spreading across his face as he extended a hand to Elmer. "Hey there, buddy! What do you think about playing some fetch tomorrow?"

Elmer responded with a playful bark, bounding forward to nudge Jake's hand with his nose. "Looks like he's ready for a game!" Jake laughed, clearly smitten.

Olivia watched the interaction, a smile tugging at her lips. It was comforting to see her family embracing Elmer so wholeheartedly, especially after the events of the night.

Once the introductions were over, Jake turned to Olivia, a hint of concern in his eyes. "Hey, are you okay?"

"I'm fine," Olivia reassured him, her voice steady. "Or, I guess I will be. It's just a lot right now, you know? But having Elmer to take care of gives me a sense of purpose."

With that, she called to Elmer from the base of the stairs, "Come on, boy, let me show you where you'll be staying."

Elmer bounded over eagerly, following her up the creaky wooden stairs, his large paws thudding against the steps while Olivia lugged his things behind her. The scent of sandalwood and rose greeted them at the top of the stairs, the warm, earthy smell intertwining with the sweet floral notes to create an atmosphere of peaceful retreat.

The loft opened into a spacious bedroom, bathed in the soft, golden moonlight streaming through the large, arched windows. Olivia stepped inside and felt an immediate sense of calm wash over her, like the room itself was exhaling in welcome. The space hadn't changed much since she was younger—there was still the familiar creak of the floorboards, the light scent of lavender that lingered from sachets tucked into drawers, and the cozy, slightly mismatched furniture that spoke of a home built on stories and memories.

What struck Olivia most was the way she saw her old room now. Returning as an adult, it felt more than just a cherished relic from her past; it had transformed into a refuge. The armchair in the corner, plump with colorful cushions and draped with her grandmother's well-loved knitted throw, seemed to be waiting for her with open arms. The shelves, lined with framed family photos, delicate trinkets, and thriving potted plants, whispered of continuity—a bridge between then and now.

The bookshelves, overflowing with worn paperbacks and vintage editions, were like old friends offering solace. Each title held memories of her childhood, of nights spent curled up by the window, losing herself in stories as the wind rustled through the trees outside. She glanced at the large window seat, cushioned and inviting, and imagined herself there again, remembering the tranquility that space brought her. Olivia felt a warm rush of gratitude that her mom had kept the room just as it was. It was a beautiful reminder of her childhood, a testament to the love that surrounded her. This space, untouched by time, made her feel cherished and welcomed home. In that moment, as she took in the familiar surroundings, she felt a sense of grounding and comfort, knowing that some things hadn't changed. Perhaps that stability was exactly what she needed right now.

Elmer's paws clicked softly on the hardwood as he entered behind her, his eyes wide and curious. He trotted over to the window seat, sniffing it tentatively before giving a small, approving wag of his tail. Olivia couldn't help but smile. His presence made this return feel complete, transforming the room from a wistful memory into something vibrant and real. It wasn't just a space from her past—it was now a space they shared.

As Elmer explored, Olivia felt a deep sense of comfort wash over her. He brought with him a piece of Emily, a tangible reminder of their friendship that made everything feel just a little brighter. The thought of Elmer curled up beside her, just like he had with Emily, filled the room with a sense of love and connection. Together, they were weaving new memories, blending the past with the present, and in that moment, Olivia knew that they would carry Emily's spirit with them wherever they went.

She walked over to the fairy lights strung across the beams, their soft glow casting playful patterns on the ceiling. It felt magical, warm, and hopeful. The vintage vanity by the window, cluttered with an assortment of perfumes and old jewelry, seemed to glimmer with quiet promise as if to say, *Welcome back. You're safe here.*

Olivia drew in a deep breath, letting the feeling sink in. Maybe this unexpected return was more than a pause; maybe it was a chance to find her footing again, to remember who she was before life's twists and turns pulled her in so many different directions. With Elmer at her side and the comfort of this familiar space around her, she felt a spark of confidence. Here, in this loft filled with memories and light, she could believe that everything was going to be okay.

Elmer's eyes scanned the inviting space as he took in the new sights and smells. Every corner seemed to whisper promises of peace and safety. His nose twitched as he inhaled the comforting scents, his tail wagging slowly as he moved deeper into the room.

This place feels...nice, he thought, his anxiety starting to melt away. *Like a big, warm hug.*

Elmer's paws sank into the soft rug, and he let out a deep, contented sigh, finally relaxing for the first time since meeting Olivia. He glanced up at her, his brown eyes filled with trust and quiet gratitude.

Maybe things will be okay, he mused. *Emily's gone, but Olivia's here. And this place...it feels like home.*

Olivia placed his dog bed in the cozy corner by the window, where the morning sunlight would pool, and set his food and water dishes against the wall. Elmer's watchful eyes followed her every movement, his ears flicking as he observed.

"Is this good, buddy?" she asked, taking one last look at the setup.

Elmer glanced around, then let out a contented sigh, laying his head back down on the rug, *Yes, this will do*.

Elmer curled up on the rug, his head resting on his paws as the tranquility of the loft seeped into his bones. For the first time that night, he felt a flicker of hope. *We'll be all right,* he thought as his eyes grew heavy with sleep. *We've got Olivia, and we've got this place. We'll make it through.*

Olivia noticed how Elmer was settling in, a small smile touching her lips. Seeing him adapt, even a little, was a victory amidst the overwhelming grief. The one thing she could focus on now was making this transition as smooth and gentle as possible for him.

Olivia sat beside him on the floor, leaning against her bed, and began to softly stroke his fur. "It's going to be okay, big boy," she whispered. "It may not feel like it right now, but I promise, it will be."

Elmer shifted, his tail thumping softly against the floor. His warm brown eyes met hers, and for a moment, they shared a quiet understanding. "You miss her too, don't you?" she asked, her voice cracking with emotion.

Elmer gave a small woof in response, nudging her hand with his nose.

She chuckled softly, blinking away the tears. "Yeah, I know. She was the best. But we've got each other now, right?"

He licked her hand, a small gesture that meant the world. The room fell quiet again, save for the occasional rustle of leaves outside and Elmer's soft breathing.

For the first time in hours, Olivia felt a flicker of hope. They were both grieving, both lost in their own way, but they had each other. And maybe, just maybe, that would be enough to get them through.

As Olivia watched Elmer drift off into sleep, the worries that had clung to him seemed to fade, replaced by dreams of a new beginning in the safety of her cozy, welcoming loft.

CHAPTER 7

By the next morning, Elmer had charmed everyone in the house and seemed to be settling in quite nicely. When Olivia woke up and didn't see him in the loft, she peeked out the window. Down in the garden, Elmer chased butterflies with an enthusiasm that only a young dog could muster, his golden coat glistening in the morning light. Her mom was nearby, tending to her garden, carefully arranging the soil while the dog joyfully dug up another patch not far from her. It was a peaceful scene—a stark contrast to the turmoil swirling inside Olivia.

As much as she didn't want to keep reliving the nightmare of Emily's death, she knew she needed to get out of the house. The same nagging feeling that had troubled her last night returned, a whisper of doubt suggesting Emily's death wasn't simply an accident. It tugged at her, urging her to dig deeper. If she was going to find answers, she had to hear what others in town were saying. Olivia stuck her head out the back door.

"Mom, I'm heading to Perks and Peaks to grab some coffee. Do you want me to bring you anything?"

Her mom looked up from her garden, a knowing expression crossing her face. She always sensed more than Olivia ever voiced. "No, I'm good, hon. Thanks, though," she replied, brushing dirt off her hands.

Olivia glanced over at Elmer, now engrossed in digging what seemed to be a hole to China. "Do you mind keeping an eye on Elmer while I'm gone?"

Her mom smiled, watching the dog with amusement. "I don't mind at all. He seems to have himself pretty well entertained."

With a quick kiss on her mom's cheek and a thank you, Olivia grabbed her bag and headed out the door. The familiar sight of Perks and Peaks greeted her as she pulled into the back parking lot. The small-town coffee shop seemed busier than usual, but maybe that was just her nerves making everything feel off. The birds were chirping, the air fresh and crisp, like any other summer morning. Yet Olivia knew this wasn't any normal day.

She pushed open the door, the bell above it jingling a welcome, and immediately caught sight of Ashley behind the counter, juggling orders and handing out drinks. There was a low hum of conversation, and Olivia could hear snippets of talk about Emily as she made her way to the back corner of the shop. Ashley noticed her and shot her a sympathetic nod, silently agreeing to bring her usual drink over when she could.

As Olivia settled into the only available table, she couldn't help but overhear the conversations around her.

"Did you hear about Emily Harris? Isn't it tragic? I just can't believe it. She knew those mountains so well. Something doesn't add up..."

"Yeah, she was such a great therapist. I guess we'll all need to find someone new now. So sad."

"Has the sheriff's department said anything more about what happened?"

As Olivia suspected, Emily's death was the talk of the town. Several familiar faces glanced her way, their expressions filled with sympathy. She busied herself with her phone, trying to listen without looking obvious. Memories of the close-knit friendship between Emily, Ashley, and Olivia flooded her mind—how the three of them had been inseparable in high school, sharing dreams and secrets as they navigated the wild ups and downs of adolescence. They were like a trio of adventurers, tackling everything from school projects to heartbreaks together. But as life often does, it pulled them in different directions. Ashley stayed in town, working with her parents, while Emily set off for college, and Olivia? Well, she was determined to escape and explore the world beyond Emerald Ridge.

When Emily moved back after college, it was like no time had passed at all. Ashley eagerly reconnected with her, thrilled to revive their friendship and swap stories over lattes.

Before long, the scraping of a chair across from her pulled Olivia back to the present. Ashley settled into the seat across from her, placing a steaming cup of coffee in front of Olivia. Her eyes were red and puffy, clear signs that she had been crying. "I can't believe she's gone," Ashley whispered, her voice cracking. "Just yesterday she was in here to pick up her usual morning latte."

The weight of their shared grief hung in the air, but then a small smile crept across Olivia's face as she met Ashley's gaze. "Yeah, and even with all her organic obsession, she wouldn't give up her coffee for anything. I mean, she swapped creamers like they were going out of style, but the caffeine? That was sacred."

They both chuckled, the sound a bittersweet reminder of Emily's vibrant spirit. In that moment, the laughter felt like a warm embrace, a fleeting glimpse of the joy they had shared. Even in their sorrow, they could still find a thread of connection, a glimmer of Emily's essence woven through their memories.

"So...How are you?" Ashley asked gently, concern etched on her face.

Olivia wasn't sure how to answer. "In shock still, I guess."

"I'm so sorry, Liv. I know how close you and Emily were. I heard you were one of the first to find out. That must have been...awful," Ashley said, her voice barely above a whisper.

Olivia took a deep breath, fighting back the emotion that threatened to spill over. "It was definitely not the best night of my life." She hesitated for a moment before leaning closer, her voice dropping to a conspiratorial tone. "Have you heard anyone saying they don't think Emily's death was an accident?"

Ashley's eyes widened at the question, surprise flickering across her face. "I mean, there have been a couple of people saying it's strange. You know how well she knew those trails. But no one's said anything solid. People here pretty much trust what the sheriff says."

Olivia nodded thoughtfully. "Yeah, but something doesn't sit right with me." She leaned in even closer. "When I went to Emily's house last night to pick up her dog, I found her office a complete mess. But it wasn't just clutter—it looked like someone had been searching for something."

She pulled out her phone and showed Ashley the pictures she had taken. Ashley's eyes widened in disbelief as she scrolled through the images, a mix of surprise and concern washing over her face as the gravity of what she was seeing sank in.

"Whoa. This doesn't look like how Emily would leave things. Are you going to show these to the sheriff?"

Olivia bit her lip, unsure. "I don't know. Maybe I'm overthinking it. It could have been Emily looking for something before she left. Or maybe I'm just seeing what I want to see. I'm no detective, and the sheriff's department already think they know what happened. What if it's nothing?"

Ashley tilted her head, her brows furrowing. "Could be nothing, sure. But it could also be something. Don't brush it off too quickly."

Olivia sighed, staring out the window as uncertainty gnawed at her. "Yeah, maybe. I'll think about it."

Ashley softened, changing the subject slightly. "How's her pup doing?"

Thinking of Elmer playing in the garden this morning made her smile despite everything. "He's doing okay. I think he's confused, but he's settling in. He's a sweetheart—big, clumsy, but sweet. I think he'll be fine."

Ashley reached out, giving her hand a comforting squeeze. "He's lucky to have you. You're doing a good thing."

Olivia smiled faintly and returned the squeeze. "Thanks, Ash. I appreciate that." As she stood to leave, she added, "Hey, if you hear anything else, anything unusual, let me know, okay?"

"Of course. You'll be the first to know," Ashley promised.

As Olivia pushed open the door to leave, she felt it collide with something solid. "Oof!" came a familiar voice. She looked up to see Noah Wilkins rubbing his chest where the door had smacked into him.

"Oh, uh, hi," Olivia stammered, her cheeks flushing. "Sorry, I didn't see you there."

Noah chuckled, clearly unbothered. "No worries. I'll survive."

They both awkwardly shuffled to get past each other, moving left, then right in unison. Noah, with a grin, finally grabbed the door and held it open for her. "Ladies first," he said.

Olivia nodded quickly and hurried past him, hoping to escape the awkwardness as fast as possible. *Will running into him ever not be awkward?* she wondered as she climbed into her Jeep. Her phone buzzed beside her just as she was backing out of the parking lot. It was a text from Jake.

Jake: The cops are here talking to Mom about Emily. Just thought you'd want to know.

Her heart raced. *Why would the cops be talking to Mom about Emily?* she thought, her mind buzzing with questions as she drove back home.

Minutes later, she pulled up in front of the house and flung open the door, bracing herself for whatever awaited inside.

As Olivia entered the kitchen, she was met with the sight of Officer Bennett—who had delivered the heartbreaking news to her last night—sitting at the table with her mom. Elmer sat nearby, glancing between the two with wide, anxious eyes, as if he sensed that something wasn't right.

"Mom?" Olivia asked, trying to keep her voice steady.

"Oh, hey, sweetie," her mom said, her tone light, though Olivia could sense the underlying tension. "This is Officer Bennett. He's here with a few questions about Emily."

Olivia glanced at Officer Bennett and replied, "We've met." Officer Bennett gave a quick nod of confirmation.

Olivia met the officer's gaze, suspicion creeping in. "What kind of questions?"

Bennett cleared his throat. "Just routine stuff—how she'd been acting lately, if anyone noticed anything unusual."

Her mom glanced at her, then back at Bennett. "She came by a couple of days ago, actually. She wanted to ask me about an herbal tincture she was working on. I gave her some advice, told her to be careful with the ingredients she was mixing."

Her mom nodded. "It seemed like a promising project, but the combination of herbs she was using could be dangerous if mishandled."

Bennett stood, retrieved his cowboy hat from the table, and settled it back on his head. "Thank you, Ms. Morgan. I appreciate your time."

Cassandra's voice was low and steady as she thanked Officer Bennett for his time, the unspoken worry in her eyes making the gesture feel more significant. She walked him to the door, her steps calm and deliberate, as if guiding him out was a ritual that might somehow protect her daughter from the weight of his questions.

The officer nodded politely, tipping his hat slightly before stepping out into the warm morning air. Cassandra lingered for a moment, watching him climb into his Summit County Sheriff's Department-marked SUV. Once he was inside, she closed the door softly and turned back to Olivia, offering a reassuring, albeit strained, smile.

After the officer left, Olivia followed her mom back to the kitchen table, her mind swirling with questions. "You mentioned Emily's tincture yesterday, but it sounded more like something she was just dabbling in. Is there more to it?"

Her mom shrugged. "It didn't seem relevant until now. She was excited about it, though. Said it could help her patients break through mental barriers more easily."

Olivia stared at her hands, trying to process everything. "Mom, I found something strange at Emily's house last night." She pulled out her phone and showed her mom the pictures of the messy office.

Her mom glanced at them, her expression darkening. "This doesn't look like Emily's doing. You should tell the sheriff."

"Should I? Maybe it's nothing," Olivia said, her voice laced with uncertainty.

Her mom gave her a reassuring look. "Intuition is never wrong, Livy. But don't let trying to figure out if it's relevant or not consume you. Take the pictures to the sheriff. Let them decide."

Cassandra walked around the table and placed a gentle hand on Olivia's arm, her touch warm and reassuring. "You're stronger than you think, sweetheart. Sometimes, the hardest part is knowing when to step back and let others take charge." Her eyes softened as she continued, "You don't have to bear this weight alone. The people who care about you—like me—we're here for you. The sheriff's department is looking into it; it's their job. Maybe it's best to let them handle it?

Olivia looked into her mother's eyes, finding comfort in their familiar depths. The knot in her chest loosened slightly, a little of the burden she'd been carrying lifted. Cassandra continued, "You've always been brave, Livy. Trust yourself but remember it's okay to lean on others too."

The moment stretched between them, enveloping the space in a quiet understanding. It reminded Olivia of all those times her mom had said just the right thing when everything felt overwhelming. This was one of those moments, a comforting reminder that she wasn't alone in her struggles.

As her mom turned to head back to the garden, a teasing smile broke through the seriousness of the moment. "By the way, Noah still thinks about you. Maybe it's time you two had an actual conversation?"

Olivia shook her head, a reluctant smile tugging at her lips despite herself. "Thanks, Mom, but remember, you're not supposed to use your psychic powers to pry into your kids' lives!"

Cassandra laughed lightly, the sound brightening the atmosphere. "Oh, please. It's not my fault if I happen to know things!"

Watching her mother walk away, a mix of warmth and apprehension filled Olivia. She realized she had more questions than ever—and not just about Emily's death. The thought of reconnecting with Noah stirred something within her, a blend of nostalgia and curiosity. As Olivia's mom closed the back door, retreating to the garden, Olivia realized she had more questions than ever—and not just about Emily's death.

CHAPTER 8

The cold blast of stale air hit Olivia as soon as she pushed open the door to the Summit County Police Department. She had spent the entire thirty-minute drive second-guessing her decision. Was this the right move? Should she really be doing this? She'd lost count of how many times she had almost turned around. But here she was, with a mission in mind.

A receptionist, whose bored expression suggested she'd rather be anywhere else, glanced up briefly as Olivia walked in. "What can I do for you?" she asked, her tone flat and uninviting.

"Hi, uh, I was hoping to speak with Officer Bennett or whoever is handling the Emily Harris case. I have some additional information."

The receptionist nodded, pressing a few buttons on her phone. "Someone should be with you shortly." She gestured toward the metal-framed chairs against the wall and returned to her previous activity, something far more entertaining than greeting nervous visitors.

Olivia took a seat, her bag clutched tightly in her lap, her foot tapping nervously against the floor. Minutes ticked by, each one slower than the last, until a tall, graying man with a badge that read "Detective" walked into the reception area.

"You the one with information on the Harris case?" he asked, his voice a low rumble.

Olivia nodded quickly. "Yes, that's me."

"I'm Detective Reilly. Come with me." He turned on his heel, his long strides forcing her to scramble to keep up as they walked down a sterile, tile-lined hallway. At the end, he pushed open a door and motioned for her to enter.

It wasn't the office she had expected, but a room that screamed interrogation. Concrete floors, dingy white walls, a metal table bolted to the floor, and matching chairs. A camera in the corner silently recorded everything, its red light blinking like a silent sentinel. Olivia's stomach churned at the sight, but she squashed the unease. She had a job to do.

She perched on the edge of her seat, back straight and posture solid. Detective Reilly took a seat opposite her, his demeanor professional, but Olivia could see right through it. His cool detachment wasn't going to intimidate her. She had her own answers to find.

Nervousness crawled up her spine, but she shook it off. Her hands trembled slightly as she placed her bag on her lap, fingers drumming lightly on the leather. Reilly grabbed a notepad and pen, his gaze focused on the paper, but there was an edge of impatience in his posture. Ready for business. She could see the wheels in his head turning as if they were going through a routine checklist.

"Name?" he asked, his voice flat, not looking up.

"Olivia Morgan." Her voice was steady, a little more clipped than usual.

"Age?"

"Twenty-six."

"Height?"

"Five foot six."

"Weight?"

Olivia paused, almost biting back a chuckle. "Uh, 130-ish. Is this really necessary? I'm just here to give you some information on Emily's case." She didn't add that it was her case now too. The last thing she wanted was to make it sound like she was taking over. But she wasn't going to be some passive observer either. She was in it, like it or not.

"Procedure," he muttered, scribbling something down without even a glance at her. "Now, what's the information you have?"

Olivia reached for her phone, pulling up the images she'd taken of Emily's office. She handed the phone across the table, her fingers brushing the cool surface of the screen. As he swiped through the images, a furrow appeared between his brows.

"How exactly is this relevant?"

"I was one of Emily's best friends," Olivia began, each word carrying the weight of the past. "I was supposed to watch her dog while she went to a conference. After I heard about what happened, I went to her house to check on the dog."

"How did you get inside?" Reilly's voice stayed flat, his eyes finally meeting hers for the first time.

"I knew where she kept a spare key." Olivia shifted in her chair, a slight discomfort tugging at her. Not that she had anything to hide, but it felt like she was in the spotlight. She'd been in this situation before, but never for something like this.

"Go on," he prompted, his pen still moving across the page.

"While I was getting ready to leave, the dog ran upstairs to Emily's office. The door was slightly ajar, and when I looked inside, I saw the mess." She gestured toward the phone still in his hands, showing the disheveled office.

"He showed you her office?" Reilly raised an eyebrow, skepticism oozing from his voice.

Olivia's mind raced for a second. *Don't mention Elmer, don't mention Elmer*, she told herself. Keep it together. She wasn't about to complicate things by bringing up a dog that could communicate telepathically. Not now, not with Reilly already suspicious of her.

"Yes," Olivia said firmly. "He ran straight to it and sat by the door. I followed him, and that's when I saw the mess."

"Were the lights on or off?" Reilly asked, his tone still all business.

"They were on."

Reilly scribbled something else, muttering under his breath. "And you're saying this isn't how Ms. Harris normally kept her home?"

"Exactly. Emily was incredibly organized, especially in her office. She would never leave it like that on purpose."

He nodded, his pen tapping against his notepad. "Do you know what Emily was doing that evening before the accident?"

"She mentioned having a therapy session with a client around six p.m.," Olivia replied, her voice cool but the hint of a question still lingering in her mind. "She was supposed to meet with me after that."

"Did you see anyone around her house when you arrived or left?"

"No, no one. The only person I saw was Officer Bennett when he told me about the accident."

And Samuel Carter, Olivia thought, though she didn't add it out loud. She wasn't sure why his presence was still nagging at her. It felt like a piece of a puzzle that hadn't clicked into place yet.

Reilly's eyes narrowed, his gaze shifting with a new level of intensity. "Ms. Morgan, withholding information from law enforcement is a serious offense. You seem to have an opinion about Ms. Harris's death being an accident. Is there something else you're not sharing?"

Olivia swallowed hard, but she didn't back down. "No, nothing else. It's just... doesn't that mess in her office seem suspicious to you?"

"The only thing that seems odd," Reilly said slowly, "is Cassandra Morgan's daughter offering 'new information.' You know your mother was one of the last people to see Emily alive, right? We've heard they had some disagreements."

Olivia's heart skipped a beat, her breath catching in her throat. "What?" Her voice rose, incredulous. "My mom didn't have any issues with Emily!"

Reilly gave her a bored look, not the least bit phased. "That's not what people around town are saying." He slid her phone back across the table. "In my line of work, we see a lot. Sometimes a messy room is pertinent, but most often it's not. Ms. Harris could've just been in a hurry. There's nothing in these images that indicates foul play. However, if you want to send them to me, I'll have someone look into it. In the meantime, I suggest you stay away from Ms. Harris's home."

Olivia felt like the floor had dropped out from beneath her. Was he really implying that her mother might be involved in Emily's death? This was absurd.

Reilly stood up, signaling the end of their conversation. "I'm sorry for your loss, Ms. Morgan. If you come across any additional information, feel free to reach out."

Olivia grabbed her phone and purse, barely managing a stiff nod. "You can see yourself out," Reilly said, pointing down the hall, and disappeared through another door before Olivia could respond.

Back in her Jeep, Olivia sat in silence, a storm of emotions brewing inside her. Frustration, disbelief, and an undeniable determination. Reilly had dismissed her entirely, and even hinted that her mom might be involved in Emily's death. And who were these people spreading rumors about her mom? Sure, her mom had given Emily advice about the tincture, but that hardly qualified as a fight. It was nothing more than a casual conversation.

She gripped the steering wheel tightly, her knuckles turning white. Now, not only did she need to figure out what really happened to Emily, but she had to clear her mother's name. There was no way she was letting this go. As she started up her Jeep, her phone buzzed on the passenger seat. She glanced at the screen and saw a message from her mom.

Mom: *Can you swing by the pharmacy on your way home? Jake managed to cut himself while we were gardening, and we're out of bandages and antiseptic cream. Also, could you grab the vitamin D supplement I like? Oh, and some ibuprofen for Jake—he says my herbal pain remedies don't work as well. Thanks, sweetheart!*

A small smile tugged at Olivia's lips. Even with all her dedication to natural remedies and holistic healing, her mom was never one to impose her choices on others. Growing up, Olivia and Jake had learned about the benefits of chamomile for sleep, ginger for an upset stomach, and lavender for relaxation. But if Jake preferred a quick fix like ibuprofen for pain relief, their mom wouldn't make a fuss. Her motto had always been, "You know your own body best. I'm here to help guide you, but the choice is yours."

Olivia took a deep breath. This errand would be a welcome distraction after the tense meeting at the sheriff's office. Plus, it would give her a chance to keep her eyes and ears open, especially with all the recent whispers surrounding Emily's death.

"All right, Mom. Pharmacy it is."

The Emerald Ridge Pharmacy stood at the corner of Main Street, its familiar neon sign flickering in the soft afternoon light. Inside, the scent of antiseptic mingled with the faint aroma of herbal cough drops. Olivia stepped through the door, greeted by the chime of a bell and the hum of conversation.

Olivia's attention was drawn to the low voices at the counter. A couple of locals—Mrs. Tilly, the town's relentless knitter, and Mr. Hammond, who owned the hardware store—stood talking to Derek, the pharmacist. Derek's usually warm demeanor was absent, replaced by a tense frown that deepened when Emily's name was mentioned.

"It's just such a shock, isn't it?" Mrs. Tilly said, her knitting needles clutched in one hand as if even here, she couldn't bear to put them down. "Emily had so many plans, so much life ahead of her."

Derek's eyes darted from the counter to the small cluster of customers browsing in the aisles. His fingers tapped nervously against the polished wood. "Yes, well, tragic things happen. There's no use in trying to make sense of it now," he said, his tone clipped and final.

Mr. Hammond cleared his throat, shifting on his feet. "It seems suspicious though, don't you think, Derek? I mean, it's a small town, but you never know."

Derek's jaw tensed, and he turned to organize the bottles behind the counter, avoiding eye contact. "No idea, and frankly, it's none of my business. We don't need to stir up more talk around here. Let's just leave it at that," he said, the irritation clear in his voice.

Olivia pretended to browse a display of vitamins, her ears straining to catch every word. Derek's sudden defensiveness struck Olivia as unusual. She couldn't recall a time when he had ever been so short with his customers. The mention of Emily's name seemed to make him squirm, and his outright refusal to engage in any conversation about her was completely out of character for someone who usually thrived on being part of the town's gossip network. Was it discomfort at the reminder of Emily's death, or was there something more?

Mrs. Tilly huffed, exchanging a glance with Mr. Hammond. "Well, I suppose we shouldn't pry," she said, though it was obvious she was disappointed at the lack of information.

Derek finally turned, catching sight of Olivia as she approached the counter with a small smile. His eyes flicked from her to the locals, his expression softening just enough to look polite. "Olivia, what can I do for you?"

"My mom asked me to pick up a few things," Olivia said as she grabbed the requested vitamin D supplement. "I'm pretty sure I still know my way around here, so I think I've got it covered." She offered him what she hoped was a normal smile, one that didn't reveal the fact that she'd been eavesdropping. She noticed the subtle tremor in his hands before he stilled them, taking a deep breath.

"Of course," he replied, nervously rearranging items on the counter. "Just let me know if you need any help." As he turned back to fill orders in the pharmacy, Olivia's mind raced. Derek was acting suspiciously, but she couldn't quite pinpoint why. It was too early to jump to conclusions, and she didn't have enough information yet to claim that Emily's death was anything more than an accident.

The drive back to her mom's house was quiet, punctuated only by the crunch of gravel under the tires and the rustle of leaves in the breeze. As she parked and stepped inside, her mom was waiting at the kitchen table, a cup of tea steaming in front of her.

"Thanks, Livy," her mom said, taking the pharmacy bag from her with a warm smile. "Everything okay?"

"Not great," Olivia said, sitting down across from her mom. "The detective basically dismissed everything and implied you might be involved. Can you believe that?"

Her mom's eyes widened, shock and anger mixing in her expression. "Me? Involved? That's ridiculous."

"I know," Olivia said, her frustration rising again. "But I'm not giving up. There's more to this, and I'm going to figure it out. For Emily. And to clear your name."

Her mom sighed, sitting down beside her. "I appreciate your determination, but you need to be careful. This isn't a game, Olivia."

"I know it's not," Olivia replied, her voice firm. "But someone has to get to the truth. And right now, that someone is me."

They sat in silence for a moment, the weight of the situation heavy between them. Her mind returned to the scene at the pharmacy and Derek's uneasy reaction. It was something she'd file away for later, a thread to tug at when the time was right. The path ahead was unclear, but Olivia knew one thing for certain: she wasn't backing down.

Emily deserved justice, and she would get it—no matter what it took.

Chapter 9

"Liv," her mother sighed, the familiar tone of exasperation in her voice, "you know how people around here talk. And Millie is the one starting all these rumors. There's really nothing to worry about."

Millie Partridge had been a fixture in Emerald Ridge for as long as anyone could remember. With her signature floral dresses, ever-present string of pearls, and a penchant for sipping sweet tea on her porch while eyeing the comings and goings of the entire neighborhood, Millie was the unofficial keeper of the town's secrets. She knew everything—from who argued at the diner that morning to which out-of-towner had parked their car suspiciously close to the hardware store. It was said that if you wanted to know what was happening in Emerald Ridge, you didn't check the newspaper—you checked with Millie. But her information wasn't always accurate; she was prone to exaggeration and piecing together stories from pieces of overheard conversations, spinning them into rumors that often had only a grain of truth. If you weren't careful, your business could become the latest tale told with dramatic flair, whether it was true or not.

Olivia frowned. "I trust you, Mom, but I just need to be sure there wasn't anything between you and Emily that could have made people think you weren't getting along. I need to know everything that happened. It's the only way I can figure this out and make sure your name stays out of it."

Her mother crossed her arms, her gaze thoughtful as she replayed the interactions in her mind. "Emily did stop by a handful of times recently. We had one disagreement for sure—it was about some of those plants she was working with. They're volatile and hard to stabilize. I warned her that if she went ahead with using them, especially if she was planning on mass production, it could be dangerous. The supply chain for some of these plants is also fragile; we could be damaging ecosystems just to keep up. Edward Barnes has been growing some in his greenhouse, but they weren't as potent, nor could he do enough on his own to keep up with any kind of mass-marketed product."

Her mother paused, rubbing her temple as if the memory pained her. "But it was just a disagreement—a difference of opinion, really. By the time she left, we had both calmed down, and I thought that was the end of it. We didn't argue in front of anyone, and as far as I know, no one overheard us. We were here at the house so who could have? I have no idea how people twisted it into anything more."

Olivia nodded slowly, letting the words sink in. "I believe you. It's just strange—I've heard people think you and Emily had a big falling out, or at least that's what the detective suggested everyone's saying. It just doesn't add up."

"It wasn't a falling out," her mother insisted. "But this is a small town, Liv. People hear bits and pieces, and they fill in the blanks with whatever makes for a more dramatic story. A simple disagreement between two people doesn't sell as well as a juicy conflict."

Olivia managed a small smile. "That's probably true." She sighed deeply, frustration brewing beneath her calm exterior. "I feel like there's still more to find at Emily's house. I want to go back and look through her office again, but since I already told the police, and the house is taped off as a crime scene, I'm not sure how to get back in without making things worse."

Her mother pondered for a moment before suggesting, "Maybe you could call Emily's sister, Kate? She's next of kin—maybe the police would allow her access."

"That's a good idea, but Ash told me Kate's out of town right now, helping their parents with Emily's...arrangements." Olivia replied, her voice faltering on the word "arrangements."

Her mother gave her an understanding look. "Well, that was my best suggestion. Follow your gut, Liv. But whatever you do, just be careful. This could be a simple accident, or it could be something much bigger. Either way, don't take any unnecessary risks."

Olivia nodded. "I'll be careful, Mom. I promise."

Her mother glanced at her watch and sighed. "I have a client in ten minutes. I'd better get over to the shop to prepare." With that, she kissed Olivia's cheek and hurried out the back door, leaving Olivia alone in the quiet house.

As soon as the door clicked shut, a wave of determination washed over her. She couldn't sit back and do nothing. Emily deserved the truth, and her mother deserved to have her name cleared. If she couldn't get official access to Emily's house, there was always another way. She remembered the spare key to Emily's porch was in her bag. It wasn't the first time she'd used it, and the urgency of the situation made it clear she needed to use it again.

She grabbed her car keys and headed for the door, looking around to see where Elmer was. Her eyes scanned the space, and she found him, sprawled at the end of the couch, locked in an intense stare-off with Aster. The feline had cunningly claimed one of his favorite toys, holding it hostage beneath her paw like the queen of a very strange kingdom. Olivia watched, amused, as the silent battle of wills unfolded.

Do you want the toy, doggie? Aster's voice dripped with mock innocence, her green eyes sparkling with mischief.

Elmer let out a low, almost mournful woof. *You know I do, cat. We've been over this a thousand times.*

But do you really want it? Aster's tone was teasing, filled with sardonic amusement.

How many different ways can I say yes? Elmer's reply was a desperate plea. *Please, just give me Mousie McSqueakums back. He's my favorite.*

Aster lifted her paw ever so slightly, her claws flexing lazily. *You know cats like mice more than dogs, right?*

Yes, I know. But it's not even a real mouse, Elmer replied with a resigned whine, laying his head down on his paws, his big brown eyes shimmering with melancholy.

Okay, fine. Don't look so pitiful, Aster relented, her tone softening. She released the toy, letting it tumble from the couch to the floor. Elmer pounced immediately, snatching it up in his mouth with a triumphant wag of his tail. Noticing Oliva was watching, he trotted over to her, proudly presenting the toy at her feet.

"Is the kitty being mean to you?" Olivia asked, crouching down to scratch behind his ears. Elmer gave a soft, confirming woof, clearly seeking sympathy.

Aster, watching from her perch, head-butted Olivia's shoulder gently, her green eyes wide with innocent curiosity. Olivia rolled her eyes as she gave Aster a quick scratch. "Be nice to Elmer, okay?"

If cats could roll their eyes, Aster would have done so. Instead, she flopped onto her side and stretched lazily, inviting more attention. Olivia obliged for a moment, then turned her focus back to Elmer.

"Hey, buddy, I'm going to head back to Emily's house for a bit. I want to see if there's anything else we—well, *you*—might need that I forgot."

Elmer let out a mournful whine. *Liar. I have everything I need. Danger, Olivia, take me with you.*

Olivia sighed and replied, "There's nothing dangerous there now, boy. I'll be fine. You can go nap in the loft with Mousie McSqueakums."

No. Take. Me. With. You, Elmer thought, his front paws planted firmly in front of her, sitting tall with an earnest expression that was hard to resist.

"Okay, fine. It won't hurt to take you along," she said, knowing it was pointless to argue. Elmer's tail wagged furiously at his victory. Olivia grabbed her bag, and they headed for the door, Elmer trotting happily beside her.

Suddenly, Elmer barked and sprinted up the stairs. Olivia watched as he clumsily climbed, then carefully tucked Mousie McSqueakums into his bed and draped a blanket over the toy for good measure. He descended the stairs two at a time, his tail wagging in satisfaction.

Ready now, he announced proudly.

Olivia couldn't help but smile. Even with all the intelligence he's shown, Elmer was still very much a young dog at heart. His dedication to Mousie McSqueakums was endearing. They stepped outside, and when Olivia opened the driver's side door, Elmer barreled past her, diving into the passenger seat without hesitation.

He flashed her a doggie grin, his eyes twinkling. *My seat.*

"Fine, fine, it's your seat now," Olivia conceded, though she added, "Unless another human is in the car."

Elmer shot her a reproachful look. *My. Seat.*

Olivia chuckled. "We'll figure this out later," she suggested, knowing full well that arguing with a stubborn dog was futile. With Elmer's head hanging out the window, they backed out of the driveway and headed toward Emily's house.

***

Emily's house loomed in the distance, the yellow police tape fluttering in the wind like a grim flag marking a tragic event. When they reached Emily's house, Olivia parked discreetly and led Elmer through the side gate. They had taped the front of the house off but hadn't taped off the back, so sneaking in this way felt less illegal. She dug around in the bottom of her bag until she located the single key. The key slid into the lock with a soft click, and Olivia pushed the door open cautiously. The stillness inside the house felt suffocating, like a heavy blanket wrapping around her. Elmer's nose twitched as they entered, his senses on high alert, but Olivia knew they needed to move quickly before the creeping unease took hold.

"Let's go see what secrets your office is hiding, Em," Olivia said aloud, a mix of determination and anticipation building within her.

The creak of the staircase echoed through the house as they ascended. The light in Emily's office was still on, casting an eerie glow over the chaotic scene. Olivia hesitated for a moment, her heart pounding, then slowly pushed the door open.

The once-tidy office was still in complete disarray. Dried lavender and chamomile perfumed the air, the calming scents clashing with the sharp, pungent odor of freshly overturned plants. Papers were strewn across the floor like fallen leaves, and drawers hung open, their contents scattered as though someone had rummaged through them in a frenzy.

The wooden floorboards creaked beneath her feet, each sound amplified in the otherwise silent room. Sunlight filtered through the partially drawn curtains, casting a warm, golden light over the wreckage. Emily's antique oak desk—once a symbol of order and calm—was now a testament to chaos. Glass jars of herbs had toppled over, their contents mingling in a colorful tangle on the floor.

The comforting scent Emily's office normally carried that invited calm and focus was now overwhelmed by an unexpected and chaotic mix of aromas. The sharp, peppery bite of crushed rosemary mingled with the earthy scent of sage and the licorice-like sweetness of fennel. The once soothing air had turned heady and oppressive, creating an odd dissonance that made Olivia's nose wrinkle. It was as if the room itself had lost its balance, the peace shattered by the disorder.

A soft rustling drew Olivia's attention to the cracked window. A breeze stirred the lace curtains, carrying the scent of the garden. Despite the sunlight, the draft sent a shiver down her spine. Elmer stood by the door, his eyes scanning the room with a mixture of curiosity and caution.

The room felt heavy with Emily's lingering presence. As Olivia surveyed the space, memories flooded her mind. It was as though the room—or perhaps Emily herself—was trying to guide her toward something, offering answers in its silence.

Near Emily's overturned chair, Olivia spotted a delicate teacup lying on its side. A few drops of dark liquid stained its rim, seeping onto the floor. She crouched down, careful not to touch anything with her bare hands. The teacup was one of Emily's favorites, an heirloom passed down from her great-grandmother. The faint floral scent of the tea Emily loved lingered in the air, a stark contrast to the chaotic herbal aromas now filling the room.

The color of the dark liquid was unusual, yet strangely familiar. Olivia used her shirt to pick up the broken piece of the teacup, bringing it closer to her nose. She definitely recognized the floral scent of Emily's tea, but there was something else—an unfamiliar note mingled with it. The smell reminded her of summer, but she couldn't pinpoint what it was. Whatever had been in Emily's cup before it broke, it was more than just tea.

Olivia placed the piece of teacup back on the floor and stood up, moving closer to the desk. One drawer was slightly ajar, and something caught her eye—the bottom of the drawer was uneven, raised at the back. Using her shirt again to avoid leaving fingerprints, Olivia pulled the drawer open further and discovered a hidden compartment. Inside were two leatherbound journals, each embossed with Emily's initials.

Olivia sank to the floor beside the desk, the leatherbound journal cool and smooth beneath her fingertips. She hesitated, the weight of the moment pressing down on her. The room's chaotic scent seemed to amplify her unease, making her pulse quicken. What secrets lay within those pages? And did she even have the right to look?

She glanced at her hands, then at the journal again. Fingerprints. A sharp pang of anxiety flared up—what if disturbing Emily's belongings made things more complicated? The logical side of her brain reminded her it didn't matter; she was already knee-deep in this. Still, she swallowed hard, heart thudding in her chest as she reached for the first page, careful not to smudge or leave any more traces than necessary.

Emily's delicate handwriting filled the pages—personal reflections, notes on her patients, and detailed accounts of their reactions to the tincture she had been developing. Olivia's fingers hesitated as she turned the pages, a sinking feeling growing in her chest. Emily's words were raw, thoughtful, and filled with an openness that was both familiar and vulnerable. For a moment, Olivia could almost hear Emily's voice in each sentence.

The weight of Emily's words hit Olivia hard. She had always known Emily as a confident and passionate person, someone who was deeply committed to her work. But reading these private notes—seeing the personal doubts and the struggles she hadn't shared with anyone—made Olivia feel the depth of her friend's isolation. She set the journal aside, the feeling of loss pressing against her chest, and opened the second one.

This journal contained meticulous research notes—formulas, diagrams, and descriptions of each ingredient. Emily had been dedicated to her work, and as Olivia scanned the pages, she could almost feel Emily's presence, guiding her through the discoveries.

Realizing these journals might hold the key to the mystery, Olivia carefully placed them in her bag. As she stood, her eyes wandered to the window. Elmer was staring intently at something outside. Curious, Olivia moved to the window and peered out.

Samuel Carter's gray pickup truck was crawling down the street. Panic tightened her chest—had he noticed her Jeep? Quickly, she stuffed the journals into her bag and scanned the room for anything else that might be pertinent, deciding to take Emily's laptop and a few more notebooks. Just as she finished, she saw Samuel's truck disappearing from view.

"Elmer, let's go," Olivia whispered urgently.

They rushed down the stairs and slipped out the back door. The sidewalk seemed to stretch endlessly as they hurried toward the Jeep. Elmer leapt into his seat, and Olivia tossed her bag onto the floorboard. As she rounded the front of the car, her heart sank—the gray truck was coming back, moving deliberately slow.

Panic surged through her. Should she back out quickly and hope for a clean escape, or stay put and hope Samuel didn't notice? She slid into the driver's seat, clenching the steering wheel as Elmer sensed her anxiety and froze beside her.

The truck crept closer. "Just keep going," Olivia muttered, watching the rearview mirror. The truck passed behind her Jeep, but then it stopped and backed up, positioning itself to block her in. A sharp knock on her window jolted her out of her thoughts.

"Hey, Mr. Carter!" Olivia said, forcing a smile. "Is there something I can help you with?"

Samuel's stern gaze cut through her facade, his eyes scanning the inside of Olivia's Jeep with unsettling focus, as if he were looking for something—anything that didn't belong. His eyes lingered over the mess of papers and items scattered across the passenger seat, moving with a practiced, deliberate pace, before briefly flicking toward the back. Olivia's heart skipped a beat, but before he could linger on her bag, Elmer shifted subtly, positioning himself between Samuel and the bulging bag with an almost protective stance, blocking the view. Olivia couldn't help but feel a slight sense of relief.

"Olivia," Samuel finally said, his voice low, as if weighing every word. "Any particular reason you're in this area? I saw some unusual movement in Emily's upstairs window earlier." Olivia's smile faltered, but she did her best to remain composed despite the uncomfortable scrutiny.

Olivia fumbled for words. "Oh, uh, I'm taking care of her dog. We were just picking up some of his toys that he left behind."

Samuel eyed her skeptically. "You know the house is off-limits, right? How did you get in without breaking the tape?"

"I went through the back," Olivia admitted. "There wasn't any tape there."

Samuel grunted, pulling out his phone. "I'm afraid I'll need to call the sheriff. The crime scene has been breached."

Olivia slumped back in her seat, defeated. A few moments later, Samuel returned. "The sheriff will be here soon," he said.

Five minutes later, Sheriff Bennett's patrol car pulled up. Olivia braced herself as the officer approached, looking weary.

"Olivia, what are you doing here?" Bennett asked.

"We were just picking up Elmer's things," Olivia explained.

"You should have contacted us before entering," Bennett said firmly. "I know this is hard but let us handle it."

Olivia nodded. "I'll call next time."

The men gave her stern looks before driving away. As Olivia started the Jeep, Elmer sat up in his seat, wagging his tail.

"Good job, Elmer. Thanks for covering for me," she said, scratching his ears. Elmer's hopeful eyes glistened. *A treat?*

"Sure, you deserve a treat," Olivia chuckled. "What are you thinking?"

Cheeseburger, he replied eagerly.

"Cheeseburger?" Olivia asked, astonished. "How do you even know about that?"

Jake, Elmer said, wagging his tail.

Olivia rolled her eyes. "Of course, Jake would be the one to introduce you to junk food," she said, pulling onto the road. "No promises on the cheeseburger but we will find you an acceptable treat." Elmer seemed satisfied with the compromise.

As they drove home, Olivia's mind raced. The journals and notebooks might finally give her a lead. She wasn't convinced the police were seeing beyond an accident. She needed something solid to prove otherwise.

CHAPTER 10

Back at the house, Olivia rummaged through the kitchen, looking for something Elmer would actually eat. She first offered him a dog biscuit, but he sniffed it, then turned his head away with a look of disdain. She tried again with a handful of dry kibble, but Elmer stared at her as if she were offering him nothing more than cardboard. With a sigh, she finally dug through the fridge and pulled out a piece of leftover roast chicken, adding a little shredded cheese for good measure. This time, Elmer's tail started wagging as he eagerly gobbled it up, clearly much more satisfied with this treat offering.

She then prepared a quick bite for herself, settling on a simple sandwich, feeling oddly disconnected as she ate. It was hard to focus on anything with the weight of everything pressing down on her, the unease in the pit of her stomach growing stronger.

With a sigh, she wiped her hands on a dish towel and headed for the stairs, her gaze drifting to the loft above. It felt like the calm before a storm—the kind where you can almost feel the tension in the air, where you know something big is about to happen but you're not sure what yet. She hesitated for a moment at the bottom of the stairs, the quiet stretching around her like a warning.

The narrow staircase creaked under her weight as she climbed, Elmer's nails clicked rhythmically behind her like a metronome of his excitement. The late afternoon sun streamed through the skylight, casting dappled patterns on the wooden walls and giving the room a warm, golden glow. The atmosphere was cozy, almost deceptive in its serenity.

Olivia dropped her bag, heavy with the weight of Emily's journals and assorted items, onto the bed. The quilt, a thick patchwork of faded colors and memories muffled the thud of the bag hitting the mattress. Elmer, always the ball of energy, made a dramatic leap onto the bed, spinning in circles like a doggy tornado before settling down with a contented sigh. His tail thumped rhythmically against the mattress, providing a steady background beat to the unfolding scene.

Olivia ran a hand through her hair, the tension of the day pressing heavily on her. She took a deep breath and sat on the edge of the bed, feeling the mattress dip slightly under her weight. Elmer immediately nudged his way onto her lap, his warm body a comforting presence. Olivia glanced around the loft, the sunlight casting a tranquil aura over everything, and reached into the bag.

The first journal she pulled out was encased in worn leather, its surface cool and slightly textured beneath her fingertips. The familiar earthy scent that had always been Emily's signature wafted up, mingling with the faint lavender and chamomile that clung to the quilt. She flipped open the cover and started leafing through the pages, each word a fragment of Emily's passion and dedication.

Elmer, sensing her focus, nestled closer, his head resting gently against her leg. The soft hum of the ceiling fan above was a comforting drone, blending harmoniously with the distant chirping of birds outside. It was as if the room itself was wrapping them in a cocoon of calm, a sanctuary where she could piece together the fragments of this puzzle.

As she traced the lines of Emily's handwriting, a mix of anxiety and determination settled over her. The entries spoke of her meticulous observations and intricate research, each note a piece of a larger puzzle. Olivia glanced at Elmer, who looked up at her with his big, trusting eyes, as if he understood the gravity of the moment.

"All right, boy," she murmured, her voice barely rising above a whisper. "Let's see what secrets Emily left for us to uncover."

Elmer gave a soft huff and a gentle wag of his tail. Olivia took another deep breath, allowing the calming scents of the room to settle her nerves. As she delved deeper into Emily's notes, she felt a renewed sense of purpose. The loft, once a place of peace, now became her base of operations, each discovery drawing her closer to the truth about what really happened that fateful night at the Ridge.

The first journal was an ongoing log of Emily's research on the tincture—a project she'd been immersed in for over a year. Knowing Emily, she had probably been contemplating and researching long before that. She was always meticulous, never offering any new herbal treatment to her clients until she was absolutely certain of its safety. Her work was always a meticulous dance between hope and skepticism, and this tincture seemed like it was walking a fine line between herbal remedy and major pharmaceutical breakthrough.

Her early notes were filled with grand hypotheses about the tincture's potential.

Hypothesis: *The combination of herbs in the tincture will facilitate a profound relaxation response in clients, allowing them to access and process deeply buried traumas without the usual defensive barriers. Given the volatile nature of some ingredients, I will need to explore the full spectrum of side effects. My preliminary hypothesis is that while mild physical side effects (e.g., nausea, dizziness) may occur, the psychological benefits will far outweigh these risks, provided the tincture is administered in controlled doses. I theorize that the active compounds in the tincture will interact with specific neurotransmitters, potentially boosting* *serotonin levels and reducing symptoms of anxiety and depression in a significant portion of clients. Regular use of the tincture, when combined with therapy, may result in sustained improvements in mental health, including reduced recurrence of PTSD symptoms and improved overall emotional resilience.*

Reading through her meticulous notes, Olivia realized Emily had dreams far beyond her clinical practice. Her aspirations stretched into a broader vision for the tincture, one that could impact not just her patients but potentially a much wider audience. Her personal thoughts followed:

The brain is such a beautiful and messy space. It has the ability to create things beyond our wildest imaginations, but it can also lock us into our nightmares, preventing many people from living the lives they were meant to live. I dream of a world where people can confront and heal from their traumas without the debilitating fear that often accompanies such journeys. This tincture, I believe, can be a key to unlocking that potential.

My deepest hope is that this tincture will revolutionize the mental health field. If successful, it could provide therapists with a powerful tool to help clients break through their emotional barriers and achieve lasting healing, far more quickly than traditional therapy alone. While not all professionals may agree on its efficacy, those who genuinely care about helping people will. The goal should be to restore lives in the shortest amount of time possible. If this tincture can help me achieve that, I'll have more time to assist others.

I want this to extend beyond just my clinical clients or a small subset of therapists. If it works as I hope, it could benefit veterans, the elderly struggling with dementia, and even the homeless community, offering hope and healing to those who have long been neglected.

After witnessing the cognitive decline of Grandma Lou and working with children in the state system, I've longed to contribute something meaningful to the mental health world. Though I'm not a fan of traditional pharmaceuticals, if this tincture can make a significant impact while remaining organic and properly regulated, it would be worth pursuing. It could pave the way for new, natural treatments for psychological conditions, reducing reliance on synthetic drugs.

More than anything, I want to leave a legacy of compassion and innovation. This tincture isn't just a product; it's a testament to the power of nature and the human spirit to heal and transform. If I can help even one person reclaim their life, all my efforts will have been worth it.

As she read Emily's heartfelt words, tears streamed down her face, leaving watermarks on the pages. Startled, she quickly wiped her eyes, trying not to smudge Emily's notes. Elmer looked up at her with concern, asking, *Are you okay?*

"I'm okay," she reassured him, giving him some gentle pets. "I just miss Emily."

Elmer rested his chin back on her leg with a soft sigh. *Me too* came his silent reply. Emily's words were so quintessentially her—articulate, passionate, and filled with hope. She had never been one for pharmaceutical treatments, often dismissing them as quick fixes with too many side effects. Instead, Emily had spent years delving into herbal remedies with Olivia's mom, absorbing everything she could from the woman who had become a second mentor to her.

Olivia remembered those afternoons in high school when Emily would come over after school, eager to help her mom in the garden or around the house, always asking questions about the different plants and their healing properties. Emily had a genuine curiosity about everything Olivia's mom taught her, her sharp mind soaking up the knowledge like a sponge. From making tinctures and salves to understanding the intricate balance of nature, Emily was fascinated by the idea of natural healing, and Olivia's mom had been more than happy to pass on her wisdom.

The two of them spent hours experimenting with different herbs, often testing combinations to treat everything from headaches to sleep problems. Olivia couldn't count how many times she'd found them in the kitchen, carefully weighing out dried lavender or grinding up fresh ginger for tea blends, all while laughing and sharing stories. At the time, Olivia hadn't understood Emily's deep dive into the world of alternative medicine—it all seemed like a lot of fuss over things that didn't work. But Emily had never been one to follow the status quo. Olivia had felt like a bit of an outsider when it came to their common passion. She didn't share Emily's passion for herbs and potions, and it stung a little to see how easily the two of them connected over something Olivia didn't fully understand. It wasn't that she didn't love her mom—it was just that she often felt like she couldn't quite live up to the shared space they had created.

That's why Olivia had been so surprised when Emily chose to pursue a career that seemed rooted in traditional psychology, a field so intertwined with pharmaceutical treatments. It had felt like a departure from everything Emily had once championed. But as time went on, it became clear Emily had found a way to blend her knowledge of herbal remedies with modern mental health treatment. She wasn't just looking to work within the system—she was determined to revolutionize it. Olivia had to admit, the idea of Emily pushing for a more holistic approach to mental health was both bold and inspiring. Emily's decision made perfect sense now, even if it had surprised Olivia at the time. If anyone could have made this work, it was Emily.

Reading on, Olivia's eyes caught a section dedicated to the starling berry, its name underlined with a flourish, as if Emily had pressed her pen harder with excitement. The entry, dated nearly a year back, outlined the berry's history—both botanical and social. The starling berry was more than just a local legend. It was a point of pride and contention for Emerald Ridge, a town that had both revered and whispered about its unique properties for decades.

Emily's notes described how the berry's deep, inky hue was said to hold powerful healing qualities. It had been an open secret in the community that the starling berry's properties were first discovered by the area's indigenous people, who had long used it in their traditional remedies. However, what caught Olivia's attention was the name that appeared in the margins, circled several times: *Dr. Larry Stevens*.

Dr. Stevens had been the town's revered doctor and scientist-turned-pariah. Emily's scribbles traced the tale of how he had claimed the discovery of the berry's potential benefits, a move that had caused an uproar. While he initially basked in the glory of being the doctor who might revolutionize holistic medicine, the narrative shifted when it emerged that he had taken credit for knowledge shared with him in confidence by the indigenous community. The backlash had been fierce, and Dr. Stevens left Emerald Ridge under a cloud of disgrace.

Emily had written, *It's impossible to talk about the starling berry without acknowledging Dr. Stevens's fall from grace. But it's equally important to remember that the berry's potential doesn't belong to one man's story. The truth deserves to be explored, and this time, with integrity.*

Olivia recalled how Emily had often mentioned Dr. Stevens in their conversations. As a student of Liz Stevens, Emily had learned the basics about Larry Stevens and his involvement with the starling berry, but any time she pressed Liz for more details, Liz would clam up, refusing to talk about it. Emily, ever persistent, had always found Liz's reluctance curious, but she respected the boundaries Liz set.

The journal entry revealed Emily's determination not just to reclaim the berry's reputation but to honor those who had first understood its power. Olivia could almost hear Emily's voice, that spark in her eyes when she was on the brink of a breakthrough. The passion was palpable, filling the room like a warm glow.

A sudden memory surfaced: sitting under the maple tree in Emily's backyard, the scent of crushed starling berries and sun-dappled leaves surrounding them. "It's like the town's best-kept secret," Emily had said, fingers stained purple as she held up a berry. "But secrets never stay buried forever."

Elmer shifted beside her, sensing her agitation. He nudged her with his snout, drawing her out of the spiral of thoughts.

"I'm okay, boy," Olivia said, rubbing his head absently. But the truth was, she wasn't sure she was okay. Emily's notes had just added another layer to a puzzle that was growing more complicated by the minute.

CHAPTER 11

While Emily was away at college, Olivia remembered receiving a slew of passionate rants from her. She'd call, her voice bubbling with frustration, about how everyone was fixated on pharmaceuticals. "Why can't they see?" she'd exclaim. "The Earth has everything we need for healing. We don't need to concoct crazy chemicals!" Olivia often thought how proud her mom would have been to hear her voice those sentiments.

Back in Emerald Ridge, Emily had taken her philosophy into practice, regularly advising her clients on local herbs and natural remedies to supplement their treatments. Some embraced her advice, others did not, but Emily never missed an opportunity to share her knowledge. She was a fervent advocate for nature's medicine, even if it wasn't always well received.

Emily and Olivia had been inseparable since elementary school, a bond forged over shared secrets and countless sleepovers. Back then, Emily was just like any other kid—content with eating sugary snacks, using store-bought lotions, and playing with plastic toys. They were both carefree, basking in the simplicity of their childhoods.

But something changed around the beginning of high school. Emily's mother was diagnosed with a severe illness, a turning point that rocked her world and made her question everything. As her mother underwent treatment, Emily delved into the world of natural remedies, desperate to find alternatives that might help. She became obsessed with the idea that nature held the key to true healing, and that the synthetic world we lived in was slowly poisoning us.

Her transformation was gradual but unmistakable. By sophomore year, she was carrying homemade herbal teas in mason jars and packing her lunches with ingredients from the local farmer's market. She shunned anything processed or artificial, believing that nature offered the best ingredients for our bodies and minds.

In the beginning, her passion was endearing. Olivia admired her dedication to living an organic lifestyle, even if it meant a few extra trips to the co-op or spending weekends concocting her own skincare products. It was a quirky, charming trait that set her apart from the rest, who were content with store-bought solutions and convenience foods.

But in the last few years, Emily's advocacy for natural living had intensified. What was once a gentle encouragement to try organic shampoo had become fervent lectures on the dangers of chemicals and the benefits of natural remedies. She had taken up the mantle of an activist, tirelessly promoting her beliefs to anyone who would listen—and even to those who wouldn't.

Olivia remembered one particular conversation they had over coffee at Perks and Peaks. She was on a tear about the preservatives in common medications, her eyes flashing with the kind of passion that could either inspire or alienate, depending on the listener.

"Do you know what's in those pills?" she asked, leaning forward, her voice low but insistent. "Half of the ingredients are unpronounceable chemicals that do more harm than good. We're poisoning ourselves, Olivia. There are natural alternatives for almost everything. We just need to be willing to seek them out."

Olivia had nodded, sipping her coffee, half-wishing it was something stronger. She supported her friend's ideals, but sometimes her intensity was overwhelming. "I get it, Emily. I really do. But not everyone is ready to switch their entire lifestyle. It's a process."

Emily had sighed, frustration evident in the tight lines around her mouth. "It's just...we're running out of time. People need to wake up. If I don't push, who will?"

Emily had always been relentless, a force of nature who believed in doing what was right, no matter the cost. It was one of the things Olivia admired most about her—the way Emily could stand tall, unwavering, even when everyone else backed down. But that same quality had a sharp edge. There were times when Emily's conviction turned into stubbornness, and her determination became a double-edged sword.

She would challenge anyone who stood in her way, often without considering how far she was pushing. Olivia had watched it happen more than once: a tense board meeting where Emily's passionate speech silenced the room, or a heated conversation where her directness left people shifting uncomfortably, unsure whether to support her or step back.

There were whispers, too, of colleagues who once stood in Emily's corner but had gradually drifted away, unable to keep pace with her relentless pursuit. Olivia sometimes wondered if Emily saw it, the way people slowly retreated, their admiration turned to wariness. It wasn't that Emily didn't care—she did, deeply—but her eyes were always so focused on the bigger picture that she sometimes missed the cracks forming in her relationships.

"Emily," Olivia had once said, half-joking, half-serious, after a particularly fiery community meeting, "you've got to remember that people need to feel like they're in this with you, not just watching you charge ahead."

Emily had laughed, brushing it off with a wave of her hand. "If they can't keep up, maybe they're not meant to."

But Olivia saw the cost, even if Emily refused to. The isolation. The small fractures in trust. The allies turned skeptics. And now, with everything unraveling, Olivia couldn't help but wonder: had Emily's fierce pursuit of the truth finally caught up with her?

But Emily's zeal had also given her a steady stream of critics. People like Derek Collins, the local pharmacist, who tired of her relentless pestering to carry more holistic remedies in the pharmacy. Or Raymond, the diner owner, who was tired of her crusade against non-organic ingredients. And then there were the personal conflicts, like the one with Liz Stevens, her former mentor.

As Olivia delved deeper into Emily's research notes, she couldn't help but feel a pang of guilt. Had she done enough to support Emily? Could she have helped her navigate her battles more effectively? Emily's dedication was undeniable, but her approach had often been confrontational, something that both inspired and provoked.

Now, as Olivia pieced together the fragments of Emily's life and work, she realized that understanding Emily meant understanding her uncompromising commitment to her ideals. It was a commitment that had driven her to great heights but had also, perhaps, led her into dangerous territory. And it was up to her to uncover the truth, no matter how painful it might be.

As Olivia pored over Emily's journal, she saw her evolving views. It was evident she'd started to entertain the idea of pharmacological applications for her tincture, albeit with cautious parameters. The pages detailed her meticulous research, cataloging every plant she considered—where they were sourced from, their therapeutic uses, and potential side effects if not used correctly. Her notes were interspersed with hand-drawn sketches of plants and elaborate formulaic diagrams. She had clearly spent countless hours perfecting her approach, documenting every possible chemical reaction and how slight deviations in ingredients could lead to wildly different effects.

The journal's subsequent pages revealed proposed formulations, including precise measurements and detailed notes on what worked and what didn't. It seemed Emily had been her own guinea pig, testing various concoctions on herself before she deemed them ready for others. The next section was dedicated to her meetings with Edward Barnes, the local botanist. Their discussions on formulation were described with a palpable sense of tension, hinting at spirited debates about whether to distribute the tincture more widely. The passion in Emily's words was almost tangible.

Despite the treasure trove of information, Olivia was still left without a clear motive for why someone might have wanted to harm Emily. She stretched, glancing over at Elmer, who had fallen asleep, drooling contentedly on one of her pillows. The sunset was painting the room in warm hues, and the aroma of something delicious wafted up from downstairs. She was about to set the journal aside and head for the kitchen when she noticed the next section of notes titled, "Case Studies and Patient Feedback."

A flicker of hope sparked. This could be where she might find something useful. Hesitant, she felt a pang of guilt about delving into Emily's patients' personal lives. But Emily had been meticulous about confidentiality. Each patient's identification was coded to maintain privacy. Emily had logged consent forms and documented each patient's experiences with the tincture, including start and end dates. Some patients had stopped using it—marked with end dates—and Olivia assumed this was due to either a lack of efficacy or adverse effects.

The initial entries for most patients showed a standard pattern: everyone started on a low dosage. These early stages revealed minimal effects. It was only when Emily increased the dosages that responses began to diverge. Her notes meticulously tracked dosage adjustments and timelines, though Olivia struggled to discern her rationale for the varying schedules.

The journal was a goldmine of insight into Emily's dedication and the careful experimentation she had conducted. But more than that, it hinted at a deeper complexity in her work—and perhaps, in the motivations of those around her. Olivia took a deep breath, determined to unravel the layers of Emily's research and uncover the truth behind her tragic end.

Realizing Edward Barnes might hold crucial pieces of the tincture puzzle, she decided a visit to him was in order. She rummaged through her nightstand drawer, pulling out a pad of sticky notes and a pen. Scribbling "Timeline?" on one note, she slapped it onto a patient case that seemed to be progressing faster than the others. Emily's journal was a mix of triumph, frustration, and outright dread.

One entry practically sang. "Patient made great strides today! We accessed the root of her core trauma without a single tear or panic attack. She reached out later, saying she felt lighter than she had in years!"

Another was more subdued. "No progress with patient despite increased tincture dosage. No change in trauma access. Patient reports feeling no different."

But some entries were downright chilling. One read, "Patient fell unconscious during the session. Called 911. By the time they arrived, she was conscious, but she was taken for testing. I detailed everything used and ensured her written consent was on file. No follow-up yet."

Another noted, "Patient experienced vivid hallucinations, leading to hyperventilation and a panic attack. Managed to calm her with breathing exercises and water. Kept her in the office until the effects wore off. Patient canceled all appointments later that evening."

Olivia's heart began to thud in her chest as she read the entry. The coded label, "47136LS," felt clinical, and detached, but the details beneath it painted a picture that hit too close to home. She gripped the edge of the desk, feeling a shiver trace down her spine. The entry wasn't just unsettling—it was alarming. Emily had been monitoring someone who seemed to be spiraling, someone stubborn enough to refuse to stop the treatment despite clear signs of distress.

Patient feels the tincture isn't helping, though I've observed otherwise. She's been having vivid memories of her grandfather and childhood, which she doesn't recall having before. She seems agitated. Works in science and has started asking detailed questions about the tincture, which feels a bit unsettling. Reports mood swings, difficulty concentrating, and increased anxiety. Suggested a break from the tincture, but she refused, insisting this is her best progress yet. I'll monitor her closely, and if her condition worsens, I'll halt treatment, regardless of her wishes. Also, her current boyfriend is a patient of mine. I've informed him of her volatile moods and suggested he give her extra space.

The mention of vivid memories, agitation, and mood swings made Olivia's stomach clench. She could almost picture the patient, pacing a room, eyes wild with restless energy, questions tumbling out in rapid succession as they demanded answers. The insistence on continuing despite the risks, the desperation for progress—it all felt uncomfortably familiar, like the stories Emily used to tell after working with certain patients who pushed too hard.

And then, there was the boyfriend. A quiet, icy realization spread through Olivia. Whoever this woman was, she had someone close to her who knew about her volatile state. Did Emily's caution reach him, or had her warning been ignored? The thought of Emily navigating such delicate situations, juggling not just the physical well-being of her patients but their emotional entanglements, made Olivia's chest ache.

As she reread the line "feels a bit unsettling," Olivia's fingers twitched. The words were calm, clinical, but the implication was anything but. Emily must have sensed something deeper was wrong, something more dangerous lurking beneath the surface. The idea that Emily might have been caught in a web spun by this patient or someone close to her made Olivia's pulse quicken.

She took a shaky breath, trying to push down the questions battering her mind. Had this situation boiled over in a way Emily hadn't anticipated? And more importantly, had it come back to haunt her?

That entry was a red flag. It seemed this patient's volatility was severe enough for Emily to involve her boyfriend—a drastic measure for Emily, who usually kept patient matters strictly confidential.

With this new perspective, Olivia felt it was imperative to speak with Edward Barnes to grasp the full extent of the tincture project. Emily had conveniently jotted down his contact details in her notebook. Olivia grabbed her phone and tapped out a quick email to him.

Subject: Request for Meeting Regarding Emily Harris's Tincture Project

Hi Mr. Barnes,

This is Olivia Morgan. I'm one of Emily Harris's best friends. In light of her recent passing, I'm looking into her tincture project and its implications. Emily was incredibly passionate about her work, and I'd like to understand more about it. Could we schedule a meeting to discuss the tincture? My schedule is quite flexible, so please let me know a time that works you.

Looking forward to your response.

Best,

Olivia Morgan

As she hit send, she heard her mom's voice calling from downstairs, "Dinner's ready, everyone!" At the sound of "dinner," Elmer leapt off the bed, practically flying down the stairs. Olivia chuckled at his enthusiasm and set Emily's notebooks aside. As she headed downstairs, she hoped Edward Barnes would get back to her soon. He might hold the key to unraveling the mystery behind Emily's death and the role her tincture played in it.

Olivia descended the stairs, the scent of her mom's famous roasted vegetables filling the air, mingling with the warm, familiar smell of home. Elmer was already waiting at the bottom, tail wagging and eyes wide with anticipation. She reached down to give him a quick scratch behind the ears before making her way to the dining room.

After dinner, Olivia cleared the table absently, her mind still consumed by Emily's notes. The words swirled around in her head, each one raising more questions than answers. She glanced out the window, taking in the soft glow of the evening sky. The summer air was warm and inviting, and the tranquil beauty of the night stirred something inside her. She longed to step outside, to clear her head, if only for a little while.

Elmer, her ever-faithful companion, stretched out on the living room rug, his belly full and his breathing deep and steady. Olivia couldn't bring herself to disturb him. He deserved the rest after all of the emotional support he'd been providing. *I'll go this one alone,* she thought.

"I'm going out for a bit," Olivia called to her mom, her voice carrying easily through the house.

From somewhere in the distance, her mom responded, "Okay, sweetie, be careful."

Olivia nodded to herself, grabbed her bag, and headed for the Jeep. The night air would do her good, she decided. Maybe a walk through downtown—just enough to shake off the weight of the evening—and a quick stop at Perks and Peaks for a coffee would help settle her mind. It was a simple plan, but in that moment, it felt like just what she needed.

The cozy coffee shop was alive with its usual warm buzz. The scent of freshly brewed espresso mingled with the faint sweetness of pastries, and the low hum of conversations added a comforting backdrop. Olivia settled at a corner table, sipping her drink and letting the warmth spread through her, grounding her in the moment.

Just as she felt herself begin to relax, a sudden flurry of movement outside caught her attention. Through the wide front window, she saw a crowd gathering in the town square across the street. The familiar figure of Samuel Carter stood out, his authoritative presence unmistakable even from a distance. A sign above the crowd read: **Town Hall: Conservation Efforts Debate—The Future of the Ridge**.

Curiosity sparked, Olivia leaned forward, her eyes narrowing as she recognized another familiar face—Liz Stevens. The science teacher stood opposite Samuel, arms crossed and eyes sharp, but there was a subtle tension in her posture that Olivia hadn't noticed before. It was as if Liz were trying to hold her ground, but something beneath the surface was giving way.

Olivia's mind raced. She hadn't expected to see Liz involved in a conversation with Samuel Carter, the former sheriff and head of the neighborhood watch. There was always a certain... animosity between the two, though neither had ever said anything outright. Olivia had picked up on it over the years—something about the old guard, the town's history, and the reluctance to change. But this? This exchange felt different. The tone wasn't just casual; it was loaded with something unspoken, a simmering undercurrent of conflict that neither one was willing to back down from.

Unable to resist, Olivia picked up her cup and made her way outside. As she approached the edge of the gathering, the voices became clearer, and she instinctively slowed her pace, staying out of direct sight. She didn't want to be obvious, but she needed to hear more.

"...preserving local traditions is more than just a nostalgic dream," Samuel's voice rang out, commanding and stern. His eyes swept over the crowd before landing on Liz with a pointed intensity, as though he was daring her to challenge him. "It's about maintaining respect for what this town has always stood for."

Olivia could feel the weight of his words—he wasn't just talking about traditions. This was about power, control, and the history that Samuel thought he could dictate. There was an edge in his voice that made her skin prickle. Was this about more than just the town's history?

Liz's expression wavered, just for a second, before she straightened her shoulders. "No one's suggesting we forget our history, Samuel," she replied, her voice steady but strained, like she was choosing her words carefully. "But moving forward means adapting, not staying stuck in the past."

Her reply was sharp, but Olivia caught the subtle catch in Liz's tone—a crack in the armor, a sign that Liz was feeling more pressure than she was letting on. Olivia wondered what had sparked this particular confrontation.

Had something happened between them that she didn't know about? And why was Liz so defensive, when her argument seemed like it should have been a simple point?

A murmur passed through the crowd, a mix of agreement and skepticism. Olivia noticed a few familiar townsfolk exchanging glances, their brows furrowed as they absorbed the charged exchange. Some seemed unsure, while others—those with more history in the town—nodded knowingly, clearly reading between the lines. Samuel's ability to command the room was undeniable, but it was clear that Liz was a force to be reckoned with, too. The way the crowd responded said more than the words ever could.

Olivia's pulse quickened. There was more at play here than she realized. What were these two really fighting over? And, more importantly, what role did Emily's work—and death—have in all of this? Whatever was going on, it was far more complicated than it appeared.

Samuel's lips pressed into a thin line. "Progress shouldn't come at the expense of what's right," he said, each word deliberate. "We've all seen what happens when ambition overshadows respect."

A flicker of unease crossed Liz's face, and for a moment, Olivia could have sworn she saw the slightest hint of fear. "We're straying from the topic," Liz said quickly, her voice tight. "This debate is about preserving the Ridge while ensuring it remains a space for everyone to enjoy."

The crowd shifted, the focus of the conversation moving on to other voices raising questions about trail maintenance and conservation funding. But Olivia's mind stayed with that brief, loaded moment between Samuel and Liz. The way they sparred, the undercurrent of something unsaid, made her wonder.

Why did it feel like this was more than just a community debate? What history did Samuel and Liz share, and what did it have to do with the Ridge?

The evening air felt heavier now, laced with more than just the chill of an approaching night. With her coffee cup forgotten in her hand, Olivia knew one thing for sure—there was more to uncover, and she was just beginning to scratch the surface.

CHAPTER 12

E dward Barnes's reply came faster than Olivia expected, confirming their meeting for the following evening at six p.m. Anticipation buzzed inside her like a low hum, and she decided to clear her head before diving back into Emily's journals. She clipped Elmer's leash on, hoping a run might help sort through the jumbled thoughts swirling in her mind.

Running had never been Olivia's favorite activity—given the choice, she'd likely choose watching paint dry over it. But when her thoughts were tangled like wires, a run in nature offered a reprieve. The trail Olivia chose at the Ridge was one of the quieter paths, a lesser-used loop that meandered through groves of pine and wildflowers. Unlike the steep, treacherous section where Emily had fallen—which was now sealed off with police tape and guarded by warnings—this trail was open, safe, and wrapped in the gentle whispers of rustling leaves.

It had always been a place where she and Emily would walk when they needed to talk without interruption, a place filled with the scent of warm earth and the sound of chirping birds.

As Olivia made her way along the familiar path, the dappled sunlight filtering through the branches above, she felt a small measure of calm settle over her. The trail was peaceful, offering the illusion that everything in Emerald Ridge was as it once was. But with each step, the weight of the investigation and the unanswered questions about Emily's death pressed harder on her, making her wonder if this serene space held any clues she had overlooked before.

It wasn't about finding peace anymore; it was about finding the truth.

Elmer leapt eagerly into the Jeep, his mental chant of *Car ride!* clear in his every movement. His excitement was contagious, easing Olivia's tension just a little. They parked in the small lot reserved for trail-goers, the surrounding trees casting long shadows that danced in the late afternoon light.

"Ready, boy?" Olivia asked, though Elmer's impatient pacing at her feet already answered the question. She started into a light jog, the leash slack in her hand, while Elmer trotted alongside her. His long legs kept pace easily, his gait shifting from a brisk walk to a smooth, eager trot as they moved deeper into the woods.

The path wound through familiar terrain, the earthy smell of damp leaves and pine filling the air. Normally,

the forest brought Olivia a sense of peace, a refuge from everything. But today, something about the stillness felt different—tinged with an unnamable unease. She shook it off, pushing forward, determined to focus on the run.

They crested a hill just below the spot where she and Emily used to meet, a place brimming with shared memories. Olivia stopped, catching her breath, as the air around her seemed to shift. A strange sensation prickled at the back of her neck. Elmer, ever attuned to her emotions, perked up, his ears twitching as his gaze scanned the area.

A rustle of movement caught her attention, but when Olivia looked, she only saw a squirrel scurrying up a nearby tree, indifferent to their presence. Then, suddenly, a disjointed voice hit her ears—Emily's voice. It was faint, like a distant echo, yet unmistakable. Olivia froze, her heart thudding in her chest as the fragmented sounds faded, leaving behind an unsettling silence.

"Find out. Find out." The words echoed in her mind, persistent and eerie, as if Emily was reaching out from the past. Olivia pressed her fingers to her temples, struggling to shake the feeling of confusion and disorientation.

Elmer's cold nose nudged her leg, pulling her back to the present. His wide eyes reflected his concern, asking, *Are you okay?*

"Yeah, buddy, I'm fine," she whispered, though the tremor in her voice betrayed her uncertainty. Elmer, sensing her discomfort, stayed close, his body tensed as if on alert.

Just then, the sharp snap of a twig broke the quiet. Olivia glanced up in time to see a small branch tumble down the hill, landing near her feet. Her eyes darted toward the trees, where the branches swayed as if something—or someone—had just passed through. But there was no one in sight.

A chill ran down her spine. Olivia swallowed hard, the sense of unease now gnawing at her insides. "Let's get out of here," she muttered to Elmer, already feeling the urgency to leave. Elmer seemed to agree, and they quickened their pace, hurrying back to the safety of the Jeep. The woods, once her sanctuary, now felt full of secrets she wasn't ready to uncover.

Back home, the anxiety from the strange encounter lingered. Olivia stood under the hot spray of the shower, hoping the water might wash away the unsettled feeling that clung to her like a second skin. She replayed the events in her mind—the eerie echo of Emily's voice, the rustling branches, the snapping twig. Was it just a coincidence, a random stir of nature? Or had something more sinister been lurking on the trail?

Despite the warmth of the shower, Olivia's heart raced with unanswered questions. How would she ever find peace without knowing the truth? Edward Barnes might have the answers she needed, but until their meeting tomorrow, the mystery would weigh heavily on her.

After drying off, she slipped into her favorite soft shorts and an oversized high school t-shirt, worn to comfort.

She made her way up to the loft where Elmer lay curled on the rug, his beloved Mousie McSqueakums clutched protectively in his paws. The room was dimly lit by the soft glow of a single candle. Olivia flipped off the light, blew out the candle, and smiled at Elmer's expectant gaze.

The pup's big eyes silently asking, *Am I really sleeping on the floor tonight?*

"All right, come on up," Olivia relented, patting the bed beside her. Elmer didn't hesitate, bounding onto the bed with his toy still in his mouth. He circled a few times, finding just the right spot, before flopping down with a contented sigh, his warm body pressed close against hers.

The familiar comfort of the bed and Elmer's presence offered some reprieve from her troubled thoughts. As she nestled into the blankets, the steady rhythm of Elmer's breathing beside her lulled her into a sense of calm, even as her mind buzzed with the mysteries left unsolved. Tomorrow's meeting with Edward Barnes was her best hope for clarity, and she would need every ounce of her focus to uncover the truth.

The next morning, instead of heading to her usual spot at Perks and Peaks, Olivia found herself in the warm, bustling atmosphere of the Miner's Diner. It was the kind of place that hadn't changed in decades, where locals and tourists alike gathered for a hearty breakfast and the latest gossip. If there was any chatter worth hearing, it would be here.

A few of the regulars, seated in their usual booths by the window, nodded or raised a hand in greeting.

"Hey, Liv," called Mr. Thompson from the corner booth, his weathered face lighting up with a smile. He was always there at this hour, sipping his black coffee and reading yesterday's newspaper as if it were today's breaking news.

"Morning, Olivia!" chimed in Marge, the waitress, as she balanced a tray of pancakes and eggs. "Haven't seen you here in a bit."

Olivia returned their greetings with a quick smile and wave, her heart swelling slightly with the comfort of familiarity. Even amidst the uncertainty of everything that had happened, the diner and its regulars were a small reminder that some things stayed the same.

The small town diner had been around for decades, its wooden booths worn but still comfortable, each table a little memory of the past. The place had changed ownership a time or two over the years, but the essence of it had remained the same—the worn checkered floor, the bright yellow and green signs that hung on the walls, and, most importantly, the menu. The rocky road pancakes were still the same, thick and fluffy with gooey marshmallows, crunchy nuts, and ribbons of chocolate swirled through each bite. Olivia smiled to herself. She'd been eating them since she was a little girl, sitting in the same corner booth with her mom and Jake, debating which toppings to add. Every year, without fail, this was the meal she'd request for her birthday—rocky road pancakes, a tradition that never grew old.

Her stomach rumbled in anticipation as she slid into a booth by the window. The pancakes were a treat—one she could always count on, no matter how much had changed around her. The simple, comforting meal felt like a small anchor, a reminder that not everything in this town had moved forward too quickly.

The waitress arrived a few moments later, placing the steaming plate in front of Olivia with a warm smile. The scent of the rocky road pancakes hit her first—sweet, with the faint scent of melting chocolate and the rich aroma of butter that filled the air. The pancakes were stacked high, their golden brown edges just slightly crisp, with gooey pockets of marshmallow peeking out from beneath the soft, fluffy layers. A drizzle of chocolate syrup cascaded over the top, pooling at the bottom of the stack, and a dusting of powdered sugar gave it the perfect finishing touch.

Beside the pancakes, the eggs were perfectly scrambled—light and airy, with just a hint of butter. The bacon, crisped to perfection, had that irresistible salty aroma, slightly charred at the edges but still tender in the center. Olivia could hear the faint sizzle of the bacon and feel the warmth rising from the plate as she picked up her fork, her stomach growling in eager anticipation.

She took a bite of the pancake first, the chocolate and marshmallow melting in her mouth, the sweetness balanced by the lightness of the fluffy batter. It was just as good as she remembered—comforting, familiar, and a little indulgent. She followed it with a bite of the eggs, the smooth creaminess providing the perfect contrast to the richness of the pancakes. Then, a crispy piece of bacon, salty and satisfying, rounded out the bite, leaving her with the comforting feeling of home, the taste of something unchanged.

As she ate, her ears perked up at the low murmur of a conversation from the booth behind her. A group of older men, their voices gravelly from years of hard work, were speaking in hushed tones. One of them, a familiar face, mentioned Emily's accident, saying they had been sent up to the site to check the area and make it safe for hikers again. Olivia's fork paused halfway to her mouth, the sound of her heartbeat rising as she leaned in a little closer, trying to catch every word.

The men, part of the forestry maintenance crew, had seen the aftermath firsthand. Knowing this was enough to pull her focus completely away from her breakfast. Her pancakes, once comforting and nostalgic, now sat untouched, forgotten as she strained to hear more of their conversation.

"It's a shame about that girl," one of the men said, his voice rough with age and disillusionment. "Think it was really an accident?"

Olivia's grip on her fork tightened as she looked down at her food, trying to hide the tension that suddenly crept into her shoulders. She could feel her pulse quicken, but she tried to stay calm, pretending to be absorbed in her plate while her attention was fully on the men.

Raymond Filtch, the diner's owner, shuffled past, his eyes narrowing slightly as he overheard the conversation. He lingered for a moment, arms folded over his chest, before muttering, "You never know. This town ain't as innocent as it used to be."

Olivia's stomach flipped at the cryptic words, the weight of them pressing into her chest. She didn't know if Raymond was just being his usual grumpy self or if there was something more behind his statement, but it didn't matter. What was clear was that something about Emily's death wasn't adding up.

Raymond, with a final glance at the men, retreated into the kitchen, leaving behind an air of suspicion that lingered like smoke. Olivia's appetite evaporated. Her breakfast, which had once been a source of comfort, now seemed like a reminder of the mystery she had to solve. Without another thought, she wrapped the remaining bacon in a napkin for Elmer and paid her bill, her mind buzzing with new possibilities. Every word she overheard made her more certain: nothing about Emily's accident was as simple as it seemed.

As she arrived back home, Elmer greeted her with his usual enthusiasm, his tail wagging furiously as he sniffed the air. His nose twitched in delight when he caught the scent of bacon, and Olivia couldn't help but chuckle as she handed him the treats, one by one. His joy was contagious, and for a brief moment, it brought some comfort to her restless mind.

"I've got a lot to figure out, buddy," Olivia murmured, scratching behind his ears as she set the napkin down for him to finish. With a deep sigh, she walked up to the loft, grabbed her notebook, and started scribbling down every new detail that had emerged. Tomorrow's meeting with Edward Barnes couldn't come soon enough.

CHAPTER 13

The late afternoon light filtered softly through the loft windows, casting long, slanted shadows across the room. Olivia glanced at the clock—five p.m. already. She had lost track of time, her thoughts still spinning from the events of the day. Elmer, always intuitive, sat at her feet, his steady gaze reminding her of the ticking clock.

With a deep breath, Olivia pushed herself up from the cozy chair she had been sitting in, a surge of anticipation rising in her chest. The meeting with Edward Barnes was finally here, and she couldn't afford to be late. She grabbed her bag, her phone, notebook, and Emily's journal in a rush, her mind already racing with the questions she planned to ask. She could feel the weight of the moment, the answers she needed just beyond her reach.

"All right, Elmer," she muttered, as she slid her phone into her pocket, "time to go."

Elmer bounded down the stairs with the kind of enthusiasm only a dog could have. Instead of heading toward the front door, he veered toward the back, tail wagging furiously, eyes fixed on a freshly turned patch of dirt in one of her mother's planters. *Potty?* he asked.

Olivia rushed to open the door. "Okay, but make it quick!" she urged, watching as Elmer leapt into the dirt with the enthusiasm of a child diving into a pile of autumn leaves, completely ignoring her request. He rolled around joyfully, his golden fur quickly turning the color of a dusty wheat field.

"Elmer!" she groaned. "We're going to be late!" He trotted over, thoroughly satisfied, his coat dusted with dirt. Olivia brushed off what she could, fully aware she'd be vacuuming her Jeep later. Elmer beamed up at her, his goofy grin full of pride *Fun!* he said.

"For one of us, maybe," she muttered, unable to hold back a small laugh as Elmer hopped into his seat in the Jeep, ready for their next adventure. Gravel skittered beneath the tires as Olivia reversed quickly and sped off toward Edward Barnes's home.

***

When Olivia pulled up in front of Barnes's property, she felt like she had driven into a botanical wonderland. The house was surrounded by lush greenery, with two large greenhouses standing sentinel on either side. Exotic plants, some unfamiliar, lined the path, and the rich perfume of flowers hung heavily in the air. Behind the house, more greenhouses loomed, each hiding a world of rare flora.

Elmer and Olivia got out of the Jeep and walked up the gravel path. She couldn't help but admire the meticulous arrangement of the plants, each tagged with scientific names and care instructions. The atmosphere felt alive, humming with the quiet energy of nature.

Barnes greeted them at the door with a warm smile, the scent of the garden still lingering around him. "Olivia, Elmer! So glad you could make it," he said, gesturing them inside. Olivia hesitated, realizing she hadn't asked if bringing Elmer was okay.

"Oh, Mr. Barnes, I'm sorry. Is it all right if Elmer joins us? He's been my constant companion lately."

Barnes chuckled. "Of course. Elmer is always welcome here. He was as much a part of Emily's life as any of us." At the sound of his name, Elmer's ears perked up, his tail wagging in approval.

They walked down a long hallway adorned with botanical prints, heading toward the back of the house. Barnes led them to one of the greenhouses. "This is where we did much of our work," he explained as he unlocked the door and let them inside.

The greenhouse was a jungle of vibrant, exotic plants, their lush leaves and bright colors creating an otherworldly scene. Elmer's nose went into overdrive, sniffing every inch of the humid space.

"These plants"—Barnes gestured—"are key to the tincture Emily and I were working on. We sourced flora from all over—Amazonian rainforests, Himalayan mountains, and other remote places. Each one has unique properties, and when combined correctly, they can help individuals confront and heal from deep emotional traumas."

He paused, his fingers brushing over the leaves as though contemplating the plants' potential. "I've been trying to cultivate some of these species myself, but it's been...challenging. I'm struggling to reach the potency levels that the original plants held in their natural environments. The conditions here just aren't the same—it's proving harder than I expected. Still, I'm determined to make it work." He glanced up, eyes briefly meeting Olivia's, a flicker of frustration crossing his face.

Olivia's gaze fell on a plant that looked oddly familiar. "Is that a starling berry bush?" she asked, surprised.

Barnes nodded. "Yes, Stellarubus memoria. It's not as exotic as some of the others, but it has neuroprotective properties. It's great for stress relief and overall brain health. Plus, it tastes good."

Starling berries had been a staple of her childhood, but now, seeing them in the context of this groundbreaking work, they seemed so much more significant.

"What makes these other plants so special?" Olivia asked, running her fingers lightly over the deep purple leaves of a striking vine.

Barnes smiled. "This one is Solus Vine, *Solifera tranquilla*. In small, controlled doses, it can induce vivid, therapeutic visions. The challenge is to balance the effects so patients don't experience hallucinations. It's delicate work, but the results have been promising."

The scientific complexity of Barnes's work was fascinating, though Olivia's mind kept circling back to the strange events she'd experienced. As Elmer nudged her leg and the scent of exotic plants filled the air, she felt a strange mixture of calm and unease. Could this tincture be the key to understanding Emily's death?

They moved into Barnes's lab, a cluttered but functional space filled with vials, notes, and various scientific instruments. The air was thick with the sharp scent of herbs and chemicals. "The potential for mental health treatment is immense," Barnes said, his voice growing serious. "We've seen patients make breakthroughs in a single session—progress that would take years with traditional therapy."

His expression darkened. "But I've been worried lately. Emily mentioned feeling watched, and I've noticed strange occurrences here, too. Plants that were thriving have suddenly withered. Notes have gone missing. I've even found doors left unlocked when I was certain I'd locked them."

A chill ran down Olivia's spine. "Do you think someone's trying to sabotage the project?"

Barnes nodded slowly. "I think it's possible, but I can't think of anyone locally who would have any reason to do something like that."

His brow furrowed as he continued. "There was an actual break-in here last week. The security footage showed a shadowy figure, but we couldn't make out who it was. Whoever it is, they're trying to stop us—or steal our work."

Suddenly, a vibrant parrot swooped down from the rafters and landed on Barnes's shoulder. "Meet Archibald," Barnes said with a chuckle. "He's quite the character."

Archibald eyed Olivia with interest. "Hello, pretty lady! Secrets, secrets!" he squawked, flapping his wings.

Despite the tension, Olivia couldn't help but smile. "Does Archibald know any secrets?"

"Emily! Emily!" the parrot squawked. "Danger! Danger!"

Barnes stroked Archibald's feathers, amused. "He picks up on everything. He was very fond of Emily."

While Barnes delved deeper into the complexities of the tincture, Olivia noticed an odd interaction between Elmer and Archibald. Elmer lay on the floor, casting occasional glances at the parrot, who preened himself on his perch.

Elmer was curious. *Bird must know a lot, seeing everything from up there.*

Archibald cocked his head, his bright eyes narrowing as he observed Elmer. Though he was a talking parrot, Archibald could understand Elmer's thoughts without any effort, just as animals often communicated with each other in ways humans couldn't fully grasp. His voice was loud and clear as he responded, "Doggie looks confused. Emily's gone, doggie sad. Archibald knows things." He puffed out his chest, clearly proud of his insight.

Elmer's ears perked up. *You know things? Like what?*

Archibald fluttered down to a lower perch, closer to Elmer's level. "Emily's secrets, Emily's friends. Watch, listen, learn."

Elmer's gaze widened. *Can you help us find out who hurt her?*

Archibald bobbed his head excitedly. "Yes, yes! Find bad ones! Together, yes!"

Barnes, who had been quietly watching the interaction between the two, looked both amused and slightly uneasy. His gaze flicked from Archibald to Olivia, then back to the parrot. There was something in his expression—a mixture of surprise and a touch of wariness. As if he were trying to decide whether he should find this whole thing endearing or unsettling.

"Is that... normal?" Olivia asked Barnes, raising her eyebrow. Edward cast a gaze at the parrot, "Well, he talks all the time. That's normal." His voice betraying a trace of discomfort, though he quickly masked it with a half-smile. He didn't seem to know how to react to Archibald's cryptic words. "But I'm not sure what he thinks he knows about Emily..."

Olivia chuckled lightly, glancing at the parrot. "Sometimes it's the ones who aren't human that pick up the most important details."

Barnes raised an eyebrow, clearly unsure how to take the conversation. "Right...". He tried to brush off the oddness of the situation, but the way his eyes flicked back to Archibald suggested that he wasn't fully convinced.

Olivia smiled, feeling an unexpected surge of gratitude for Archibald's antics, even as she recognized the way Barnes seemed to be processing the situation—half incredulous, half skeptical.

Barnes quickly turned the conversation back to his explanations and Olivia felt a strange sense of hope. As bizarre as it sounded, if this parrot was as perceptive as he seemed, perhaps he could help unravel the mystery surrounding Emily's death.

Barnes looked up from his notes and met Olivia's gaze, his brows knitted and eyes tinged with worry. His voice, though steady, carried an undercurrent of unease. "Do you really think Emily's death wasn't an accident?"

The question hung in the air between them, heavy and expectant. Olivia felt a chill run down her spine as she searched his face for any sign of disbelief or doubt. She took a deep breath, choosing her words carefully. "I don't know, Edward. But something about it just doesn't add up. Emily was too cautious, too experienced on that trail. It feels...off."

Edward's fingers tightened around the pen in his hand, tapping it anxiously against the edge of the notepad. "I knew she could be intense, always pushing herself and others, but I never imagined it would come to this," he said, a flicker of uncertainty crossing his features.

Olivia nodded, a determined glint in her eyes. "That's what I'm trying to figure out. Whatever it was that led to her being out there that night—it wasn't random."

Barnes's gaze shifted, the hint of curiosity deepening the lines around his eyes. "Be careful, Olivia. Digging up secrets in this town can bring out the worst in people."

"I know," Olivia replied softly, the weight of his words pressing on her. But deep down, she was sure. Emily's death was no accident, and she wouldn't rest until she uncovered the truth.

Olivia shrugged, the weight of uncertainty settling heavily on her. "Too many things don't add up. The more I learn about this tincture, the more I realize how many people might have had a reason to want Emily...silenced." She hesitated, unsure if "silenced" was the right word, but the truth was, she wasn't yet sure if anyone had a motive to kill Emily—or if they simply wanted to get rid of her.

Barnes sighed, his expression turning somber. "If you're right, we need to be careful. Whoever is behind this is dangerous, and they won't stop until they get what they want."

Elmer, ever vigilant, gave a soft bark. *We'll protect you.*

Olivia glanced back at Barnes, considering another thought that just popped up. "Do you think any of this ties into the conservation debate the other day?" she asked, shifting her focus. "I overheard some heated arguments about preserving the land and local flora. Samuel Carter seemed especially invested, which felt strange. I mean I know he's always been invested in all things Emerald Ridge, but I can't ever remember him being especially interested in conservation or plants."

Barnes's expression darkened, the lines on his face deepening as he let out a heavy sigh. "Conservation has always been more than just a discussion about nature here. It's about control—control over the land, resources, and the stories we tell. The starling berry, for example, is more than just a plant; it's woven into the town's legacy. And really all those things lead to power."

"Power?" Olivia echoed, tilting her head in curiosity. She reached out and ran her fingers over the familiar leaves of the starling berry bush, the memory of childhood treks with Emily coming to mind. They'd always pick berries, their hands stained purple as they giggled and dreamed about wild, impossible futures.

Barnes nodded, his eyes catching the flicker of recognition in Olivia's expression. "Exactly. That power is what people like Samuel Carter and even Liz Stevens care about. It's not just about the berries' properties; it's about what they represent. Dr. Stevens, Liz's grandfather, claimed the discovery as his, but the truth runs deeper. The Indigenous communities knew the starling berry's potential long before any so-called 'pioneering scientist' ever set foot here. It's a symbol, and symbols are worth fighting over—sometimes at any cost."

The mention of Liz made Olivia's chest tighten. She remembered Emily's excitement when she first spoke about the starling berry's potential for the tincture. It wasn't just another ingredient to Emily; it was the key to her vision of holistic healing. Olivia's mind flashed back to the way Emily's eyes would light up, her voice speeding up as she shared her latest findings, not caring if Olivia fully understood or not. It had been one of the many times Emily's passion made her seem larger than life.

"But why now?" Olivia pressed. "Why would tensions over something like this lead to—" she swallowed, the words catching in her throat. "To what happened to Emily?"

Barnes glanced around, as if confirming they were alone. "Because now, more than ever, people know that whoever controls the starling berry controls a lucrative opportunity. Emily's research could have upended the entire pharmaceutical market if she proved what she was onto. But she also stirred old wounds—Liz has a family legacy that she's always been so determined to reclaim."

Olivia's pulse quickened, this just added more pieces to the puzzle surrounding Emily's death. The pieces weren't falling into place but leaving jagged gaps that refused to connect. She sensed the layers of the town's quiet history, now disturbed and shifting beneath the surface. As Elmer's ears twitched and he cast a glance toward the greenhouse door, Olivia knew one thing: this was just the beginning. The deeper she dug, the more tangled this story became.

And in Emerald Ridge, stories weren't just told; they were guarded.

As Olivia and Elmer stepped away from Barnes's home, a chill crept over her, despite the warmth of the evening air The world seemed quieter now, as though the weight of what she'd just learned had shifted the air around her. Every step she took felt heavier, the path ahead lined with uncertainty and potential danger. But even as doubt whispered at the edges of her mind, there was no turning back. For Emily's sake, she wouldn't back down.

She glanced at Elmer, who walked beside her, his head held high, and for a moment, she felt a surprising sense of comfort from his presence. It was as though he had been with her forever, though he'd only been around for a few days. In that short time, he had become her steadfast companion, offering a quiet, unwavering loyalty that was more familiar than she could have imagined. His simple, trusting nature seemed to steady her, guiding her through the whirlwind of thoughts and emotions that had been swirling in her mind.

With Archibald's cryptic words, Barnes's troubled revelations, and the nagging feeling that more secrets were hidden beneath the surface, Olivia knew the road ahead wouldn't be easy. But as she looked toward the horizon, determination welled up inside her. Together with Elmer, Archibald, and Barnes, she was resolved to uncover the truth—no matter how dark and winding the path became.

CHAPTER 14

Leaving Edward Barnes's house, Olivia was weighed down by more questions than answers. Her mind was a whirlwind of thoughts, but she tried to push them aside as she drove, her knuckles gripping the steering wheel a little too tightly. Elmer, ever the companion, occasionally glanced up at her from the passenger seat, his wide eyes filled with unspoken curiosity. *What now?* his gaze seemed to ask.

The silence stretched between them, only broken by the occasional hum of the engine. Olivia barely noticed the road, lost in the puzzle she was trying to piece together. Then—*pop!* A loud noise jolted her back to the present. The Jeep sputtered, its engine jerking as the dashboard lit up with warning indicators, flashing in frantic succession. Elmer's ears pricked up, his tail freezing mid-sway as he sensed something was wrong.

"It's fine, I got this," Olivia muttered under her breath, trying to reassure both Elmer and herself, though she wasn't sure she believed it. The car had never made a sound like that before. She gripped the wheel tighter, her eyes scanning the dashboard, willing the engine to keep going. But, deep down, she knew something wasn't right.

Luckily, a familiar landmark appeared up ahead—the Ridgeway Garage. Relief flooded through her, and she focused on coasting the Jeep as smoothly as possible. If she could just get there, even though the garage was probably closed for the night, it would be a safe place to leave the car until morning. With a final groan of protest, the Jeep lurched forward, and Olivia steered it into the lot.

She yanked the emergency brake just as the engine sputtered its last breath, the Jeep coming to a halt just inches from the shop's front door. The lot was dark, the garage itself closed for the night, and Olivia sighed in frustration. "Great," she muttered to herself, reaching down to rummage through her bag for her phone.

Before she could get a grip on the situation, a sharp knock on her window startled her, and she slammed her head against the steering wheel with a yelp. Rubbing the sore spot on her forehead, she looked up to see Noah standing outside.

She blinked, still a little disoriented, and fumbled to open the door manually, the electric windows now useless. "Noah! What are you doing here?" she asked, her voice flustered as she tried to recover her composure.

Noah scratched the back of his neck, glancing away for a moment, clearly unsure of how to respond. "I, uh, work here. Actually, I own the place now."

Olivia's eyebrows shot up in surprise. "Really? That's great!"

"Yeah," he said, a small, proud smile tugging at the corners of his mouth. "Old man Wrigley sold it to me before he passed. Said it only made sense to leave it to the best mechanic in town."

Olivia smiled, sharing in his pride for a moment before Noah gestured toward the Jeep. "Looks like you're having some car trouble."

She nodded, feeling a knot of frustration twist in her stomach. "Yeah, I was coming back from Edward Barnes's place when it made this loud popping noise, and then all the lights came on. It sputtered and just...died."

Noah frowned, his brow furrowing as he thought it over. "That doesn't sound good. I can't take a look at it tonight, but if you leave it here, I'll check it out first thing in the morning. Same number?"

"Yeah, it hasn't changed." Olivia let out a soft laugh, trying to ease the tension, but the silence that followed felt heavy and awkward. She was the first to break it. "I should probably call someone to pick me and Elmer up."

Noah hesitated for a moment, then blurted out, "I can drive you home, if you want. It's no trouble."

Olivia blinked, surprised by the offer. "I don't want to be a burden. I know you live on the other side of town."

"You're not a burden," he cut in quickly, almost too quickly. "I'll grab my truck. Give me a sec." He disappeared around the corner of the building before she could respond.

Olivia watched him go, her lips curving into a small smile despite herself. Elmer, sensing the shift in her mood, wagged his tail excitedly, eyes bright with anticipation. "Looks like we've got a ride, buddy," Olivia whispered to him. Elmer woofed softly in agreement.

A few minutes later, Noah returned in his old but dependable truck. Olivia climbed in, squeezing onto the bench seat beside him. Elmer immediately claimed the passenger window, his head sticking out to catch the breeze, his ears flapping in the wind. The truck creaked as they settled in, and the drive started off in comfortable silence, the winding mountain road bathed in the dimming twilight.

"So, what were you doing at Barnes's place?" Noah asked, breaking the silence. His voice was casual, but there was a subtle edge of curiosity behind it. "With all the police activity around town lately, people are starting to talk."

Olivia hesitated, her fingers tightening around the seatbelt as she looked out the window, unsure how much to share. She had a feeling Noah already knew more than he was letting on. "I was following up on some things about Emily," she said, her voice as neutral as she could manage, though her stomach tightened with the weight of the truth she wasn't yet ready to reveal.

Noah nodded, his expression softening with sympathy. "Yeah, I heard about Emily. I'm sorry. She was a good person." His words hung in the air, filled with a sincerity that made Olivia's chest tighten. He didn't say more, but the unspoken understanding between them was clear. Emily had touched both their lives in ways words couldn't fully capture.

Their eyes met for a brief moment, and in that fleeting exchange, a flood of memories rushed through Olivia—her and Emily in high school, the late-night talks, the hikes, and all the unspoken things they'd never said to each other. Noah's presence beside her seemed to anchor her to the present, but the past lingered, both comforting and haunting. Olivia looked away first, focusing on the winding road ahead, trying to steady her breath and the rising lump in her throat.

She needed to change the subject, needed to find a way to ground herself again. "Do you remember how she used to drag us all up to the Ridge for those weekend hikes?" Olivia asked, her voice softening with the warmth of the memory. A small smile tugged at her lips, a rare moment of nostalgia breaking through the haze of her grief. "She was always so enthusiastic about nature. No one could ever say no to her when she got that look in her eyes."

Noah chuckled softly, the sound familiar and comforting. "Yeah, and those weird trail mix blends she'd make us eat. 'Best snack for the trail,' she'd always say. Peanut butter chips, almonds, pretzels...it was like she threw in whatever she had left in the cupboard. But we ate it anyway." His laugh faded into a smile, his gaze softening as they both shared in the memory of simpler times.

They both laughed together, the banter easing the tension that had built between them. The warmth of the moment, the lighthearted exchange, seemed to fill the space in the truck, washing away the heaviness of the day, if only for a moment. And for just a split second, it was as if the years hadn't passed—like they were back on those hikes, as carefree as they had been when the world hadn't been quite so complicated.

As Noah turned onto the road leading to Olivia's house, the truck jostled over the uneven gravel, causing Olivia to steady herself by reaching out—and accidentally landing her hand on his leg. She froze, her cheeks flushing with heat as she quickly pulled her hand back. Noah glanced at her, then back at the road, a smile tugging at the corner of his mouth.

"Well, here we are," he said, pulling to a stop in front of her house.

Olivia nodded, flustered. "Yeah, thanks again, Noah. I appreciate it."

"No problem," he replied, giving her a small, sincere smile. "I'll take a look at the Jeep first thing tomorrow and give you a call." He hesitated, his voice dropping a little. "If you hear anything strange about Emily's case or need help, let me know, okay?"

She smiled, grateful for his sincerity. "I will, and the same goes for you."

Noah paused, his eyes locking with hers for a moment before he spoke again, the weight of his words clear in his expression. "Liv...Sarah was seeing Emily for some counseling. This whole thing with her has really shaken her up."

Olivia's heart sank at the mention of Sarah. She'd always known Noah's little sister as the bright, energetic girl she had been, but she'd heard whispers about her struggles lately. Emily had been helping Sarah through some difficult times, and the loss now felt even more personal.

"I didn't know," Olivia said softly. "I'm so sorry, Noah. If Sarah ever needs someone to talk to, she can reach out to me. I'm here."

"Thanks," he said quietly, his smile small but grateful. "I'll let her know." He gave her one last look, then glanced back at the road. "Take care of yourself, all right?"

"I will," Olivia promised, giving him one last look before stepping out of the truck.

CHAPTER 15

Olivia pushed the front door open and spotted her mom sitting on the couch, reading glasses perched on her nose as she sipped a steaming cup of tea. "Kind of late, isn't it?" her mom asked, raising an eyebrow. "Your meeting was at six, and now it's almost ten."

Elmer trotted off, his nails clicking against the hardwood floor, making a beeline for his food bowl. Olivia ran her hand through her hair, feeling the weight of the evening's stress. "Yeah, the meeting ended a while ago, but my Jeep started acting up. I had to take it to the garage."

A flicker of concern crossed her mom's face. "Oh no! You should have called me. Wait—if your Jeep's still there, how did you get here?"

Olivia hesitated, not wanting to get into too much detail about Noah. "Uh, turns out Noah works at the garage now. He was there when I pulled in and offered to drive Elmer and me home."

Her mom's expression shifted into something playful, a knowing smile creeping across her lips. "Well, wasn't that nice of him?"

"Yeah, it was," Olivia admitted, though she tried to downplay it. Her mom continued to give her that teasing look, and Olivia sighed, exasperated. "Quit looking at me like that! He was just being nice, that's all."

"Whatever you say," her mom chuckled, turning back to her tea and book. "There are leftovers from dinner in the fridge if you're hungry. Elmer's food bowl is already taken care of."

"Thanks, Mom." Olivia dropped her bag by the door and wandered into the kitchen, pulling a plate from the cabinet and rifling through the fridge. She found the leftover roasted chicken, a few herb-crusted potatoes, and a container of buttered green beans—all lovingly packed into glass containers. She scooped generous portions onto her plate, piling up slices of chicken, a couple of crispy potatoes, and a handful of beans before popping it into the microwave. As she waited for it to heat, the comforting aroma began to fill the kitchen, and she leaned against the counter, momentarily lost in thought. The warmth of home and the simple, familiar meal was grounding, giving her a small but needed sense of stability.

Once her food was ready, she sat at the kitchen table with her plate and a glass of water. The quiet of the house wrapped around her like a blanket, giving her room to think about Noah and the unexpected stir of emotions the evening had brought. She couldn't help but smile, remembering their shared memories from high school, the laughter, and the easy camaraderie they used to have. And now, there was something more—a spark she hadn't expected. Would reconnecting with him be a complication or a source of comfort amidst the chaos surrounding Emily's death?

Finishing her meal, Olivia rinsed her plate and left it in the sink. The living room was now empty; her mom had retired for the night, and the curtain around her space was drawn. With a sigh, Olivia grabbed her bag and trudged upstairs to the loft, exhaustion settling in from the day's events. Elmer lay sprawled contentedly on the rug beside the bed.

"Good dinner?" Olivia asked, smiling as he responded with a sleepy, *Yum.*

She quickly changed into pajamas, too tired for her usual bedtime routine. As she climbed into bed, she patted the space beside her. "Come on, Elmer," she called softly. With a wagging tail, he jumped onto the bed, pouncing playfully before flopping down beside her.

"What now?" she asked as Elmer nudged her arm persistently.

Friend? Man friend? he asked with an innocent gleam in his eyes.

Olivia rolled her eyes, feeling a blush creep up her neck. "You mean Noah? Yes, he's an old friend. We can trust him. Now go to sleep."

Elmer gave her a knowing look before circling a few times and settling down. *More than a friend,* he murmured sleepily, satisfied that he had uncovered something important.

Olivia groaned into her pillow. "First Mom, now Elmer. I can't win."

***

The next morning, Olivia was jolted awake by the sound of her phone ringing. Groggy, she fumbled for it on the nightstand. "Hello?" she croaked.

"Hey, Liv, it's Noah," came Noah's overly cheerful voice. "Sorry, did I wake you?"

Olivia cleared her throat, trying to sound more awake. "No, no, you didn't."

Noah chuckled. "You're still a terrible liar."

She rolled her eyes, grateful he couldn't see her. "What's up?"

"I took a look at your Jeep," Noah explained. "Your fuel pump's shot. I can fix it, but it'll take most of the day. I'll give you a call this afternoon when it's ready."

"That sounds great, thanks again, Noah."

"All right, see you later," Noah said before hanging up.

Olivia rolled out of bed and headed for the shower, leaving Elmer still sprawled out in a deep sleep. After getting ready, she fed Elmer and let him outside to run around while she made herself a cup of coffee. She took her notebook and coffee out to the porch swing, where she could watch Elmer zoom around the garden with his usual morning energy.

Flipping open her notebook, Olivia stared at the list of suspects that she had started writing down, tapping her pen in frustration. No one on her list stood out really, she had just listed out the people that might have had any bad blood with Emily. There had to be more to this. Her gut told her she was missing something, but what?

With a sigh, she called Elmer back inside and climbed up to the loft, where she rummaged through the pile of items she had taken from Emily's office. She pulled out another one of the journals, and flipping it open, she realized it Emily's personal journal. She sat down on the rug, Elmer now curled up on his bed, watching her closely. Combing through the pages, Olivia felt the familiar pang of loss as she read Emily's handwriting.

Most of the entries were mundane—details about work, food, and her latest organic experiments. But then she stumbled upon a smudged entry from two months ago, the ink streaked with what looked like dried tears.

Matt broke up with me today. Out of nowhere. I had no idea anything was wrong. He said my 'intensity' was too much for him. I've been focused on the tincture and Elmer, but I was still making time for him. He couldn't handle me being passionate about my work, I guess. He's a park ranger, maybe he just doesn't get it. I thought he might be the one...but I guess not. I have clients all day, and I'm going to be a mess. I should apologize to them. Maybe I'll drink some wine tonight...not organic, but my body will have to cope.

Olivia read the entry twice, frowning. Emily had mentioned the breakup, but she hadn't seemed this upset when they'd spoken. Maybe there was more to it than Emily let on. Could Matt have something to do with her death? Olivia made a note to speak with him.

Continuing through the journal, another entry two weeks later caught her eye:

Matt showed up drunk tonight. Or something was off. He forced his way inside, saying he needed to talk. I had to hold Elmer back. He ranted about me being paranoid, too wrapped up in my work to be a good partner. I called the cops, but he left before they arrived. I hope they caught him.

Olivia's pulse quickened. This was more than just a breakup. Maybe Matt had a grudge against Emily, something worth investigating. As her mind spun with possibilities, her phone buzzed. It was Noah.

"Hey, Liv. The Jeep's ready to go whenever you are."

"Great, I'll see if someone can drop me off," Olivia replied, already planning her next move.

After a quick conversation with her brother, they were on their way to the garage. The silence between them was comfortable, but Olivia couldn't help but feel the weight of the new information from Emily's journal pressing on her mind. It was like something was just out of reach, like a word on the tip of her tongue. She needed to figure it out—she needed to get to the bottom of it.

The hum of the engine was a steady companion as they drove, the cool air coming through the window mixing with the soft scent of pine from the trees that lined the road. Her mind kept spinning in circles, processing the details she'd uncovered. Emily's notes had been filled with urgency, hints of something darker lurking behind the surface. And the idea that someone might have been after Emily...well, that was a whole new level of concern.

Jake broke the silence, his voice soft but steady as he glanced over at Olivia, his brow furrowing slightly. "Sarah's been really upset about Emily," he said, his tone careful. "She kept saying people had it out for her. Thought you might want to know."

Olivia raised an eyebrow, surprised by the mention of Sarah. Jake and Sarah had always gotten along, though they hadn't been as close as Olivia and Noah had once been. Sarah, Noah's younger sister, had always been the lively one—full of energy, a bit of a troublemaker at times. Her heart tightened at the thought that Emily's death could have hit her so hard.

Jake glanced at her again, clearly concerned. "She was pretty shaken up when I saw her last week," he continued. "She kept saying someone was after Emily, even before the accident. It sounded like more than just a hunch."

The words hit Olivia like a slap in the face. Her chest tightened, a heavy weight settling in her stomach. The air around her seemed to grow thinner, and she had to swallow hard to push past the lump in her throat. *Had*

Emily confided in Sarah? If so, why hadn't Sarah said anything sooner? She felt a wave of unease wash over her, each new piece of information adding to the storm brewing inside her. The idea that Emily might have been targeted wasn't just a theory anymore—it was becoming all too real. And with it, the fear that her own search for the truth could be putting her in danger.

"Thanks, Jake," Olivia said, trying to keep her voice even, though her heart was pounding in her chest. Her mind was racing, the puzzle pieces scattered everywhere. She couldn't stop now. *I have to keep digging.*

When they arrived at the garage, Noah greeted her with his usual warm smile, but there was something different about the way he handed her the keys—like he knew something she didn't.

"All set," he said, his tone professional but laced with a hint of concern.

Olivia felt a wave of relief wash over her, and she took the keys, grateful for his help. The Jeep was still in one piece, and for the first time in hours, her nerves settled just a little.

Noah's voice cut through her thoughts. "Liv," he said cautiously, his expression shifting from friendly to serious. "I just want you to be careful, okay? I know you're determined to find the truth but promise me you'll watch your back." He hesitated, his eyes flicking to the side before returning to hers. "The, uh, damage to your fuel pump didn't look...normal. I'm concerned someone may have tampered with it."

The news hit Olivia like a ton of bricks. She'd known that Emily's death had a dark side to it, but the thought that someone might have deliberately tried to hurt her—*tried to hurt her*—was a cold, hard reality she hadn't fully grasped until now. It was one thing to be cautious. It was another to face the possibility that someone had meant her harm.

Noah's protectiveness sent a rush of warmth through her, and for a brief moment, Olivia felt her heart flutter, the mix of gratitude and something deeper catching her off guard. "I will," she assured him, her voice more steady than she felt. "But I can handle myself, Noah. I've learned a lot through all of this." She said it with more confidence than she truly had, but she had to convince herself of it.

He nodded, but his gaze didn't soften. It was filled with that quiet concern that made Olivia's chest tighten. "I know you're strong," he said, his voice firm but gentle, "but that doesn't mean you have to do it alone. If you ever feel overwhelmed, just call me, all right?"

Olivia met his eyes, and in that moment, she saw the sincerity there, the quiet promise of support. "I appreciate that, really. It means a lot to know you're looking out for me," she replied, her voice catching slightly. There was something deeper there, something she couldn't quite name, but it was enough to stir something inside her.

"Always," Noah said softly, his expression earnest, his gaze not leaving hers. "Just remember, I'm here for you. Whatever you need."

As she got into the Jeep and drove away, the engine humming steadily beneath her, Olivia couldn't shake the feeling that the puzzle pieces were slowly starting to fall into place. But with each new detail, the stakes kept rising. She had more questions than ever, and the more she uncovered, the more she realized how dangerous it might be to keep digging. But she couldn't stop now.

For Emily.

For the truth.

CHAPTER 16

The sky hung low and overcast, perfectly mirroring the somber mood that settled over the small cemetery. Olivia stood on the outskirts of the crowd, feeling disconnected from the faces she had known all her life. Familiar, yet now they felt distant—strangers, enemies, suspects. Trust had become a fragile concept, slipping further from her grasp with each passing day.

Emily's funeral was a quiet affair, set in a quaint cemetery just outside of town, nestled among ancient oaks whose gnarled branches stretched like solemn sentinels. The crowd gathered was a testament to how deeply Emily had touched Emerald Ridge. Friends, family, and clients came to pay their respects, their grief a shared weight. But Olivia could only focus on the uncomfortable knot in her chest, a gnawing unease that had taken root.

Elmer sat beside her, his warm presence a small comfort amid the overwhelming sadness. He was unusually quiet, his expressive eyes reflecting an understanding that seemed too profound for a dog. His head rested gently on her foot, as if grounding her to the present. The minister's voice droned on, blending with the soft rustling of leaves and the occasional sniffle from the crowd. "We gather today to honor the life of Emily Harris, a healer, a friend…"

Olivia's eyes scanned the crowd, searching for something—or someone—that didn't belong. The voices and laughter around her seemed hollow, masking a tension she couldn't quite pinpoint. Maybe it was the way certain people avoided eye contact or how whispered conversations hushed as she walked by. The air was thick with something unsaid, like a shared secret everyone knew except her.

Her mind flickered back to snippets of gossip she'd heard over the past few days, subtle shifts in behavior, and the guarded expressions of people she thought she knew. The unease wasn't just paranoia; it was a warning bell, a silent alarm that something was wrong—something beyond the tragic loss of Emily. The scent of fresh earth mingled with the bittersweet aroma of flowers that adorned Emily's casket—white lilies and daisies, her favorites. The sight tugged at Olivia's heart, reminding her of their coffee dates at Perks and Peaks, Emily's laughter always filling the space. But now, Emily was gone, and the world felt emptier for it.

Elmer nudged her leg with his nose, his dark eyes questioning, asking, *Is everything okay?* Olivia offered a faint smile and patted his head, but her mind was miles away, tangled in the mystery of Emily's death and the pieces that still didn't make sense.

A gentle touch on her arm startled her, and she turned to see Noah standing beside her. His presence was steady, a small comfort amid the sorrow. "You holding up?" he asked in a low murmur.

"As much as I can," she replied, managing a weak smile. "Thanks for being here."

"Wouldn't be anywhere else," he said, his hand resting briefly on Elmer's head. "He looks just as heartbroken as the rest of us."

Olivia nodded, knowing Noah was right. Elmer had been Emily's companion as much as hers, and the dog's grief was palpable. "Dogs know more than we give them credit for," she said softly, glancing at Elmer, who gave Noah a gentle nudge of acknowledgment.

The silence between them grew thick with unspoken words. Noah's sister, Sarah, had been one of Emily's clients, and the loss had hit her hard. Sarah was attending the funeral with Noah, her eyes red and her posture stiff with grief. The weight of the loss was evident in the way she clung to him, seeking comfort in the only family she had left. Emily had been helping Sarah through some tough times, and now, without her, the rawness of that absence was even more painful. Noah, ever the protective older brother, was carrying the weight of his sister's pain along with his own, doing his best to hold it all together, though Olivia could tell it wasn't easy. There was history between him and Olivia—complicated and unresolved—but now wasn't the time to unpack it. Still, his presence meant more than Olivia could express.

As the minister concluded, people began to step forward to place flowers on the casket and share their memories. Olivia watched as the high school science teacher Liz Stevens approached with a bouquet of wildflowers. Her face was somber, but something about her expression didn't sit right with Olivia. Guilt? Or was it Olivia's paranoia looking for answers in the wrong places? Liz's name had been mentioned in the conversations swirling around Emily's death, but mostly because she had been a mentor to her. But there was something about her presence, the way she carried herself at the funeral, that made the hairs on the back of Olivia's neck stand up.

A shiver ran down her spine as she surveyed the crowd. Somewhere among them could be the person responsible for Emily's death. The thought made her stomach churn. She turned to Elmer, who pressed closer against her leg, sensing her distress.

The silence around them was heavy, broken only by the soft murmur of people sharing their thoughts or memories of Emily as they laid flowers on her casket. Some spoke quietly, others with more emotion, but all of them seemed to carry the weight of her loss in their own way. Olivia stood beside Noah, feeling a deep ache in her chest. She wanted to say something, to offer her own words, but the weight of the moment was too much. Her mind raced with memories of Emily, but they all felt tangled and too big to express in front of everyone.

Noah, sensing her hesitation, turned to her, his voice soft but steady. "Do you want to say something?"

Olivia swallowed hard, feeling the lump in her throat grow. She shook her head, unsure how to begin. "I don't know if I can," she whispered, her voice tight with emotion.

Noah nodded, understanding. He glanced toward the others who had spoken, then back to her. "It might help. She meant a lot to you."

Taking a deep breath, Olivia stepped forward. The crowd blurred around her as she approached the casket, placing a single white daisy on the lid. Her hand trembled as she turned to face the gathering. "Emily was more than a friend," she began, her voice cracking. "She was a confidante, a healer, and someone who always saw the best in people. She dedicated her life to helping others, to making the world a better place."

Her gaze swept over the faces, lingering on Liz for a heartbeat. "Emily believed in the power of nature to heal. Her work held so much promise. I just hope we can continue her legacy and find the truth about what happened to her."

A murmur spread through the crowd and Olivia could feel the ripple of unease. Most didn't know there were questions surrounding Emily's death, but now they did.

As she stepped back, her eyes met Liz's again. The tension between them was palpable, and Olivia couldn't shake the feeling that Liz knew more than she was letting on.

After the service, Olivia found herself standing next to Millie Partridge, who dabbed at her eyes with a lace handkerchief. "Such a tragedy, isn't it, dear?" Millie said, her voice thick with emotion. "Emily was such a bright light."

"She was," Olivia agreed, her voice tight.

Millie leaned in, her voice lowering. "You know, I heard Emily was working on something big before she died. Some kind of special project. Do you think there's more to her death than an accident?"

Olivia's pulse quickened, but she kept her expression neutral. "I'm not sure. She was always passionate about her work."

Millie nodded, her gaze shifting toward Liz. "And did you see Liz Stevens? Acting like she cared when everyone knows she couldn't stand Emily."

"Really?" Olivia asked, feigning casual interest. "I thought they were friends."

Millie scoffed. "They weren't. She may have been a mentor to her in high school but ever since Emily struck out on her own, started her practice here in Emerald Ridge, Liz has been jealous of her. Something about their work overlapping. You didn't hear it from me, but I wouldn't be surprised if Liz had something to do with...all this."

Olivia's mind raced. Liz's presence, her suspicious behavior, and now Millie's cryptic words—there was too much to ignore. She filed the information away for later, her resolve strengthening.

As the service ended, people began to drift away, lost in hushed conversations. Olivia lingered, her thoughts swirling with unanswered questions. Elmer remained by her side, a steady presence amidst the chaos.

From the corner of her eye, she spotted Samuel Carter, the head of the neighborhood watch, watching her. He approached slowly, his expression unreadable. "Olivia," he said, his voice low, "I'm sorry for your loss. Emily was a good woman."

"Thank you, Samuel," Olivia replied, the weight of his words settling heavily on her shoulders.

He hesitated before speaking again. "You've been looking into Emily's death. Be careful. Whoever did this...they might be closer than you think."

A chill ran down her spine at his warning. The thought of him watching her that evening from across the street came tumbling back into her mind. Samuel's words echoed in her mind long after he walked away. The killer could be anyone—someone she knew, someone she trusted. The thought made her sick.

Noah found her again as the crowd thinned. "Need a ride home?" he asked, his hands shoved into his pockets.

"I've got my car," she replied, nodding toward her Jeep parked down the road. "But thanks."

"Anytime," he said, hesitating before adding, "If you need to talk, or just...not be alone, you know where to find me."

Olivia nodded, grateful for his offer. "I might take you up on that."

As she drove home, Elmer resting his head on her lap, Olivia's mind raced. Emily's journals had given her glimpses of the truth, but there was so much more to uncover.

***

Later that evening, Olivia sat in her loft, the soft glow of a lamp casting shadows on the walls around her. Emily's journal lay open in her lap, its pages filled with the careful, elegant handwriting that had once been so familiar. Elmer was curled beside her on the floor, his head resting on her leg, his gentle breathing providing a comforting rhythm that helped ground her in the midst of the chaos swirling in her mind. She skimmed the entries, but one section caught her attention, a part she had missed during her initial read-through. Now, it stood out like a beacon, pulling her focus with an intensity she couldn't ignore.

"Day one," she read aloud, her voice barely more than a whisper in the quiet of the room. "The tincture shows promise. The combination of solus vine, memory blossom, calm lotus, and starling berry is proving effective. Patients report calm and improved memory recall. The potential is immense."

Olivia's fingers traced the edges of the page as her mind raced with the implications. She glanced at Elmer, who looked up at her with wide, trusting eyes. "We're going to figure this out, for Emily," she murmured, her voice firm despite the uncertainty gnawing at her insides.

His tail thumped softly against the floor in response, as if reassuring her, grounding her in the moment. Olivia took a deep breath, letting the sound of Elmer's quiet presence settle her nerves. She turned the page, her eyes scanning the next set of notes with increasing determination.

Every word in Emily's journal now felt heavy with significance. The combination of ingredients—each one so carefully chosen, each one so potent—held a mystery that Olivia couldn't walk away from. There was something deeper here, something more dangerous than she had originally thought. The answers were out there, she was certain of it, and as she continued to read, her resolve hardened. She wouldn't stop until she found the truth—no matter what it cost.

CHAPTER 17

The sun had barely begun to rise when Olivia clipped Elmer's leash onto his collar. The air was cool and crisp, the first hints of light filtering through the trees, casting long shadows over the quiet town. Elmer's tail wagged with excitement, blissfully unaware of the gravity of their task. He was ready for his morning walk, as he always was, but today was different. Today, Olivia was stepping into unfamiliar territory, and she needed his calming presence more than ever.

It had been days since Emily's death, and Olivia's mind had been running in overdrive. She'd spent hours reading through Emily's journal, connecting the dots between the tincture and the strange occurrences surrounding her friend's passing. The questions were piling up, and Olivia knew she couldn't wait any longer. The time had come to start talking to people, to press for answers. She couldn't do it alone, though. There was something about this investigation that felt more personal than anything she'd ever tackled before, and she needed all the help she could get.

As much as she hated the idea of dragging people into this, Olivia knew the key to unlocking Emily's secrets lay in the people around her—those who had known her best. But she couldn't approach them alone. Not yet. Not with the way things were unfolding. That's where Elmer came in.

Though some might question the wisdom of bringing a dog along on something as serious as this, Olivia knew better. Elmer wasn't just a comforting presence; he had an uncanny way of reading people. She had seen it time and time again—how he could sense emotions others tried to conceal, how he seemed to know when someone was nervous, anxious, or hiding something. His friendly demeanor could disarm even the most guarded individuals, putting them at ease in a way Olivia herself couldn't always manage. She was certain his presence would make the interviews feel less like interrogations and more like conversations, giving her the chance to uncover the truth without raising suspicion.

Today was just the beginning. As they headed out together, Olivia felt a mixture of determination and apprehension settle in her chest. She wasn't sure what she was about to uncover, but she knew it was time to face whatever lay ahead.

Emerald Ridge was known for its charm, not just in its quaint shops and picturesque views, but in how warmly it welcomed its four-legged residents. Dogs were a staple sight on the town's sidewalks, trotting happily alongside their owners or lounging under café tables with bowls of water set out by thoughtful shopkeepers. Most establishments, from the small boutique on the corner to the bakery that made dog-friendly scones, had signs welcoming pets. It was part of what made Emerald Ridge feel like home, where the community extended beyond its human inhabitants.

Olivia knew she might be pushing her luck taking Elmer into the Miner's Diner, though. The diner was more old-school than most places in town, with a cranky owner who had a soft spot for pets when they were well-behaved. Still, as she pushed through the door, the familiar aroma of coffee and sizzling bacon wafted around her, and she felt Elmer's excitement ripple up the leash. His tail wagged furiously, and he glanced up at her with hopeful eyes. *Are we really doing this?*

"Behave, Elmer," Olivia whispered, offering a gentle scratch behind his ears as they stepped inside. She scanned the room, noting a few of the regulars giving her amused nods, their gazes shifting to Elmer with knowing smiles. The waitress gave them a questioning glance but said nothing—small towns had a way of accepting quirks without much fuss. Elmer padded beside her, scanning the room with curious eyes. Today, Olivia thought, he was more than just her companion; he was her partner in unearthing the truth. Olivia felt the weight of the notebook in her bag, filled with fragments of conversations and half-buried clues, each name a potential lead in the mystery surrounding Emily's death. The task before her was daunting, but she had to push forward. Too much was at stake.

Raymond Filtch stood behind the counter, polishing a coffee pot with a rag. Olivia approached him, Elmer trotting obediently beside her, his eyes wide and nose working overtime to catch every scent floating in the air.

"Morning, Raymond," Olivia greeted. "I was hoping I could ask you a few questions about Emily."

Raymond looked up, his face a picture of calm indifference. "Sure thing. I've got nothing to hide," he responded, a comment Olivia filed away as odd. She hadn't mentioned anything about hiding, after all.

"Rumor has it Emily wasn't too happy with some of your ingredient choices," Olivia said, keeping her tone casual. "Did that ever cause any tension between you two?"

Raymond snorted, his tone a mix of annoyance and defensiveness. "Emily was a tough critic, no doubt about that. She was always pushing that organic nonsense. But people don't come here for fancy salads and healthy food—they come for a hearty meal." He glanced at Olivia, then back at his work, his words becoming more pointed. "Look, I wasn't thrilled with her poking her nose in my business, but it wasn't worth killing over if that's what you're getting at." His answer was straightforward, but Olivia sensed something lingering beneath the surface. She pressed on, undeterred. "Where were you on the night of Emily's accident?"

Raymond paused, his fingers drumming on the counter as he recalled the night. "I was at home with Lisa and the kids. We had one of our family movie nights. The twins insisted on watching that new animated film with the singing animals, so we all squeezed onto the couch with bowls of popcorn. Lisa can vouch for me—she was right there trying to keep the boys from spilling their snacks everywhere. I didn't even know anything had happened to Emily until a customer came in the next morning and mentioned it."

Olivia nodded. His alibi seemed solid enough, though she could always verify it later if needed.

Ever since Emily's death, her questions had started to stir the pot. As much as Olivia had grown up in Emerald Ridge, been a part of this community her entire life, people still noticed when she started asking too many questions. And Emily—well, Emily had been a figure that some didn't quite understand, especially with her penchant for pushing the limits on things like organic food and alternative remedies. That had earned her both loyal followers and those who were skeptical, if not outright dismissive.

Olivia could feel the undercurrent of suspicion, the town's uneasy whispers following her wherever she went. In a place as tight-knit as Emerald Ridge, it didn't take much for word to get around, and her digging into Emily's death was beginning to raise eyebrows. She wasn't a stranger, and yet, her curiosity—her persistence—had people wondering why she was pressing so hard. Some didn't want to see the truth uncovered, and some were worried about what the truth might mean for them. The harder Olivia tried to get to the bottom of things, the more she realized that the town wasn't just mourning Emily—they were holding their breath, waiting to see how this would all play out.

"People are talking, you know," Raymond added with a lower voice, shifting uneasily behind the counter. "They're wondering why you're asking so many questions. Some of 'em think you know more than you're lettin' on."

Olivia's stomach tightened as she processed his words. It wasn't just Raymond; there had been subtle hints from others, too. Her involvement in trying to figure out what happened to Emily was starting to cast a shadow over her, despite the fact that she had every right to seek answers. But in a town where secrets ran deep, even asking the wrong questions could make you a target.

Olivia didn't respond immediately, but she felt the sharp edge to Raymond's words. Before she could ask another question, Elmer nudged her leg, letting out a soft whine. Raymond chuckled, noticing the dog for the first time.

"I'm surprised Alexis didn't have a fit seeing a dog in here," he said with a grin. "But I don't mind. He's a good-looking dog. Gonna be huge when he's grown, though."

Raymond disappeared into the kitchen for a moment, reappearing with a thick slice of bacon in hand. Leaning over the counter, he offered it to Elmer, who accepted it graciously, licking his lips in delight.

"Well, you've just made a new friend," Olivia said with a laugh.

Raymond chuckled. "Bacon has that effect on people and dogs alike."

"Thanks for chatting with me," Olivia said, gathering her things. "I'll let you get back to work."

"Anytime," Raymond replied, his tone easy. "You know where to find me if you have more questions."

Back in the Jeep, Elmer settled into the passenger seat, looking content after his impromptu snack. Olivia pulled out her notebook and jotted down a few notes from their conversation. Raymond's alibi seemed solid, and while he admitted to some tension with Emily, it felt like typical business disagreements, not something that would lead to murder. Elmer hadn't indicated anything off either, so Olivia felt confident moving on to the next person on her list.

The next stop was Wags and Whiskers, the local pet grooming salon owned by Shana Evans. Olivia didn't know Shana well, but the rumors swirling about a heated argument with Emily over Elmer, as well as whispers of Shana's criminal past, put her on the list of people to talk to. She wasn't convinced Shana was the person she was looking for, but due diligence demanded she at least check in.

They parked on the street in front of the salon. Olivia hopped out and moved around to Elmer's side to let him out. But Elmer didn't budge. Olivia patted her leg, calling him with an encouraging tone. "Come on, Elmer, let's go."

He glanced at the shop's sign, then back at Olivia with a pointed look. *No bath*, came his unspoken but very clear answer.

With a sigh, Olivia crouched down and rubbed his head. "Oh, Elmer. We're not here for a bath. I just need to talk to Shana for a few minutes."

His response was equally firm. He lay down on the seat, resolute. Olivia groaned, "Fine," and left him in the car. After rolling down the window for fresh air, she gave him a command. "Stay here, and no barking at people."

Elmer gave a soft woof of agreement, settling into his vigil by the window.

Pushing open the door to Wags and Whiskers, Olivia took in the cheerful decor. The salon was colorful and lively, with a playful animal theme. A vase of flowers sat on the reception desk, a small sign reading *Paws and Smell the Roses* perched next to it. Through a clear window separating the front area from the grooming room, she saw Shana working on a large poodle. Catching Olivia's eye, Shana quickly finished up and released the dog into a play area. Wiping her hands on her apron, she stepped into the reception area.

Shana's appearance was striking, definitely not what you would envision as the typical Emerald Ridge resident. Ripped jeans, a black T-shirt, turquoise hair framing her face, and piercings in places most people wouldn't have thought to pierce. Tattoos peeked out from under her sleeves, and her nails were painted black. Shana wasn't the typical resident of the sleepy town, but she had carved out her place here.

"Hey, Olivia. Busy day, huh?" Shana greeted her with a friendly smile.

"Seems like it," Olivia replied. "Always busy is good, right?"

"Pays the bills," Shana agreed with a nod. "What brings you by?

Olivia glanced out the window at Elmer, who was sitting in the Jeep, clearly relieved to be avoiding a bath. "Elmer's with me, but he's avoiding any potential surprises you might have for him."

Shana laughed. "Smart boy. He's sweet, but I don't think I'm his favorite person—probably because of the whole bath thing."

Olivia smiled, feeling the tension ease a little. "I wanted to ask you a few questions about Emily. Do you have a moment?"

Shana glanced at the grooming area to ensure everything was under control, then turned back to Olivia. "Sure. Shoot."

"I've been hearing some things around town," Olivia began carefully. "Some people seem suspicious about your past."

Shana's expression darkened slightly, her smile fading as she tucked a lock of turquoise hair behind her ear. "I figured that would come up sooner or later. Look, I did some dumb stuff when I was a kid. Who didn't? I shoplifted, skipped school. Ended up in juvie, but that was years ago. I did my time, and I've moved on. That's not who I am anymore."

Olivia nodded, trying to ease the conversation. "I figured it was something like that, but I had to ask. Also, I heard there was some disagreement between you and Emily about Elmer."

Shana rolled her eyes in frustration. "Yeah, that was a recent thing. When she first brought Elmer in, everything was fine. But lately, she'd been on this all-natural kick and started insisting I use natural products for him. Problem is, some of those aren't as effective for grooming, and they're expensive. I couldn't justify ordering a whole new line of supplies for one customer. I run a business, and no one else ever complained. Emily was the only one who had an issue."

"Did it ever get heated between you two?" Olivia asked.

Shana shook her head. "Not really. Sure, it was frustrating, but I'm not going to kill someone over dog shampoo. Emily was passionate about her ideas, and yeah, she could get under your skin sometimes, but that's just how she was."

"Where were you the night of Emily's accident?"

"I was at home, binge-watching TV. It had been a long day, and all I wanted was to sit on the couch and relax. My neighbor saw me through the window, so you can check with her if you want. Here," Shana said, scribbling a phone number on a sticky note and handing it to Olivia. "That's her number."

Olivia glanced at the note. Shana's defensive tone was noticeable, but it felt more like exasperation than guilt. If her alibi checked out, Shana could be crossed off the list.

"Thanks for your time, Shana. I appreciate your honesty," Olivia said.

"No problem. Look, I know I'm not exactly Emerald Ridge's favorite person, but I didn't have anything to do with Emily's death. Maybe if you tell people that, they'll stop giving me the side-eye every time I walk into a room."

Olivia smiled, crossing her heart. "I'll do my best."

Shana chuckled and glanced out the window at Elmer. "Just let me know when you're ready to set up his next appointment—unless you're brave enough to tackle it yourself."

The thought of wrangling Elmer through a bath made Olivia grimace. "Oh, I'll definitely be calling you."

With a wave, Olivia headed back to the Jeep, where Elmer was watching her, happily panting. He seemed to sense the threat of a bath had passed. Olivia sat down in the driver's seat and pulled out her notebook, scribbling down a few notes from the conversation. Shana's alibi seemed credible, and her frustration with Emily felt like the kind of professional disagreement that was more annoying than dangerous.

"All right, Elmer," Olivia said, starting the engine. "Another one off the list. But we're still no closer to figuring this out."

Elmer gave her a supportive nudge with his nose, as if to remind her that they were in this together.

CHAPTER 18

A fter reviewing the list of potential suspects, Olivia knew her next stop was the pharmacy to visit Derek Collins, the local pharmacist. There had been whispers that Emily had pestered him about stocking more natural remedies, and though Derek seemed like the friendly, helpful type, he was now on Olivia's radar.

She parked her Jeep outside the pharmacy, and Elmer gave her a look saying, *Again? Really?* Olivia chuckled, ruffling his ears. "Don't worry, this won't take long." Elmer didn't seem convinced.

As Olivia made her way into the pharmacy, Elmer padded beside her, his leash slack as he sniffed curiously at the air. The town's animal-friendly reputation made it easy to bring Elmer along without raising eyebrows. His presence was comforting, grounding her as she prepared to speak with Derek, the pharmacist. While Olivia knew this conversation could reveal something important, she also understood the subtle power Elmer brought into these encounters. People tended to lower their guard around animals, and Elmer's friendly, unassuming nature often helped smooth the way in tense situations.

The bell above the pharmacy door chimed softly as Olivia entered, the familiar scent of antiseptic and herbal teas filling the air. The store was quiet, the mid-morning lull leaving only a couple of customers browsing the aisles. Derek was behind the counter, arranging a display of vitamins. When he looked up and saw her, a polite smile crossed his face.

"Olivia, what a surprise," he greeted, his tone as smooth as always. "What brings you in today? Need something for Elmer?"

Olivia returned the smile, keeping her voice casual. "Actually, I was hoping to ask you some questions about Emily. I know how people talk when they're picking up their meds, so I was just wondering if you've heard anything unusual."

Derek raised an eyebrow, his expression shifting slightly. "Emily, huh? Well, you're right—people do love to chat. What specifically are you looking to know?"

Though his tone remained calm, Olivia noticed a flicker of something in his eyes. Before she could respond, Derek gestured toward the aisle with the over-the-counter meds. "Let's step aside, away from any potential eavesdroppers."

They moved a few steps away from the counter, and Olivia could sense Derek bracing himself. She decided to get straight to the point.

"I've been talking to a few people who had...disagreements with Emily. I'm not saying they're suspects, but I'm trying to understand what was going on with her before she died. Did she ever mention anything to you? Or maybe you heard something?"

Derek frowned thoughtfully, leaning against a shelf. "She didn't talk to me directly about anything serious, but I did overhear a conversation she had with someone. She was talking about some research she was working on, and it sounded important. She seemed a bit on edge, like she was worried about something."

Olivia's interest piqued. "Do you remember who she was talking to?"

Derek rubbed his chin, his gaze distant as he recalled the memory. "I'm not sure, but it was someone who comes in regularly. Could've been Edward Barnes or maybe Liz Stevens. They're both frequent customers—Liz especially. She's always picking up something for her headaches."

At the mention of Liz, Olivia felt her heart skip a beat. "That's helpful, Derek. Thanks. Anything else you remember?"

He shook his head. "Nothing specific, but if I think of anything, I'll let you know."

Olivia nodded, then decided to probe further. "I heard Emily was pretty vocal about wanting you to stock more natural remedies. Did that create any tension between you two?"

As the conversation deepened, Elmer remained a quiet presence, his soft gaze on Derek as though he could sense something important lurking beneath the surface. Derek, perhaps unwittingly, let down more of his guard, the weight of Elmer's calm presence seeming to coax out truths that might have stayed hidden otherwise.

Derek sighed and ran a hand through his hair. "Tension might be putting it strongly, but yeah, she was persistent. Emily was all about natural products and thought they'd be good for the community. She'd come in once a week with flyers and suggestions, even offering to help with suppliers. It was frustrating at times, but nothing I couldn't handle."

There was a hint of exasperation in his voice, though he quickly masked it with a neutral expression. "A pharmacy has to carry what people will buy, not just what one person insists on."

Olivia studied his face, looking for any sign of discomfort or guilt. "Where were you the night of Emily's death?"

Derek met her gaze, his eyes steady and calm. "I was here, doing paperwork and inventory. My assistant, Carla, was with me for part of the evening, and we have security footage from the store if you need to check."

His alibi seemed solid, but something about his calmness nagged at Olivia. She couldn't put her finger on it, but there was a sense that Derek might be holding something back.

"Thanks for your time, Derek. I appreciate the help," she said, offering a smile.

Derek's smile wavered, his eyes flicking away for a fraction of a second before landing back on Olivia. He shifted his weight, folding his arms across his chest. "No problem. If you need anything else, just let me know."

Olivia nodded, studying him carefully. As he turned to adjust a row of bottles on the shelf, he made an offhand comment, almost as if he couldn't help himself. "You know, sometimes people get too involved in things they don't understand. It makes them...reckless."

The words hung in the air, their weight pressing down on Olivia's chest. Derek's tone was casual, but there was a hardness beneath it that made her stomach twist. Was it frustration? Annoyance? Or something darker?

"That's true," Olivia said, keeping her tone light even as her mind raced. "But I suppose that's the risk when you're passionate about what you believe in."

Derek's jaw clenched subtly, a muscle ticking just below his cheekbone. He didn't respond but gave a tight nod.

Elmer, who had been lying quietly by Olivia's feet, shifted and let out a soft whine, drawing her attention. His gaze was locked on Derek, ears slightly back as if he sensed something more.

Olivia filed the exchange away in her mind, the unease settling deeper. She might not have anything solid, but

Derek's subtle shift in demeanor when Emily's name came up—and that strange comment—left her with more questions than answers.

As Olivia and Elmer left the pharmacy and returned to the Jeep, she couldn't help but feel that Derek's answers shed some light on a few things, especially with Liz Stevens's name coming up again, but she couldn't shake the feeling that there was more to his story.

Climbing into the Jeep, she scratched behind Elmer's ears. "One step closer, buddy. Let's go see Matt, Emily's old boyfriend, and see what he has to say."

Matt lived on the outskirts of town, his cabin nestled close to the edge of the vast state park where he worked as a ranger. The drive out there was scenic, with the landscape gradually shifting from the bustle of the streets to the quiet solitude of forest-lined roads. The dense trees and distant calls of birds offered a peaceful contrast to the noise of town life. As Olivia drove, she could sense Elmer relaxing, his nose twitching as he took in the scents of nature.

By the time they arrived, the sun had begun to dip below the horizon, casting a golden glow over the area. Matt's house was a modest cabin, its rustic wooden structure blending seamlessly into the surrounding greenery. The place exuded a quiet serenity as if it had always been part of the forest.

As Olivia pulled up to Matt's cabin, Elmer sat up in the passenger seat, his ears perked and his head tilting slightly as he stared out the window at the dense forest surrounding the house. His nose twitched, as if trying to pick up on something. Olivia glanced at him and noticed how still he had become, his usual playful energy muted. It was almost as if he sensed the significance of the visit, the weight of the moment hanging in the air. He had been here before, on visits with Emily, and though he wasn't one for lingering memories, something about this place felt different now.

Elmer's eyes swept the cabin and the surrounding woods, his gaze narrowing in that familiar, knowing way that Olivia had come to trust. He'd been with Emily enough times to recognize Matt and his cabin, but now—now there was an unfamiliar tension. Elmer's ears flicked, and he let out a soft whine, a subtle sign of unease that Olivia couldn't ignore. It wasn't like him to react this way, but she couldn't shake the feeling that Elmer knew something was off, something beyond the peaceful setting of the cabin. She gave him a reassuring pat, trying to settle him, but his eyes stayed alert, as though he were waiting for something.

"Don't worry, buddy," she murmured to him as she shifted the gear into park. "We'll get some answers."

Elmer's tail wagged briefly, but the tension didn't ease from his stance. His body was still, his eyes scanning the cabin and the surrounding forest with an intensity that sent a prickling sense of unease crawling up Olivia's spine. She gave him a soft, reassuring pat, but it didn't help—his behavior was off. The usual excitement of a new place, a new scent, was absent, replaced by an alert, almost wary posture.

Olivia's thoughts flashed back to the journal entries she had read earlier. Emily had mentioned Matt had shown up at her house under the influence of something after their breakup, a night that had ended in a heated argument. Olivia's heart had clenched when she read that part—Matt, who Emly had always described as controlled and calm, had lost himself that night. And Emily had written about how unnerved she had been by his behavior, how his presence had made her feel vulnerable.

Could it be that Elmer, with his finely tuned instincts, was picking up on something in the air connected to that night? Perhaps Matt's actions—or the energy he left behind—had stayed with him and now Elmer was reacting to it. She couldn't deny the possibility. Dogs like Elmer had a way of sensing things that humans couldn't, picking up on emotions, scents, and the faintest hints of tension that went unnoticed.

Her gaze flicked back to the cabin. She had to admit that there was something unsettling about the way Elmer was behaving, something that mirrored the unease she'd felt when reading Emily's words. Could there be more to Matt's involvement in Emily's death than she'd initially thought?

***

When Olivia opened the Jeep door, Elmer hopped out and stretched, but his usual playful energy was subdued. He padded alongside her, his leash slack, as they approached the front door. Olivia felt a twinge of anxiety creeping in—this wasn't just any conversation. Matt had once been close to Emily, and any hidden emotions from their relationship might come to the surface now.

Elmer nudged Olivia's leg gently, almost as if sensing her apprehension. She looked down at him, grateful for his quiet, steady presence. "You ready for this, boy?" she murmured. Elmer's tail gave a slow wag, his eyes focused on the door ahead.

She knocked lightly and waited, her gaze drifting over the wildflowers growing along the edge of the cabin. A moment later, the door opened, and Matt appeared. He looked rugged and a bit tired, his ranger uniform slightly disheveled, as if he'd just come in from a long day of work. He greeted her with a small, friendly smile, though there was a hint of weariness in his eyes.

"Hey, Olivia," he said, his voice carrying a note of surprise. "What brings you all the way out here?"

"Hi, Matt. Hope I'm not intruding," Olivia replied, offering a sympathetic smile. "I wanted to talk to you about Emily."

Matt's expression flickered for a moment, his eyes briefly revealing a mix of exhaustion and sadness that seemed to weigh heavily on him. His gaze drifted to the half-empty coffee mug on the table and the framed picture of him and Emily during a happier time. The photo's corner was smudged, as if it had been handled too many times in recent days. He quickly stepped aside to let her in. "No problem. Come on in. I've just gotten home, so now's as good a time as any." Elmer padded inside cautiously. He wandered the edges of the room, sniffing around as if he was investigating just as much as Olivia was.

Inside, the cabin was cozy, with the scent of pine lingering faintly in the air. The living room had a personal touch—photos of scenic trails and nature-themed décor, with a large map of the park pinned prominently on the wall. Matt grabbed two glasses of water from the kitchen and motioned for Olivia to sit at the dining table, where some trail guides and reports were spread out.

As they sat down at the table, Elmer settled at Olivia's feet, his large eyes watching Matt with calm intensity. Olivia noticed how Matt occasionally glanced down at the dog, perhaps unconsciously lowering his defenses in the process. Matt reached down to give Elmer a few soft pets.

"Hey, bud, remember me?" he asked. Elmer didn't react, just accepted the pets. Matt seemed a little confused by his reaction but shrugged it off and turned back to Olivia.

Matt leaned back in his chair, his posture relaxed but his expression serious. "So, what do you need to know?"

Olivia took a deep breath and met his gaze. "I've been looking into Emily's death," she began, her voice steady but soft. "I know you two were together recently, and I wanted to hear your side of things. Can you tell me about your relationship and whether anything significant happened leading up to the breakup?"

Matt sighed deeply, his gaze drifting toward the window. "Yeah, you know that Emily and I were together for a few years. It was good at first, but things got complicated. She was so passionate about her work—about everything she believed in—but sometimes it felt like that passion took priority over us."

Olivia studied Matt's face, noting the way the lines around his eyes deepened, hinting at sleepless nights and lingering grief. His gaze drifted momentarily to the framed photo of him and Emily, a candid shot where they were laughing, carefree. The memory seemed to hang between them, heavy and silent.

"What do you mean?" Olivia pressed gently, sensing the turmoil behind his words, the way his voice caught on the edges of something unsaid.

He sighed, rubbing the back of his neck, a habit that spoke of frustration mixed with regret. "We had a few rough patches, especially near the end," he admitted, his voice quieter now, as if each word took more effort than the last. "She was really focused on her activism, her research. It became everything to her, almost an obsession.

I wanted to be supportive, but it felt like I was trying to hold onto someone who was already halfway gone."

Olivia nodded, absorbing the weight of his confession. She could picture Emily in her element, eyes alight with passion as she shared her latest discovery, the fervor that made her impossible to keep up with. Emily had always been like that—pouring herself into her work until everything else faded into the background.

"Did she ever mention any conflicts or issues she was dealing with?" Olivia asked, her voice softening with understanding. "Any recent arguments or things that seemed to be bothering her more than usual?"

Matt's brow furrowed as he stared at the floor, his fingers tracing invisible patterns on the edge of the table. "We argued about her work a couple of times, yeah. I didn't always understand what kept her up at night or why she seemed so restless, like she was searching for something just out of reach." His eyes met Olivia's, a glint of guilt lingering there. "But it wasn't just us. There was something else...something that weighed on her, something she never talked about, even when I asked. It was like she was carrying a secret she couldn't—or wouldn't—share."

The room felt heavier with the revelation, the silence between them dense with unspoken fears. Olivia's mind raced, piecing together the fragments Matt offered. Emily's relentless drive, her secretive nature, the unknown burden she'd carried. The details didn't align neatly, but they pointed to something deeper, something that had overshadowed her last days.

Matt's voice pulled her back. "I don't think whatever was bothering her was personal, not between us at least. It was more like...she was caught in something bigger than either of us could understand."

Olivia leaned back, a chill running down her spine. Emily's determined spirit had always been a beacon, but maybe it had also been a warning—a signal that something more dangerous lurked beneath the surface of her passionate pursuits.

Olivia noted the strain in his voice. "Where were you the night Emily died?"

Matt straightened up, his expression serious. "I was at home, working on reports. It was a late shift for me, and my neighbor can back me up on that. I didn't hear about what happened to Emily until the next morning."

His alibi seemed plausible, but Olivia knew she'd need to confirm it. "I'll check with your neighbor, just to be sure."

Matt nodded, his gaze softening. "I understand. Look, Emily was important to me, and this whole thing has been...tough. If there's anything else I can do to help, just let me know."

"Thanks, Matt. I appreciate you taking the time to talk," Olivia said, rising from her seat.

As she made her way back to the Jeep, Olivia felt a mix of relief and unease. Matt had been honest, but their relationship had clearly been strained before

Emily's death. Whether that tension played a role in what happened to her remained to be seen. She'd need to confirm his alibi, but there was still something that felt unresolved.

"On to the next," Olivia muttered to herself. There were still more suspects to talk to, and with each conversation, the web around Emily's death grew more complex. But Olivia was determined to untangle it, no matter how far she had to go.

CHAPTER 19

As Olivia guided the Jeep back onto the road, the tension from the day's discoveries weighed heavily on her. Liz Stevens was her next and final stop before she could finally call it a day. The thought of wrapping up the day's investigation should have felt like progress, but instead, it sparked a growing sense of frustration. She was following all the leads she could find and still none of them seemed to go anywhere.

Her stomach interrupted her thoughts with a loud growl, so loud it even caught Elmer's attention. He turned his head, tilting it with concern.

"What do you think about a snack, boy?" she asked, offering him a smile. At the mention of the word "snack," Elmer's ears shot up, his head snapping toward her in eager anticipation. Olivia chuckled at his enthusiasm, finding comfort in his lighthearted reaction.

"All right, let's make a quick stop," she agreed, scanning the road ahead for a suitable place to take a break.

It wasn't long before she spotted a small food truck park on the edge of the road. It was the perfect spot—a few open areas where Elmer could stretch his legs, and judging by the delicious scents wafting through the air, something greasy to satisfy her own hunger.

Elmer had his nose pressed against the window as soon as they parked, taking in the tantalizing aromas from the various trucks. Olivia could almost hear his thoughts—*Is this heaven?*

They exited the Jeep, Elmer trotting beside her, his tail wagging with excitement. As they strolled through the food truck park, Olivia scanned the options. Her gaze settled on a taco truck with a line of customers waiting eagerly for their orders. Tacos, she thought, would do the trick.

"I'll take two fully loaded tacos," she told the vendor, watching as they were piled high with toppings. Turning to Elmer, she added, "And can you do two plain chicken tacos for my friend here?" The vendor raised an eyebrow but nodded in silent agreement.

With their food and a sweet tea for herself, Olivia found a sunny patch of grass near the trucks. Elmer followed eagerly, his eyes bright with anticipation as she set down his paper tray of tacos. He lay down with a contented huff, nibbling at his tacos while glancing at Olivia saying, *This is exactly what I needed.*

Olivia let the warmth of the sun and the soft breeze settle her nerves. She tore into her own tacos, trying to relax for the first time that day. It was a much-needed moment of peace, but her mind couldn't fully let go of the day's interviews. Liz Stevens had come up more than once in her conversations, and Olivia couldn't shake the nagging feeling that Liz was key to understanding what had really happened to Emily.

Elmer, now finished with his meal, stretched out beside her, enjoying the rare moment of calm. His presence always grounded her, reminded her that even in the midst of chaos, there were small, simple joys to be had. But as much as she wanted to savor this break, Olivia knew Liz's house awaited. And there, she hoped to find answers.

Back on the road, Olivia and Elmer soon arrived at Liz Stevens's modest brick home. The sun was dipping low, casting long shadows across the lawn as they approached the front door. Elmer padded beside Olivia, his ears perked, alert as always.

Liz opened the door, surprised to see Olivia. Olivia took in the sight of Liz and was surprised for her own reasons. The usually composed science teacher looked disheveled, her hair falling loose from its bun, and her eyes carried a frantic energy.

"Olivia," Liz greeted with a weak smile, her voice laced with tension. "I wasn't expecting you. Come in."

"Sorry to drop in on you like this," Olivia said, following Liz into the house. "I was just hoping to chat with you about Emily for a few minutes.

As Olivia stepped into the cozy living room, she noticed Liz's orange tabby cat, sitting on the back of a chair. The cat's green eyes fixed on Elmer with an intensity that set both Olivia and Elmer on edge.

"Newton, behave," Liz said, her voice cracking slightly as she hurried to usher them in. Olivia's eyes darted between Elmer and Newton, a prickle of unease tickling the back of her neck. Elmer's fur bristled slightly, and his ears twitched as if trying to catch some inaudible signal. The calm, dependable dog was now visibly on edge, and Olivia felt a twist of worry in her chest. Elmer's tail flicked with nervous energy, tapping the floor in an irregular rhythm that only added to her sense of disquiet.

Newton, perched regally on the arm of the chair, didn't move an inch. His eyes, sharp and knowing, stayed locked on Elmer, unblinking and intent. The cat's posture was tense, his ears slightly angled back—not quite aggressive, but far from relaxed. The silence stretched, taut as a wire, the room heavy with an undercurrent Olivia couldn't quite name. She caught nothing passing between the animals, aside from tension. Elmer hadn't had the best of luck with cats recently, so maybe it was just that. She hoped it was only that.

The cat's eyes shifted to her, holding her gaze for a brief, unsettling moment before flicking back to Elmer. It was as if Newton was making a silent assessment, weighing something Olivia couldn't see.

She reached down to rub Elmer's head, hoping the touch would reassure him—or maybe herself. His muscles were taut under her fingers, a sign that whatever tension crackled in the air was very real to him.

"Easy, boy," she whispered, glancing at Newton, who remained poised and silent, an unreadable sentinel. The cat's tail flicked once, as if punctuating an unspoken warning. She made a mental note to keep an eye on Newton—and to listen closely if Elmer had anything to say about him later.

"Sorry about him," Liz said, brushing off the awkwardness with a nervous laugh. "He's been a bit...edgy lately."

"No worries," Olivia replied, though she kept an eye on Newton.

They sat down, and Liz picked up a mug of tea from her side table, holding on to it like a security blanket. Olivia wasted no time easing into the conversation. "I've been thinking about Emily a lot lately, Liz. Her death has shaken the whole town. I wanted to talk to you because your name has come up a few times. And I know, at least at one point, the two of you were close."

Liz's smile faltered, her hands tightening around her mug. "I don't know what there is to say. It's all been so overwhelming."

Olivia watched Liz carefully as she asked, "You two had a relationship, right? Not just as student and teacher, but outside of school too, once Emily graduated?"

Liz's eyes darted to the side, her fingers tapping nervously on her mug. "Yes, well, we had a...complicated relationship."

"Complicated how?" Olivia pressed gently.

"She was my student first," Liz said, her voice tight. "But later, we reconnected. She was helping me with some...personal issues." Olivia raised an eyebrow.

"Personal issues?"

Liz hesitated, then sighed, as if resigning herself to the conversation. "She was my therapist, all right? I don't usually tell people that, but she was helping me through a tough time. I recently broke up with someone, and well, Emily was involved."

"Involved how?" Olivia pressed.

"She didn't mean to," Liz said quickly, her eyes wide with a mix of guilt and anger. "But she said something during one of our sessions that made me realize I needed to end it. She didn't even know what she had done."

This was nw. Could it be that Liz's resentment towards Emily wasn't just about jealousy—it was personal?

"And now, with Emily gone, it must be hard not having that support anymore," Olivia said, watching Liz closely.

Liz nodded, but there was a hardness in her eyes that Olivia couldn't ignore.

"Emily was always ahead of me," Liz continued, her voice taking on a bitter tone. "Even when she didn't mean to be. With the tincture, with her work, it was like she overshadowed everything I did. I've worked for years on making headway with the starling berry. My family has ties to it that go back generations, and Emily was able to take it and make it into more than I ever imagined. And now Alicia, one of my students, is involved with Edward Barnes, learning from him. It's like I can't escape Emily's shadow, even now."

Before Olivia could respond, Newton leapt down from his perch and padded over to Elmer. The two animals stood nose to nose for a moment, and Olivia could sense the exchange happening between them. Newton's thoughts were sharp, filled with images of Liz pacing the house, muttering to herself, her hands wringing a piece of paper—something that looked like notes. There was frustration, anger, and something darker—a plan forming.

Elmer looked up at Olivia, his brown eyes wide with concern. *She's been hiding something,* he said. *Something important.* Olivia gave a subtle nod, acknowledging Elmer's warning.

Olivia leaned forward, her voice soft but firm. "Did something happen between you and Emily, Liz?"

Liz blinked, as if snapped out of a trance. "Happen? No, no...I just wish she would have given me some credit, you know? I spent extra time working with and tutoring her in high school. She learned it all from me."

Newton gave a low, warning growl. Elmer, sensing the rising tension, nudged Olivia gently, a silent signal that they had what they needed.

"Thank you for talking with me, Liz," Olivia said, standing up. "I know this hasn't been easy."

As they left, Elmer stayed close by her side, his eyes alert. Once inside the Jeep, Olivia turned to him. "What did Newton say?"

Elmer let out a low whine, his ears flattening. *Liz is hiding something big*, he said. *Something dangerous.*

Olivia tightened her grip on the steering wheel, her mind racing. Liz Stevens was no longer just a mild-mannered teacher in her eyes—she was a suspect, and possibly a dangerous one at that.

***

As twilight fell over Emerald Ridge, the quiet hum of the town shifted into the stillness of night. Olivia found herself wandering near the pharmacy, her thoughts restless after her unsettling conversation with Liz earlier in the day. The streets were almost empty, save for the glow of streetlamps casting long shadows and the occasional car passing by. Elmer trotted at her side, his ears flicking as if listening to the whispers of the evening.

She was about to turn back toward her Jeep when the sight of Liz entering the pharmacy caught her attention. The neon "Open" sign in the window blinked with a tired persistence, but the rest of the store was dim. Olivia hesitated, lingering near the entrance of a closed bookstore a few doors down, her instincts telling her to stay out of sight.

Peering through the pharmacy's large front window, she watched as Derek stood behind the counter, his posture rigid and his expression tense. Liz, still in the same disheveled state Olivia had seen her in earlier, was leaning over the counter, her voice low but animated. Olivia couldn't make out the words, but the energy between them was unmistakably charged.

Elmer sat quietly at her feet, his eyes trained on the scene inside as if he, too, sensed the tension. Olivia's heart quickened when Derek reached beneath the counter and pulled out a brown paper bag. He held it for a moment, his fingers clutching the edges tightly as if he were reconsidering whatever was happening. Liz's hand shot out, taking the bag with a sharp motion, her eyes darting nervously toward the door and the darkened street beyond.

Derek said something then, his mouth moving in a hurried, clipped way, but Liz didn't respond. She tucked the bag under her arm, gave a terse nod, and hurried out of the pharmacy, the bell above the door chiming softly in her wake. Olivia pressed herself further into the shadow of the bookstore as Liz strode past, her eyes downcast and focused. For a split second, Olivia thought Liz's gaze might flick up and catch her, but she swept by without pause.

When Liz disappeared down the street, Olivia turned her attention back to the pharmacy. Derek stood motionless behind the counter, his face pale and drawn. He ran a hand through his hair, looking exhausted. Olivia's pulse raced as she noted the way he stared at the door Liz had just exited through, as if it might burst open at any moment and reveal something he'd rather keep hidden.

"Elmer," she whispered, a hint of resolve tightening in her chest, "we might be onto something."

The dog glanced up at her, his eyes sharp with curiosity, as though he understood that the evening had taken an unexpected turn. Olivia took one last look at the pharmacy before backing away from the window and disappearing into the night. The questions in her mind multiplied with every step, each one demanding to be answered.

CHAPTER 20

As soon as Olivia collapsed into the Jeep, it felt like all the energy drained out of her, like a balloon slowly deflating. Her head throbbed, and every muscle screamed for rest. Interviewing suspects all day had left her feeling as if she'd been spinning in circles, chasing threads that led nowhere. Yet, something about Liz Stevens nagged at her—a mild-mannered science teacher involved in murder? It seemed far-fetched, but Olivia couldn't shake the feeling that she wasn't done with Liz, especially after Elmer's subtle warning earlier and then the tense interaction they had witnessed at the pharmacy.

She glanced at Elmer, who was slumped against the passenger window, eyes half-closed and looking as exhausted as she felt.

"Let's head home, bud," Olivia murmured, stifling a yawn. "I think we've done all we can for today."

Elmer gave a low grunt of agreement, barely lifting his head. Even the mention of food wouldn't have stirred him at this point, a clear sign of how tired he was. Olivia briefly considered stopping at Perks and Peaks for a coffee, but the thought of engaging in small talk felt like more effort than it was worth. All she wanted was her bed.

As they crested the last hill before home, the sun dipped behind the mountains, casting a soft golden glow over the landscape. Normally, it was the kind of moment that brought Olivia peace, but today, all she could think about was how this beautiful town hid something dark—something that had taken Emily away.

She turned onto the familiar road leading to her mom's house, the weight of the day growing heavier with each passing second. Her body longed for rest, but Olivia knew her mind wouldn't let her off that easily tonight. Elmer let out a soft whine as they pulled into the driveway, a sound that mirrored how she felt—completely spent.

Inside, Elmer collapsed in the entryway like a sack of potatoes, and Olivia made her way into the house behind him, her movements sluggish. Her mother's voice floated over from the couch, where she sat curled up with a book.

"Long day?" her mom asked, her brow creasing in concern as she took in Olivia's exhausted appearance. "You look wiped. Can I make you something to eat? A sandwich?"

Olivia offered a weary smile. "A sandwich sounds perfect, thanks."

Elmer's lack of response to the word "sandwich" earned him a concerned glance from her mom. "Wow, even Elmer's too tired for snacks? You both must have had quite the day."

"I'll get him something, too," she added, making her way to the kitchen.

Olivia dropped her bag by the door and sank into a chair, watching as her mom moved about the kitchen with her usual calm efficiency. The soft hum of the fridge and the clinking of dishes provided soothing background noise.

"Liv," her mom said, glancing over her shoulder, "I'm worried about you. This whole murder investigation is taking a toll on you. You're still grieving, and you're throwing yourself into this headfirst. Maybe you need to give yourself a break. What if it really was just an accident?"

Olivia sighed, feeling the weight of her mom's words. "It wasn't an accident, Mom. I'm sure of that now. But...I don't know what my next move is. I have suspicions, but no hard evidence. It feels like I'm running in circles."

Her mother turned, giving her that familiar, serious look. "Just be careful. Don't push too hard."

She slid a sandwich across the counter, along with a small bowl of leftovers for Elmer. Olivia stared at the food, realizing she wasn't even hungry anymore—just drained. "Thanks, Mom. I think Elmer and I are going to eat in the loft. It's been a long day."

"Get some rest, Liv," her mom called after her, though the worry in her voice lingered.

Olivia picked up the sandwich and leftovers and motioned for Elmer to follow her upstairs. He let out a world-weary huff before hauling himself up and trudging after her.

Once they were in the loft, she flicked on the fairy lights, their warm glow casting the room in a soft, calming light. Olivia set her sandwich on the nightstand and poured the leftovers into Elmer's bowl. He looked at the food, then at her, as if deciding whether it was worth the effort. In the end, hunger won, and he lazily nibbled on his meal, his tail thumping against the floor.

Olivia kicked off her shoes and climbed into bed, nibbling on her sandwich while her thoughts raced. The day had left her without any major revelations. Liz had mentioned that one of her students, Alicia, was working as Edward Barnes's assistant. Olivia wondered if she might have some additional insight on the tincture project—and Liz. She made a mental note to reach out to Edward tomorrow and see if there was a good time to stop by and speak with Alicia.

As she finished the last bite of her sandwich, Olivia glanced at Elmer, already curled up beside her, fast asleep. The weight of the day finally caught up with her, dragging her deeper into the mattress. The investigation could wait until tomorrow. Right now, she needed sleep.

The next morning dawned bright but cool, an unusual chill for summer. Olivia rummaged through the front closet for an old hoodie, wrapping it around herself as she waited for Edward to respond to her text. She had messaged him earlier, hoping to speak with Alicia about Emily's work. The silence felt heavier than it should have, but Olivia told herself not to overthink it.

Elmer shuffled into the room, stretching lazily before plopping down at her feet with a disgruntled sigh. His eyes darted to his empty food bowl, clearly waiting for breakfast.

"Sorry, boy. No gourmet breakfast today," she said, dropping some kibble into his bowl. Elmer sniffed at it, then gave her a look that could only be described as withering disappointment.

Just then, her phone buzzed, drawing her attention. Edward had finally replied.

Alicia will be here at noon. Totally fine if you come by.

Olivia let out a sigh of relief when she saw the next line, but as her eyes scanned the words, her stomach twisted into a knot.

There was another break-in last night. Someone hacked into my computer and got into the safe. A lot of Emily's work is missing.

The blood drained from Olivia's face, and for a moment, she couldn't breathe. Her mind raced, trying to process the significance of what she was reading. A break-in? After everything that had happened, Emily's work was being stolen? It didn't make sense. Who would do such a thing? And why? Was someone trying to cover their tracks, or were they looking for something specific?

"Crap," she muttered under her breath, rubbing her temples as the weight of the new revelation sank in. The headache that had been quietly building behind her eyes flared, and she felt a sense of helplessness wash over her, mingled with frustration. Emily had been careful—so careful—about her work. This wasn't random; someone had intentionally gone after her research. What were they hoping to find? What was so important about Emily's notes and files?

Elmer, ever attuned to her mood, perked up at the sharpness in her tone. He tilted his head, his eyes questioning, as if trying to understand the cause of her unease. She could feel his concern, his unspoken desire to comfort her, but she needed to process this on her own. For a brief moment, she felt like she was standing at the edge of a cliff, unsure if she should jump in or pull back.

"Looks like our day just got a lot more interesting," she said, forcing a smile as she looked down at Elmer. Despite the unease bubbling in her chest, she was determined to stay focused. There was a larger puzzle to solve now—one that involved not just Emily's death, but the theft of her work. Whoever had done this was desperate, and Olivia was more committed than ever to finding out why.

They arrived at Edward's house around noon, Elmer hopping out of the Jeep, ready for the day ahead. As they approached the front door, it swung open, and Edward waved them in, his expression tense.

"Come in! We've had quite the morning," he said, his voice hurried.

As they entered, Archibald swooped down from the rafters, landing on Elmer's back. "Hello, Pretty Lady!" the parrot squawked, tugging at Elmer's fur playfully. Elmer tolerated the bird's antics with a sigh, his patience clearly better than Olivia's.

Edward led them into the lab, where Alicia was sweeping up shards of broken glass. She glanced up, her eyes widening with surprise at seeing Olivia. There was something nervous in her expression.

"Alicia," Olivia greeted, offering a friendly smile. "I'd like to talk with you if you have a moment."

Alicia hesitated, then nodded. "Sure. Let's go outside."

They stepped into the garden, the air filled with the scent of fresh herbs and blooming flowers. Alicia seemed to relax a little in the open air, though her fingers still fidgeted nervously. They sat down together on the edge of one of the rock walls that encased the botanical chaos that was Edward's landscaping.

"I just want to ask a few questions about Emily," Olivia began. "I know you worked with her and Edward on the tincture. Did Emily ever mention any concerns to you? Maybe about someone trying to sabotage her work?"

Alicia paled, her gaze flicking toward the lab before she finally spoke. "She did, but I thought she was just stressed. She mentioned someone from a pharmaceutical company being interested in her research, and she was worried they might try to take it." Alicia paused for a moment. "And there was something else, not that she said so much, but how she was acting. She seemed to be looking over her shoulder all the time. I don't think that had anything to do with the pharmaceutical reps."

"Did she ever say who specifically?"

Alicia shook her head. "No, but after Emily died, Liz Stevens started asking more questions. She was curious before, but after, she became...pushy."

"Pushy how?" Olivia pressed.

"She wanted details—about the tincture, about the research. I didn't tell her much, but I think she figured out more than I realized."

Alicia stood abruptly, her face pale. "I need to get back to work. I don't like talking about this."

Before Olivia could stop her, Alicia rushed back toward the lab, leaving Olivia standing alone in the garden with Elmer at her side. Feeling like there wasn't much more she could accomplish there, Olivia bade goodbye to Edward and Alicia.

As they walked back to the Jeep, Olivia noticed a piece of paper flapping under her windshield wiper. Frowning, she pulled it free, unfolding the note.

Stop asking questions, or you'll regret it.

Her heart pounded as she scanned the quiet surroundings, suddenly feeling exposed. Elmer growled low, sensing her unease.

"Well, that's not ominous at all," Olivia muttered, shoving the note into her bag.

Whoever had left it knew she was getting close—and they didn't like it.

"This just got a lot more dangerous," she whispered, her eyes scanning the trees as Elmer's ears twitched in alertness.

Whoever was behind this wasn't just after Emily's research—they were willing to do anything to get it.

CHAPTER 21

After leaving Edward Barnes's house and stuffing the menacing note into her bag, Olivia needed a break. The tension of the morning still clung to her like a heavy weight, and despite her best efforts, she couldn't shake the unsettling feeling from the threatening message. Elmer, ever her trusty companion, seemed ready to move on, his tail wagging slightly, asking, *What's next?*

"Let's grab some food, boy," Olivia said, trying to lighten the mood. Elmer's nose twitched, his ears perking up in anticipation.

They headed toward Main Street and stopped at a local sandwich shop. Olivia ordered her usual—a turkey sandwich—while Elmer got some chicken bites. They found a picnic bench outside and settled in. Olivia glanced down at her phone, which buzzed with a text from Noah.

I know you've been busy, but I was wondering if you'd want to come over tonight. Maybe decompress a little. Catch up. I'll be in the garage, but we could grab dinner if you're up for it.

A grin spread across her face as she quickly typed back, *How about I bring dinner? Jim's Pizza, same as always? Around 7?*

Sounds perfect. See you later.

After finishing their meal, Olivia felt the tension from the morning begin to ease. The idea of seeing Noah and returning to something normal made her feel lighter. As she and Elmer wandered back to the Jeep, Olivia noticed something different on Main Street. The quiet summer afternoon had given way to the buzz of an impromptu local art market.

"Let's check it out, boy," she said, her curiosity piqued. Elmer trotted beside her, his nose to the ground, sniffing the air filled with new scents.

Colorful stalls lined the sidewalks, displaying paintings, pottery, jewelry, and handmade crafts. Olivia loved these markets. It was nice to soak up the positive energy after such a stressful day. As they passed booth after booth, Olivia's eyes landed on a stall filled with stunning landscape paintings. The images depicted the mountain views around Emerald Ridge, the golden light of the sunrise hitting the peaks in a way that made them almost glow.

"These are beautiful," Olivia murmured as she stepped closer.

The artist, a man in his late twenties with tousled dark hair and an anxious smile, looked up. "Thanks," he said quietly. "I just moved here a few months ago. Still trying to get used to the place."

"Really? Your work makes it seem like you've been here forever," Olivia commented, admiring a canvas showcasing the Ridge bathed in golden light. "Where are you living?"

The man hesitated briefly, his eyes flickering with what seemed like nervousness. "Over on Maplewood," he replied, quickly waving off the question.

"Maplewood's a great street. Welcome to town," Olivia said, extending her hand. "I'm Olivia, and this is Elmer."

The man glanced at Elmer and gave a tight smile. "Lucas. Thanks. You probably won't see much of me—I mostly keep to myself and paint."

Olivia noticed how his gaze shifted as though checking his surroundings. Something about his demeanor felt off, but she decided not to press further. "Well, your work is amazing. I might just have to buy one of these pieces."

Lucas nodded but seemed distracted. The uneasy vibe lingered as Olivia moved on with Elmer. Once they were out of earshot, she whispered, "That guy was...a little strange, right?" Elmer gave a soft whuff in agreement.

They strolled through the market a little longer before heading back to the Jeep. As Olivia and Elmer made their way past the last of the art stalls, a low, tense voice caught her attention. She paused, straining to hear over the chatter and music drifting through the market. The voice came from the narrow alley between the old bookstore and the bakery.

"Don't forget who helped you when no one else would, Liz," came the sharp tone of a male voice, his words laced with a threat that sent a shiver down Olivia's spine. Peeking around the corner, she spotted Liz Stevens speaking with someone who was against the building wall where he couldn't be seen. His posture was rigid, arms crossed over his chest as he loomed over Liz.

Liz's eyes blazed, her jaw clenched in defiance. "I never asked you for your help. You just inserted yourself in my business. I need control over it. That's all that matters to me."

The man leaned in, his shadowed face mere inches from hers. "You think you are the only one with secrets, Liz? I know people, important people, and if you don't follow through, I'll make sure everyone knows just how deep in this you are."

Liz's eyes darted around, catching Olivia's attention as she instinctively ducked behind a display of pottery. Her pulse quickened, heart pounding in her chest. She held her breath as Liz's voice dropped, quivering slightly. "I'm already taking risks for you. Don't push me further. I can't afford it."

The man straightened, a smile that didn't reach his eyes curving his lips. "You've been saying that a lot, Liz.

Remember, I've helped you enough. It's time you deliver on our agreement, or I'll start collecting in other ways."

Liz's shoulders slumped, and the hard edge in her voice softened. "I understand."

Satisfied, the man stepped out of the alley, his gaze briefly sweeping the market. Olivia quickly turned away, pretending to study a booth filled with beaded necklaces. Her mind spun with questions as she watched the man, leave Liz standing alone, her fists clenched at her sides and her expression a mix of anger and desperation.

Elmer nudged Olivia's leg, sensing her tension. "We'll figure this out," she whispered, absently scratching behind his ears. But one thing was clear: whatever Liz was involved in, it sounded deep—and dangerous.

Later that evening, after picking up a pizza from Jim's—half pepperoni, half veggie, their high school favorite—Elmer and Olivia drove toward Noah's place. Olivia felt a mix of excitement and nerves building. Things between her and Noah had been tentative since she had been back in town, but tonight felt different.

When they pulled into Noah's driveway, the garage door was already open, and he was tinkering under the hood of an old car. Elmer bounded out of the Jeep and immediately found a spot on the porch to lounge.

"Hey," Olivia called, holding up the pizza box as she walked over. "Dinner's here."

Noah wiped his hands on a rag, a grin spreading across his face. "Jim's Pizza. It's been years since I've picked one up. I've tried to make healthier choices as I've gotten older, but holy cow this smells amazing," he said, taking the box from her. The warmth in his eyes made the moment feel easy, like old times.

They settled on the porch swing, the pizza box balanced between them. The cool evening breeze mixed with the scent of pine trees and melted cheese, and Elmer sprawled contentedly nearby, his earlier meal still keeping him satisfied.

They ate in comfortable silence at first, the swing gently swaying. Olivia felt a sense of calm wash over her being there with Noah, away from the investigation and the worries that weighed her down.

"So," Noah finally said, his voice soft, "you've been pretty caught up with all this Emily stuff, huh?"

Olivia nodded, finishing a bite of pizza. "Yeah. It's a lot. I just want to figure out what really happened."

Noah studied her, his brow furrowed in thought. "Sarah's been having a hard time, too. She saw Emily for therapy, and this has been rough on her."

As if on cue, the screen door creaked open, and Sarah stepped out onto the porch. Her face brightened when she spotted Olivia. "Hey, Liv! Long time no see." She eyed the pizza. "Is that Jim's? Can I steal a slice?"

Olivia laughed, holding out the box. "Help yourself."

Sarah grabbed a slice and settled on the porch step. "It's good to see you, Olivia." She paused, a wave of emotion passing over her face for a split second. Olivia wondered if her presence reminded her of Emily. Sarah sighed, "I miss Emily. She was helping me so much."

Seeing an opening, Olivia asked gently, "Did she ever mention her research? Her tincture project?"

Sarah paused, picking at the edge of the pizza crust. "A little. She thought it was going to change everything for people dealing with trauma, like me."

"Did she ever mention anyone trying to interfere with her work?" Olivia pressed, keeping her tone light.

Sarah shook her head. "Not to me. But she seemed stressed, like something was bothering her. She wasn't herself those last few sessions. I think she felt like someone was watching her."

Olivia's heart skipped a beat. "Did she say who?"

"No," Sarah said softly, her eyes clouded with sadness. "I just wish I could have done more."

Noah spoke to his sister in a comforting tone. "You did what you could, Sarah. Emily wouldn't want you to blame yourself."

The conversation faded after that, and they finished the pizza in comfortable silence. As the evening wore on and Olivia stood to leave, Noah hesitated, stepping closer to her. His hand brushed hers, a soft touch that sent a shiver down her spine.

Then, with a slight, nervous smile, he leaned in and kissed her—just a brief, gentle kiss, but enough to make her heart flutter.

"Goodnight, Liv," Noah whispered as he pulled back, his voice barely audible in the quiet evening air.

Olivia, still flushed from the kiss, smiled and whispered back, "Goodnight, Noah."

As she and Elmer drove away, the warmth of that kiss lingered, a soft glow amidst the chaos of the day. But with so many unanswered questions swirling in her mind, Olivia knew there was still so much left to uncover. This was just the beginning.

The next morning, Olivia woke with a heaviness in her chest, the weight of her swirling thoughts about Liz, Samuel, and the enigmatic painter Lucas pressing down on her. The interviews from the day before, the conversations, the veiled threats, and the secrets in the shadows all seemed to blend into a cacophony of doubt. She needed clarity, even if just on one front.

With determination settling in her bones, Olivia dressed quickly and headed into town. Elmer trotted beside her, tail wagging as they navigated the familiar path to the pharmacy. The sun was climbing higher, casting a soft golden light over Emerald Ridge. But Olivia barely noticed the beauty around her, too preoccupied with what she was about to do.

The bell above the pharmacy door chimed as she stepped inside. Derek looked up from the counter, his expression unreadable until it softened into a wary smile. He was organizing the shelves behind the counter but paused when he saw her.

"Olivia," he greeted, trying to mask the tension in his voice. "Twice in one week? To what do I owe the pleasure?"

"Good morning, Derek," she replied, forcing a small smile. She could feel her heart hammering in her chest. "You mentioned I could drop back by if I had any more questions about Emily, so here I am."

Derek's jaw tensed, and he glanced around the empty store before gesturing toward the small consultation area near the window. "All right," he said, exhaling sharply. "Let's get this over with."

They sat across from each other, the sunlight casting a stripe of light between them. Elmer settled at Olivia's feet, his gaze shifting between the two as if sensing the importance of the conversation.

"The town rumor mill keeps suggesting that recently you've been 'up to no good,' whatever that means., " Olivia began, "And Millie's been adding fuel to the fire, saying you and Emily argued constantly about natural remedies. I need to know the truth. Did you have anything to do with what happened to her?"

Derek leaned back in his chair, the tension in his body palpable. He rubbed his eyes and let out a tired chuckle. "Millie Partridge should write fiction," he muttered. "Look, Olivia, Emily and I had our differences. She was persistent—relentlessly so. Always coming in here with her flyers, telling me I should stock more natural remedies, as if I didn't know my own business. It was…annoying, I won't lie. But that's all it was. Annoyance. Like I told you the first time we talked."

Olivia searched his face for signs of deception, but he met her gaze steadily. "So, it was just her enthusiasm that got on your nerves? Nothing more?"

Derek nodded, the corners of his mouth tightening into a grim line. "She was passionate, and sometimes passion blinds you. But it was never malicious. And the idea that I'd harm her? It's ridiculous. The rumors Millie spreads—they're exhausting. I've been fending off whispers and side glances ever since Emily died. But I swear, Olivia, I had no role in what happened to her."

There was an earnestness in his voice that made Olivia's heart soften. The defensive, weary look in his eyes seemed more like that of a man overwhelmed by grief and suspicion than one hiding a dark secret.

After a moment of silence, she nodded. "I believe you, Derek."

Relief washed over his face, and he let out a breath he'd been holding. "Thank you," he said quietly. "And for what it's worth, I hope you find whoever's really responsible. Emily didn't deserve any of this."

"I will," Olivia replied, a flicker of determination lighting her eyes. She rose from her chair, Elmer following her lead. As she walked out of the pharmacy, she felt a small sense of resolution. Derek was no longer at the center of her suspicions, but the real questions—the ones about Liz, Samuel, and the secrets swirling around them—were far from answered.

As Olivia turned to leave, Derek's voice stopped her. "Wait, Olivia," he said, his tone hesitant. She paused, glancing back over her shoulder. Derek's eyes darted toward the door as if making sure no one else was listening. "I saw you outside the other night when Liz came in."

A chill crept down Olivia's spine, but she kept her face neutral. "Yeah, I was passing by," she said carefully. "Why do you bring it up?"

Derek's jaw clenched, and he rubbed the back of his neck as if trying to find the right words. "Liz is...complicated. That brown paper bag you saw her leave with? It was just some first-aid supplies. But she was agitated, more than usual. It was late, and she seemed desperate. I didn't ask questions, but I could tell something was off."

Olivia's breath caught in her chest. "Did she mention why she needed them so urgently?"

He shook his head. "No, but it wasn't the first time she's come in looking rattled. She's been in a lot recently, asking questions about pharmaceuticals and natural remedies – some of those questions Emily probably could have answered better than I did. She almost seemed like she was gathering information for some purpose, but she never mentioned what. Olivia, just...be careful. Whatever she's caught up in, it feels bigger than anyone realizes."

His words hung in the air, heavy with implication. Olivia nodded slowly, a mix of worry and curiosity taking hold. "Thanks for telling me, Derek. I'll keep that in mind."

As she stepped out of the pharmacy and into the morning sun, Olivia's mind raced. Liz's late-night visit, Derek's warning, and the mysterious bag—every piece seemed to point toward a deeper secret. One that she couldn't afford to ignore.

CHAPTER 22

Olivia pulled the Jeep into the driveway, and as soon as they came to a stop, it was clear Elmer had hit his limit for the day. The moment his paws hit the ground, he headed straight for the backyard with the single-minded determination of someone ready to clock out. Olivia followed him, feeling the cool breeze swirl around her as she sank onto the porch steps, her gaze drifting over the yard.

While the breeze promised calm, her mind was anything but peaceful. It was a chaotic storm of thoughts—an emotional tornado without the whimsical promise of landing somewhere magical like Oz. The road ahead didn't seem paved with yellow bricks; it was more like a twisting labyrinth of dead ends and questions without answers.

Olivia watched as Elmer, nose to the ground, sniffed around the yard like the diligent detective he was—only his focus was on bugs, not mysteries. She wished she could feel that carefree. Her suspect list, though thorough, had left her with more uncertainties than solutions. Liz Stevens remained suspicious, but suspicions weren't evidence. Not even close.

Frustration crept up on her as the day's dead ends echoed in her thoughts. Emily had certainly ruffled some feathers, and her work on the tincture had stirred something, but the threads Olivia was pulling weren't leading to any clear picture.

Elmer wandered back to the porch, flopping down beside her with a lazy thump. He snapped at the bees as they danced around him, content in the simple pleasure of the moment. Olivia envied his ability to disconnect. She would love to shut off the relentless loop of worry and questions in her head. She leaned back, feeling the weight of the day settle into her bones just as her phone buzzed beside her.

The screen lit up with a message from Liz Stevens. Olivia wasn't expecting that. She swiped the screen, curiosity piqued.

Hey Liv—sorry to bother you, but you mentioned to let you know if I heard anything about Emily. Not sure if this is relevant, but I overheard Mr. Carter talking about the new guy on Maplewood, Lucas something? He said he saw him painting in his garage, and the paintings looked...disturbing. Apparently, they resembled the scene of Emily's death. Thought you might want to know.

Olivia read the message twice, letting it sink in. *Disturbing paintings?* The odd interaction she'd had with Lucas at the art market replayed in her mind. He had seemed nervous, sure, but nothing about his work had screamed sinister. None of the paintings she saw had even remotely resembled anything dark or twisted. Maybe not all of Lucas's art was on public display. Should he be on her radar?

She quickly typed back, *Thanks for letting me know, Liz. I'll check it out.*

Setting the phone down, Olivia let out a long, tired sigh. Elmer, ever in tune with her moods, rolled over dramatically and plopped his head into her lap, his big brown eyes gazing up at her with that goofy, endearing expression he always wore when he sensed her stress. His ears flopped back, giving him an almost cartoonish smile.

"You're such a goofball," she murmured, running her fingers through his soft fur. "I don't know what I'd do without you, Elmer. You're probably the only thing keeping me sane."

Elmer blinked up at her, his eyes soft and reassuring, and she heard his response, *Same.* His tail thumped lazily against the wooden boards, and for a moment, Olivia let herself enjoy the simple comfort of his presence, knowing she still had a long road ahead of her.

The next morning, Olivia strolled down Maplewood with Elmer by her side, though "strolled" was a bit of a stretch. Her pace was relaxed, but her mind raced as she discreetly scanned each house. No one had given her Lucas's exact address, so they were playing detective one house at a time. Elmer trotted ahead, his nose twitching as if he, too, was on high alert.

Maplewood wasn't a long street, but as Olivia tried to keep her investigation casual, it felt like a never-ending maze. Just as she started to think they might have missed it, she spotted an open garage at the end of the road. A man stood inside, painting with a kind of intensity that drew her attention immediately. Dark colors swirled across his canvas as he moved with sharp, deliberate strokes.

"Bingo," she muttered under her breath. Elmer let out a soft whuff in response, picking up on her discovery.

As they approached, Olivia realized Lucas had earbuds in, completely oblivious to their presence. His brow was furrowed in concentration, and she took the moment to study the space around him. Canvases were scattered everywhere—some upright on easels, others leaning haphazardly against the garage walls. The painting closest to her was a moody depiction of twisted trees silhouetted against an ominous sky. It was beautiful but unsettling, as if the woods themselves were haunted.

The next canvas was even more chilling. It depicted something—or someone—lying on the forest floor, shadows creeping over the figure. Olivia's heart rate quickened as she recognized the eerie familiarity of the scene. She couldn't tear her eyes away, and a cold knot formed in her stomach.

"Uh, hello?" she called, trying not to startle him. When he didn't respond, she stepped closer. "Hey, Lucas!"

Lucas jolted, nearly dropping his paintbrush. His eyes widened as he yanked out his earbuds. "Oh! Sorry, I didn't hear you."

Olivia offered a tight smile. "Yeah, I noticed. I was hoping I could take a look around at some more of your work. "

Elmer wandered into the garage, sniffing the air, but he stopped short when Lucas's gaze flicked down to him with a frown.

"Is that your dog?" Lucas asked, his tone less than friendly.

"Yeah, this is Elmer," Olivia said, her voice light, though she could sense the tension in the air.

Lucas's frown deepened. "Kind of a mutt, isn't he?"

Elmer froze mid-sniff, shooting Olivia a wounded look. His eyes were wide with indignation. *Mutt?* He stared up at her, clearly expecting her to defend his honor.

Olivia patted his head, suppressing a laugh. "Don't listen to him, boy. You're pure awesome."

Elmer snorted in agreement, pointedly turning his back on Lucas with a dramatic huff. *You're dead to me,* his posture declared.

Lucas missed the whole exchange, too busy nervously cleaning his brushes. His hands fidgeted, his eyes darting around the garage without really meeting hers. The unease in the air was palpable.

"So, you mentioned that you're new in town?" Olivia asked, trying to keep the conversation casual while her mind raced to make sense of the situation.

"Yeah," Lucas muttered, glancing briefly at one of the more ominous canvases. "Moved here a few months ago. Needed...inspiration."

"Inspiration," Olivia echoed, her gaze drifting back to the disturbing artwork. "For paintings like these?"

Lucas's brush froze mid-wipe, his body tensing. "It's just...what comes to me. I don't really control it."

Elmer stepped closer to one of the canvases, sniffing curiously, before letting out a disgruntled huff. Olivia raised an eyebrow at the sound, sensing his unease.

"You've got some pretty intense work here," Olivia said, nodding toward a painting of a shadowy figure standing on a cliff. "That one's...unsettling."

Lucas shifted, avoiding her gaze. "It's the mountains. They bring up different ideas for me."

Olivia wasn't convinced. She gestured to another canvas, this one depicting a field of starling berries. The vibrant color of the berries seemed to bleed into the soil like droplets of blood. In the center of the field stood a shadowy figure, its face obscured. Her heart skipped a beat. Was that Emily?

"Are you familiar with Emily Harris?" Olivia asked, her tone casual but her eyes sharp.

Lucas paled slightly. "I've...heard of her. Small town, everyone talks."

His hands were shaking slightly now, and Olivia could sense the fear creeping into his demeanor. Elmer, still sniffing around, shot her a look—*This guy's scared. Something's off.*

"You paint some pretty specific scenes," Olivia continued, trying to press gently. "Do they come from anywhere particular? Or are they just dreams?"

"Dreams," Lucas said quickly, too quickly. "They're just dreams."

There was something about the way he said it—something evasive. Olivia studied him for a moment longer, trying to decide whether Lucas was hiding something or if he was simply a frightened artist caught in something bigger than himself.

"Well, if your hear anything unusual about Emily, please let me know," Olivia said, her tone lightening as she prepared to leave, "She was my best friend and I'm really trying to figure out what happened to her."

Lucas nodded too quickly again. "Sure. Yeah."

As Olivia turned to go, Elmer gave Lucas one last sniff before trotting back to her side. His tail wagged slowly, but Olivia could sense he was still uneasy.

Back at the Jeep, Olivia glanced one last time at the garage. The disturbing images of starling berries and shadowy figures weighed heavily on her mind. Lucas was clearly hiding something, but whether it was relevant to Emily's death remained to be seen.

As they drove away, Elmer stretched out in the passenger seat, clearly still miffed about being called a mutt. Olivia chuckled, reaching over to scratch his ears. "Don't worry, boy. You're a gentleman among dogs."

Elmer snorted in agreement, settling in as they headed off to uncover the next piece of the puzzle.

Olivia sat across from Jake at the kitchen table, her fingers tracing the rim of her coffee mug as the late afternoon sun streamed through the windows. The light cast a warm glow on the wooden floor where Elmer lay sprawled, his paws twitching in sleep. Olivia felt no closer to solving Emily's mystery and a nagging feeling in her gut told her she was missing something crucial—something big.

"You've been quiet," Jake said, breaking the silence. "What's going on in that detective brain of yours?"

Olivia sighed and set her mug down with a soft thud. "I don't know, Jake. I've talked to everyone on my list, but I feel like I'm just spinning my wheels. Liz Stevens keeps coming up, but I can't figure out why. She's just a science teacher, right? Why would she be involved in any of this?"

Jake leaned back in his chair, crossing his arms thoughtfully. "Maybe there's more to Liz than you think. Didn't you say she seemed off when you talked to her?"

"Yeah," Olivia agreed, her frown deepening. "There was something weird about her, but I can't put my finger on it. I just don't see any motive for her to want Emily dead."

Jake tapped his fingers on the table, eyes narrowing as he thought back. "You know her family's been tied to this town for generations, right? "

Olivia's interest piqued, her brow furrowing. "She mentioned something like that when I talked to her the other day. She mentioned something about the starling berry too."

"Yeah, her grandfather was a big-deal scientist or doctor, I think. He's the one who planted the first starling berries around here. People say he was convinced the berries had some kind of powerful healing properties. He even started researching them before...well, before some kind of scandal got him run out of town."

"A scandal?" Olivia sat up straighter, her mind racing. Some of Emily's notes mentioned that the starling berry had a past but it wasn't specific about what."

Jake nodded. "Yep. From what I've heard, his experiments went wrong, and the townspeople turned against him. It's one of those things no one talks about anymore—especially Liz. She's always been kind of defensive about her family's past."

If Liz's grandfather had been experimenting with starling berries and his reputation had been ruined, that might explain why Liz had been so secretive about her connection to them.

"So, her family has this deep history with the berries, and Liz never mentioned it?" Olivia's voice took on an edge as she tried to make sense of it all. "Emily's tincture project was all about those berries. Could Liz have felt like Emily was stepping on her family's legacy? That might explain why she's been acting so strange."

Jake nodded slowly, a glimmer of understanding in his eyes. "It's possible. Liz might have felt like Emily was overshadowing her family's legacy. If Liz had been carrying that resentment for a while, it could've eaten at her, especially if Emily's work was gaining attention."

Olivia leaned forward, the puzzle pieces shifting in her mind. "If her grandfather's work with the berries was disgraced, Liz might have seen this as her chance to restore her family's name. But instead of her, it was Emily getting all the attention."

Jake's expression grew serious. "Do you think that's enough to make Liz do something drastic?"

Olivia hesitated, her thoughts swirling. "I don't know. But if Liz felt like Emily's success with the tincture was erasing her family's history, it might've triggered something. Maybe that's why she was so invested in Emily's research."

Jake rubbed his chin, his mind turning over the new theory. "And if her grandfather's work was controversial or dangerous...Liz could be trying to reclaim her family's place in history, for better or worse. Maybe she saw this as her way to finally live up to her family's name."

Olivia leaned back in her chair, the weight of the new information pressing down on her. There was definitely more to Liz than met the eye, and now Olivia knew she had to dig deeper. Liz's family history with the starling berries wasn't just a random detail—it could be the key to the entire mystery.

Elmer stirred at her feet, letting out a low groan as he shifted positions. Olivia smiled down at him and absently scratched behind his ears. His sleepy eyes blinked up at her, asking, *Is this important?*

"Yeah, buddy," Olivia murmured. "It might be."

Jake watched her closely. "So, what's your next move? Are you going to confront Liz about her family?"

Olivia shook her head. "Not yet. I don't want to tip her off if she is involved somehow. I need more information first. I'll ask some of the older folks in town about her grandfather—see if anyone remembers what really happened with the berries. If there's more to this, I'll find it."

Jake nodded in agreement. "Sounds like a plan. Just be careful, Liv. If Liz is hiding something, you don't want to give her any reason to cover her tracks."

Olivia smirked. "Don't worry, I'll be subtle." She stood, feeling a renewed sense of purpose. "Thanks for the info, Jake. This gives me something to go on. I'll let you know what I find."

Liz's connection to the starling berries was no longer just a curious fact—it was a lead, and Olivia was determined to follow it. One thing was for sure: Liz Stevens wasn't just a quiet science teacher. There was much more to her story, and Olivia was going to figure out exactly what she was hiding.

Later that afternoon, Olivia wandered into the quiet of Perks and Peaks, the warm aroma of espresso mingling with the faint scent of vanilla from the candles placed on the windowsills. The café was bustling with the after-work crowd, but Olivia found a spot near the back, close to a bulletin board layered with town announcements, flyers, and newspaper clippings. She sipped her coffee, her eyes skimming over the collage absentmindedly until a familiar name caught her attention.

There, pinned among the flyers, was a yellowed newspaper article dated from just a few months ago. The headline read: **Town Hall Proposes Protection of Local Flora for Historical and Scientific Value.** A grainy photo of Samuel Carter and Liz Stevens standing side by side at a town meeting accompanied the article, their expressions serious. Olivia's eyes narrowed, recalling how the conservation debate had turned tense and personal.

Before she could piece together why that memory felt significant, a sudden burst of laughter came from the corner of the café. Millie Partridge was sitting with two of her friends, their voices carrying across the room.

"Can you believe Samuel? Always sticking his nose where it doesn't belong," Millie said, shaking her head. "And that meeting with Liz? Suspicious if you ask me. 'Securing what's hers,' my foot."

Olivia's pulse quickened as she listened, her ears straining to catch every word.

One of Millie's friends raised an eyebrow. "Well, if Emily hadn't been poking around in places she shouldn't have, we wouldn't be talking about this at all. But you didn't hear it from me."

Millie leaned in, her voice dropping to a conspiratorial whisper. "Word is, Samuel knows more about that night than he lets on. He's always had a hand in things around here, but this time he's in over his head."

Olivia's heart pounded as the pieces started to align. Samuel had been involved in the town's preservation efforts and was working with Liz on something related to Emily's research. If he was trying to "secure" anything, it wasn't just about conservation—it was about control. Control that could have led to desperation, even violence.

She set down her coffee, hands trembling slightly as she pushed back her chair and stood up. The chatter in the café buzzed around her, but her mind was already elsewhere. She needed to know what Samuel and Liz were up to and what they'd been hiding. And she had a feeling that whatever it was, it was tied directly to Emily's final moments.

As she stepped out of Perks and Peaks and into the cool evening air, a familiar figure caught her eye across the street. Samuel Carter was walking briskly down Main Street, his face unreadable and his eyes shifting as if looking for someone—or watching to see if he was being followed.

A chill crept down Olivia's spine. It was time to confront the secrets that had been buried in Emerald Ridge for far too long.

Chapter 23

S itting in Perks and Peaks the next morning, Olivia sipped her coffee and chatted with Ashley. Her thoughts kept drifting back to Liz Stevens and the tangled history of her family. She wondered if Ashley might have any leads on where to dig up more information on the Stevens legacy. Elmer had opted to take the day off, happily staying behind to help her mom dig holes in the garden—a task he seemed to find much more exciting than detective work.

"Hey, Ash," Olivia began, setting her mug down. "Do you know anything about Liz Stevens's family?"

Ashley looked up, a puzzled expression crossing her face. "What do you mean?" she asked. "I know the basics— like that her family has been in this area for a long time. And I think someone in her family had something to do with the starling berries." Her voice trailed off as she thought.

Olivia raised an eyebrow, exasperation creeping into her tone. "Why does everyone seem to know this stuff but me?"

Ashley smirked, her eyes glinting with humor. "Well, you never did have much of a thing for history."

Olivia shot her a playful glare. "Okay, fair point."

Ashley took a sip of her own coffee, thinking for a moment. "Hmm...you could probably find something at the library. They've got old town records, maybe even some family histories."

Just as Olivia was about to consider the idea, Ashley's eyes lit up with sudden inspiration. "Wait! What about the retirement village down in Darling Valley? I think some of Liz's older relatives might be there. Maybe her great-aunt? Let me check with my mom real quick."

Olivia's brows furrowed, curiosity piqued. "How did you know Liz has family there?"

Ashley smiled, a little nostalgic. "My great-uncle Bert used to live there before he passed. He was one of those guys who knew everyone's business—loved to chat. He used to tell me stories about some of the old-timers, including Liz's grandfather, Dr. Stevens. Apparently, the family was a hot topic back then, especially after the whole starling berry debacle. Bert mentioned Liz's great-aunt would often visit him and talk about the 'good old days' when the Stevens were still considered prominent in Emerald Ridge."

Olivia's eyes widened. "Do you think she'd know anything about the research Emily was doing or what Liz has been up to?"

"It's worth a shot. If anyone remembers the Stevens reputation or any buried secrets, it'll be her. Let me ask my mom and see what she remembers," Ashley said.

Before Olivia could respond, Ashley darted to the back of the coffee shop, leaving the door swinging in her wake. Olivia leaned back in her chair, pondering the suggestion. The library was always a good bet, but she hadn't thought about the retirement village. Maybe Liz's great-aunt could provide some firsthand insight that the records wouldn't have.

Ashley reappeared, slightly breathless, her cheeks flushed with excitement. "Mom says one of Liz's great-aunts—her grandpa's sister—lives there. Mabel or Marabelle or something like that."

Olivia's eyes widened. That was a solid lead, more than she'd expected. "That's fantastic! Tell your mom thanks for me."

She grabbed her bag and stood, the thrill of a potential breakthrough sparking a new energy in her step. "I guess I'd better get going if I want to make it there and back in time to stop by the library later. I might swing by here again for another caffeine fix afterward," she said with a grin as she headed for the door.

Pulling the Jeep onto Main Street, Olivia set off toward Darling Valley. The retirement village was about a forty-five-minute drive from Emerald Ridge, tucked away in a quiet valley just outside the bustling town limits. As the miles rolled by, she couldn't help but notice how much road she'd covered in the past few days, her Jeep seemingly becoming her second home. But with the weather warm and clear, it was a perfect day for a drive—just the kind of peaceful escape she needed before diving back into the thick of her investigation.

With the open road ahead and a potential new lead on Liz's mysterious family legacy, Olivia felt a glimmer of hope amidst the weight of unanswered questions.

***

Forty-five minutes later, Olivia pulled into the parking lot of the Darling Valley Retirement Village. She wasn't entirely sure how to approach this. Could she just walk in and ask for a Mabel or Marabelle Stevens? It felt like an odd thing to do, but she had no other choice. As soon as she stepped through the sliding glass doors, the familiar but slightly unsettling scent hit her—a mix of antiseptic cleaner, old wood, and the faint medicinal odor that clung to places like this. The air was cool enough to make her wish she'd grabbed a hoodie from home, even though it was the middle of summer.

The lobby had a faded charm. Worn carpets in an outdated floral pattern stretched across the floor, and the soft hum of medical equipment mingled with the distant sound of a TV playing a game show. Olivia noticed the framed photographs of local landmarks lining the walls—mountain vistas, old bridges, town squares. They seemed like relics of a forgotten time, just like the people who lived here.

As Olivia approached the front desk, the receptionist—a woman in her fifties with tight curls and a practiced smile—barely glanced up from her computer.

"Afternoon," the woman said, her tone mechanical, as if she'd said it a thousand times that day.

Olivia signed the guestbook with a chewed-up pen, glancing around the lobby. Hallways branched off in different directions, some dimly lit, others glowing under harsh fluorescent lights. The place felt like it was stuck in a kind of limbo, where time moved slowly, and everything just...lingered.

"Can you tell me where Mabel Stevens is?" Olivia asked.

The receptionist glanced up for the first time, her eyebrows raising slightly. "Ms. Mabel?" She pronounced it *May-belle*, drawing out the syllables. "She's probably in the community room for the painting class. But if she's not, her room's down the left hall, number 8601."

Olivia nodded, heading in the direction the receptionist pointed for the community room. As she walked down the hallway, she could already hear the soft swish of paintbrushes and the gentle murmur of conversation. When she peeked inside, she was surprised by what she saw.

Lucas, the anxious and brooding painter she had met recently, was standing at the front of the room, guiding the residents through a lesson. His usual tense energy was gone, replaced by a calm and encouraging demeanor. He moved among the seniors, offering tips and guidance as they worked on colorful landscapes. Olivia blinked, taken aback by the transformation.

"See, don't be afraid to really lean into the yellows and oranges," Lucas was saying to one of the elderly women. "The warmth of the sunlight—it's not just about what you see, it's about how it makes you feel."

The residents were absorbed in their work, smiling and chatting as they painted. The air smelled of acrylic paint and fresh flowers from a vase nearby. Olivia couldn't help but smile at the scene, but it only made her more curious. How could this be the same Lucas who had painted such dark, eerie landscapes? The contrast was striking.

As Lucas turned toward the door, his eyes lit up when he saw her. He raised a finger, asking her to wait a moment, then turned back to the class. "All right, folks, that's the end of the lesson today. Feel free to keep working or leave your paintings to dry."

He wiped his hands on a rag and walked over to Olivia in the hallway. "Olivia, hey. I've been meaning to talk to you after our last...interaction. I think I gave you the wrong impression."

His calm energy from the painting class began to waver, the anxious edge she'd seen before creeping back. "I've...been dealing with some things," he sighed. "Let me explain."

He led her down a hallway to a mostly empty sitting room. The residents seemed to be occupied elsewhere, so they sat in a quiet corner, away from prying eyes.

Lucas sank into a chair, running a hand through his hair. "I know I came off a bit strange the other day. People always expect that when they hear I'm a painter." He chuckled nervously. "Anyway, the dark paintings, the anxiety, it all started after I moved here."

Olivia leaned in, listening intently.

"I moved into that house on Maplewood about a week after Emily's accident," Lucas continued. "From the first night, I had these...intense dreams. Dark, disturbing images of the ridge and strange shapes—people, but not quite people. I have no connection to Emily or to Emerald Ridge, so I don't know why my mind is doing this. Maybe it's because I heard about the accident. My anxiety went into overdrive, and painting those scenes is the only way I've been able to deal with it."

His eyes met Olivia's, and she saw the genuine fear and confusion there. "I'm not involved in whatever happened to Emily. I don't even know her. These dreams—they're just nightmares."

Olivia nodded, her gut telling her that Lucas was telling the truth. He wasn't a threat, just a man haunted by his own mind. "Thank you for explaining. For what it's worth, I believe you. I've had some strange dreams too, ever since Emily died."

Lucas sighed in relief. "I just didn't want you to think, well, that I was dangerous. People already look at me funny, and I don't need them thinking I'm a murderer."

"I get it," Olivia said, standing up. "And for the record, I don't think you're involved. But, do you happen to know Mabel Stevens? I was told she might be around here."

Lucas smiled for the first time. "Yeah, Mabel's great. Spunky for someone in her nineties. Actually, there she is." He pointed to an elderly woman in a purple floral dress making her way down the hall with a walker.

"That's her?" Olivia asked, her brows lifting in mild disbelief as she peered down the hallway.

Lucas nodded, a smirk playing at the corners of his mouth. "Yep, that's Mabel. Good luck catching up with her. She's a tough one."

Olivia smiled and thanked him before hurrying down the hall.

Taking a breath, Olivia knocked lightly on the doorframe, bracing herself for whatever lay ahead.

"Come in, but shut that door quick!" came a raspy voice from inside.

Olivia stepped in, quickly closing the door behind her. The room smelled of cigarette smoke and leather, and there, in a worn armchair, sat Mabel Stevens. Silver hair in a messy bun, a cigarette dangling from her lips, and a glass of whiskey in hand. She looked smaller than Olivia had expected, but the sharpness in her eyes told Olivia this was not someone to be underestimated.

Mabel Stevens was nothing like Olivia had imagined. Given the stories about the Stevens family, Olivia had expected an older woman with a touch of old-world elegance—maybe coiffed white hair and a wardrobe of perfectly pressed cardigans.

Olivia hesitated for a moment, feeling the weight of unexpected nerves. This wasn't the poised, aristocratic woman she'd envisioned. Mabel looked tough, like she'd spent years fending off the world and wasn't about to let her guard down now.

"Who are you?" Mabel asked bluntly, eyeing her with suspicion. "You better start talking."

Olivia cleared her throat, her voice steady despite the tension in the room. "I'm Olivia Morgan, from Emerald Ridge. I've been doing some research on the starling berry, and your niece, Liz, keeps coming up. I was hoping you might tell me more about your family's history with the berry."

Mabel Stevens eyed Olivia with a mixture of suspicion and curiosity, her sharp gaze cutting through the smoke that lingered in the air. After a pause, she let out a dry, humorless laugh. "The starling berry, huh? That's not a family legacy—it's a curse."

Olivia took a seat across from her, sensing there was more to the story than the surface suggested. "I've heard bits and pieces about your brother, Dr. Stevens, but I don't know the full story."

Mabel took a deep drag from her cigarette, her fingers steady despite her age. She leaned forward slightly, her eyes gleaming with mischief. "Larry, my brother, he thought he was some kind of genius. He stumbled upon the properties of the starling berry, but here's the kicker—he didn't come by that knowledge honestly."

Olivia leaned in, her instincts telling her that she was about to uncover something important. "What do you mean?"

Mabel clicked her tongue, the bitterness evident in her voice. "He learned about the berry from the local indigenous people who still lived around Emerald Ridge back then. They taught him everything—how to use the berry, its properties, its healing potential. And instead of giving them credit, he claimed it as his own discovery. Took what wasn't his, and for a while, the town loved him. They thought he'd make Emerald Ridge famous. But when the truth came out?" She shook her head slowly. "Well, they ran him out of town. And good riddance, if you ask me. The scandal tainted our family for years."

Olivia's eyes widened as she processed the new information. "So, he was run out for exploiting their knowledge?"

Mabel nodded grimly. "Yep. The town turned on him fast. My brother couldn't handle it, so he packed up and left, never to return. That left the rest of us to deal with the fallout. And Liz...well, she's been trying to scrub the family name clean ever since."

"Liz has mentioned her family's legacy," Olivia said slowly, piecing things together. "But she's never talked about the scandal. How did she handle it?"

Mabel chuckled, but it lacked warmth. "How do you think? She was just a kid when it happened, but she's carried that weight her whole life. In middle school, she found out about the scandal during a family tree project. From then on, she became obsessed with restoring the Stevens name. Her mother had the same fixation, always believing the family was 'owed' something. Lizzie just picked up that torch and ran with it. She thinks the Stevens family got a raw deal, and she's been looking for a way to set it right ever since."

Olivia's thoughts raced as Mabel spoke. Liz's fixation on the starling berry wasn't just about science—it was personal. "And now that the starling berry is being used again, she must be even more interested in it."

Mabel took another sip of her whiskey, her gaze steady. "You bet. The starling berry was supposed to be our family's ticket to greatness, at least according to her. And if someone else is working with it? Lizzie's definitely got her eyes on that."

"Has Liz ever talked about doing something with the berry herself?" Olivia asked, her voice cautious.

Mabel shrugged, but there was a knowing glint in her eyes. "She's never said it outright, but I know her. She's always been jealous of anyone who gets close to that berry. That's what pushed her into science in the first place. It was never about the field—it was about proving something. She thought if she could unlock the berry's potential, she could fix everything. Her career, the family legacy...all of it. But she's too proud to admit that."

Olivia felt a chill run through her as the pieces started to align. Liz must have seen Emily's work with the starling berry as a direct threat to her family's claim to the berry. That would explain Liz's strange behavior and her obsessive interest in Emily's research.

"So, you think Liz might be interested in anything someone else was doing with the berry?" Olivia asked, treading carefully.

Mabel let out a sharp laugh. "Liz would probably try to steal whatever they were working on and make it look like her idea. She's never been one to do the hard work herself. But don't ask me to prove it—she's good at covering her tracks."

Olivia smiled slightly at Mabel's bluntness. "You've given me a lot to think about. Thank you."

Mabel waved a hand dismissively. "Ah, don't thank me, kid. Just be careful. Lizzie's been quiet about that scandal for a reason. She doesn't like it when people dig into it. And she's got a bit of a...vindictive streak."

The words landed like a stone in Olivia's chest, making her heart pound faster. *Vindictive?* The image she had of Liz—a composed and serious science teacher with an air of quiet superiority—suddenly shifted in her mind, taking on a darker hue. Olivia's stomach twisted as memories of

Liz's cool, assessing gaze surfaced, now tinged with a more sinister undertone.

"Vindictive," she repeated, the word heavy on her tongue. The room seemed to shrink around her, the musty scent of old books and lavender mingling with her sudden wave of anxiety. If Liz was capable of holding grudges and acting on them, what else was she capable of?

Olivia glanced at Mabel, whose eyes were sharp and knowing. The older woman's expression told her that she wasn't exaggerating or being dramatic. It was a warning wrapped in casual conversation, a reminder this was a path fraught with hidden dangers.

A memory of Emily's voice drifted into Olivia's mind, talking about Liz's unwavering drive and how she always sought validation. "She's intense," Emily had said once, almost offhandedly. Now, that comment felt more like a red flag that Olivia had ignored. *Had Emily known how far that intensity could go?*

The room felt suddenly stifling, the quiet hum of the hallway outside barely registering as Olivia struggled to steady her breathing. If Liz had a reputation for going after those who crossed her, what did that mean for anyone who threatened to expose her secrets now?

"Thanks for the warning," Olivia finally managed, her voice steadying, but her mind racing with questions she wasn't sure she wanted answers to.

Standing to leave, Olivia turned to Mabel, "I'll be careful. And if I find anything else, I'll keep you in the loop."

Mabel grinned, lifting her glass in a mock toast. "No need, sweetheart. I know more about that damn berry than I ever wanted to. Good luck—you're gonna need it."

As Olivia walked out of the room, the scent of cigarette smoke clinging to her clothes, unease rippled through her. Liz's obsession with the starling berry and her family's tarnished legacy was far deeper—and potentially more dangerous—than she'd realized.

CHAPTER 24

Olivia slid into the driver's seat of her Jeep, her mind still buzzing from the revelations she'd uncovered. The next step was clear: she needed to dig deeper. The library would be her next stop. She checked the clock—if she kept a steady pace, maybe bending the speed limit just a bit, she could make it to Emerald Ridge Library with an hour to spare before closing. That would give her plenty of time to search for the town records and historical details that might tie everything together.

The road back to town was bathed in golden summer light, the trees casting flickering shadows as she drove. But Olivia barely noticed the scenery; her focus was laser-sharp on the task ahead. By the time she rolled into the library's parking lot, just before four p.m., she felt like she was sprinting toward the finish line in this small-town mystery.

Emerald Ridge Library was a mix of old-world charm and modern utility, its ivy-clad brick facade looking like something straight out of a fairy tale. It stood proudly in the heart of the town, with tall arched windows glinting in the afternoon sun. The wooden door, worn smooth from decades of use, had a comforting air of permanence—much like the secrets Olivia was determined to uncover inside.

Taking a deep breath, Olivia swung open the door and stepped inside. The library's interior was a calming contrast to the chaos swirling in her mind. Polished oak floors stretched beneath rows of tall bookshelves crammed with volumes, and the soft hum of fluorescent lights filled the air. The scent of aged paper and ink, with a hint of fresh coffee from the reading area, instantly put Olivia at ease.

Sunlight streamed through the large windows, casting a warm glow on the seating nook lined with overstuffed armchairs. A stone fireplace, though rarely used, added to the homey atmosphere, and an old portrait of the town's founder hung above the mantel. The quiet was palpable, broken only by the faint rustling of pages and the occasional clink of coffee cups.

The librarian, a friendly woman in her sixties with glasses perched on her nose, sat behind an oak desk piled high with returned books. She looked up with a smile as Olivia approached.

"Hi there," Olivia began, trying to keep her voice casual. "I'm looking for some town records or anything related to the early families of Emerald Ridge. And if there's any information on the starling berry, that would be helpful too."

The librarian raised an eyebrow, intrigued by the oddly specific request. "That's quite a bit," she said, but then pointed to the staircase at the back of the room. "All the town history, archives, and old newspaper collections are upstairs. As for the starling berry, you'll want the gardening section over there." She gestured toward a corner filled with well-worn books on local flora.

"Thanks," Olivia replied, already making her way to the staircase, her footsteps soft but determined.

Upstairs, the scent of old books grew stronger, and the air seemed heavier, like it was thick with the weight of untold stories. Olivia glanced at the rows of black binders labeled by year and grabbed one marked 1952. She lugged it over to a nearby table, the yellowed pages crackling as she flipped through them. If she was doing her math right, this should have been around the time the scandal broke, give or take a few years.

She flipped through the binder bit found nothing of interest in 1952. She returned the binder to the shelf and reached for the next one, flipping through it page by page.

The further she went, the more the headlines became hyper-local—school events, farmers markets, births, and deaths. And then, there it was, May 1954: *Local Scientist Touts Properties of Starling Berry.* The photo accompanying the article showed Dr. Larry Stevens in a crisp white lab coat, standing behind a table piled high with the small, deep red berries, beaming like he'd just discovered the cure for every ailment known to man. His eyes shone with a mix of pride and fervor, the kind that only comes from a man who believes he's on the brink of changing everything.

Olivia skimmed the article. It echoed much of what Mabel had described—Dr. Stevens claiming groundbreaking medicinal properties for the berry, extolling its potential as a treatment for anxiety, pain, and various ailments. The town had once hailed him as a visionary, a local hero who was putting Emerald Ridge on the map. The article quoted town officials and local farmers who'd been swept up in the fervor, talking about how they'd never seen the town so excited.

But what Olivia found next stopped her cold. She flipped open a binder marked *Archives: 1955*, the edges worn and yellowed with age. The headline inside sent a chill through her: *Disgraced Scientist Flees After Allegations of Stolen Knowledge.* The faded photograph beneath it showed Dr. Stevens, not beaming this time, but caught in the middle of a hurried exit, eyes darting sideways as if anticipating someone shouting his name. The backdrop was the courthouse, its stone columns towering behind him like silent witnesses to his fall.

Her pulse quickened as she took in the details. Dr. Stevens had been accused of appropriating knowledge from the local Indigenous community, specifically their long-held understanding of the starling berry's medicinal qualities. Members of the community had come forward, sharing stories of their ancestors using the berry for centuries to treat ailments. Their voices, though late to be heard, were powerful and pointed, accusing Dr. Stevens of twisting their knowledge for his own gain without acknowledgment or permission.

The article outlined the fallout—how the town, once proud of their local scientist, had turned on him almost overnight. There were vivid descriptions of protests outside his home, neighbors turning their backs, and heated letters published in the local paper calling for justice. There were even mentions of tense town meetings where the community's elders spoke passionately, their words slicing through the room like blades. Olivia re-read the article, taking in the information she was seeing. It was one thing to hear town gossip about the subject, but it hit differently seeing it printed out in black and white.

Olivia's eyes caught a detail that Mabel hadn't mentioned: Liz's grandmother, a young woman at the time, had attended those meetings, noted for standing by her husband's side, chin held high even as whispers swirled around them. Her name was scribbled in the margin of one newspaper clipping, circled with notes in an unfamiliar handwriting. "Family loyalty," it read, "or blind faith?"

Her chest tightened with understanding. This scandal wasn't just a footnote; it was woven into the fabric of Liz's family. Generations had lived under its shadow. No wonder Liz never mentioned it—this was more than just a scientific pursuit. It was a deep-seated mission to redeem the Stevens name, to rewrite history in a way that cast her lineage as the rightful pioneers.

Flipping through a few more pages, Olivia found a transcript from a radio interview Dr. Stevens had given before the scandal broke. "The starling berry is a gift," he had said. "A discovery that will elevate the health and well-being of communities far beyond our town." The words now read with a hollow, ironic ring.

Olivia sat back, the weight of it all pressing down on her. Liz's drive, her relentless pursuit of recognition, wasn't just ambition—it was reparation. And that made everything far more dangerous.

After snapping pictures of the articles with her phone, Olivia closed the binder and made her way back downstairs. She had the pieces of the puzzle, but something still didn't feel quite right.

The late afternoon sun bathed the town square in a warm, golden glow as locals gathered for Emerald Ridge's Annual Conservation Fair. As Olivia had made her way back towards her mom's house, she had seen the tents and booths of the fair clustered around town square. She had decided to stop, wondering if more clues might be found there. Booths dedicated to local wildlife preservation, sustainable farming practices, and native plant conservation lined the cobblestone paths. The air buzzed with friendly chatter, punctuated by the occasional chirp of birds and the rustling of leaves from the large trees that shaded the square. Olivia smiled to herself, this was typical Emerald Ridge, especially in the Summer. There always seemed to be a fair or festival going on and there was always a booth for everything, from food to crafts, to informational flyers/

Olivia moved through the crowd, taking in the array of informational displays and community workshops. Kids laughed as they painted birdhouses at a craft station, while adults gathered around a speaker discussing the importance of protecting the town's unique ecosystem. It was the kind of event that made Emerald Ridge feel close-knit, a town that valued its history and natural surroundings.

She spotted Liz Stevens near a table adorned with pamphlets and posters about the preservation of the Ridge. Liz's posture was stiff, her eyes flitting over the crowd as though searching for someone or something. She wore a fitted blazer that looked slightly out of place in the casual setting, but her expression was one of steely determination. Seeing that expression now, Olivia knew there was more to it.

Taking a deep breath, Olivia approached, weaving between groups of chatting townsfolk and a display featuring potted starling berry bushes. "Liz," she called out, her voice level but curious.

Liz turned, her expression shifting from distracted to guarded in an instant. "Olivia. Didn't expect to see you here," she said, managing a polite, tight-lipped smile.

"I wouldn't miss it. The conservation fair has always been important to this town." Olivia's eyes darted to the pamphlets on the table, showcasing images of the native plants and wildlife that thrived in the region. "I was hoping to ask you something. I've been reading up on the history of some of these efforts, and your grandfather, I assume, Dr. Stevens's name came up quite a bit."

Liz's smile faltered, her fingers tightening slightly on the edge of a brochure. She recovered quickly, picking up a pamphlet and pretending to straighten it. "The starling berry has always been an important part of Emerald Ridge's ecosystem and its history," she said, her tone clipped but controlled. "My grandfather's contributions are well-documented."

"True," Olivia agreed, glancing at the display of starling berry products showcased nearby. "But so are the controversies. The allegations that he took credit for indigenous knowledge, the protests that drove him away. There's more to the story than most people remember, isn't there?"

A flash of irritation crossed Liz's face, quickly replaced by a neutral mask. "You've been busy, I see."

Olivia shrugged, trying to keep her tone light. "Just trying to piece things together. It's interesting how some legacies are celebrated, while others are hidden."

Liz's gaze sharpened, and for a moment, she looked past Olivia, scanning the crowd. When she spoke again, her voice was lower, almost a hiss. "Legacy is a complicated thing, Olivia. It's not just about preserving history—it's about reclaiming it, rewriting it when necessary. That kind of work requires sacrifices."

A chill ran down Olivia's spine. "What kind of sacrifices?"

Liz's eyes shifted, catching sight of Samuel Carter standing on the other side of the square, his eyes on them, watching intently. Liz's jaw tightened, and she took a step closer to Olivia, lowering her voice even further. "The kind that forces you to make choices you can't come back from."

Before Olivia could ask more, Liz pulled back, her expression turning back to one of practiced indifference. "Excuse me, Olivia. I have a presentation to give." With that, she turned on her heel and walked toward the small stage set up at the center of the square, leaving Olivia standing by the starling berry display.

Samuel's gaze followed Liz as she moved through the crowd, and then flickered back to Olivia. The weight of his stare was heavy, almost foreboding, and Olivia knew that whatever was happening, she was only scratching the surface.

The late afternoon sun cast long shadows as Olivia navigated a narrow side street, the sounds of the conservation event fading behind her. The cobblestone path felt cooler underfoot, the air heavy with the scent of honeysuckle that crept over the stone walls surrounding some of the older buildings in town. She had chosen this route as a shortcut back to her Jeep, eager to slip away and process the conversation she'd had with Liz. The unease simmering in her gut made her mind race, piecing together the fragmented clues that seemed to point in every direction.

As she approached a quiet alley, the hushed voices of a conversation caught her attention. Olivia stopped short, stepping back into the shadow of a brick storefront. Peering around the edge, she saw Liz Stevens standing a few yards away talking to someone who was obscured by the curve of an ivy-draped wall.

"I've given you plenty of time, Liz," a male voice said, low but edged with a sharpness that made Olivia's heart pound. This was the same male voice that Olivia had heard Liz speaking to last time. It sounded familiar, but she couldn't put her finger on who it might be. "Now, I want more than just a thank you and a handshake when this is all over. If you think you're going to cut me out when you secure that deal, think again."

Liz's face was pale, her arms crossed defensively over her chest. "This was never supposed to go this far," she whispered, casting a nervous glance over her shoulder as though she could feel the weight of unseen eyes. "I can't keep doing this. I'm out."

The man let out a dry, humorless laugh. The shadowed figure leaned in closer, the hard lines of his face making Olivia's blood turn to ice. "Out? You don't get to be out, Liz. Not unless you want everyone to know about that night at the Ridge—how far you went to secure the information."

Olivia's breath caught in her throat, and she had to steady herself against the rough brick wall. Emily. Whoever this man was, he knew about her death, and not just in the way everyone else did. He knew something more, something dark, and he was using it to manipulate Liz.

Liz's eyes filled with a mixture of fear and desperation. "You don't understand," she said, her voice shaking. "Emily was going to ruin everything. She didn't know how deep this ran, what was at stake. But this—this is too much. I never agreed to hurt anyone."

The man laughed, humorlessly. "Too late for second thoughts, Liz. Either you secure your end of this deal and make sure my share is substantial, or I'll make sure every whisper about that night turns into a roar. You think your name's been tarnished before? Wait until the whole town knows the truth."

Liz took a step back, her hands trembling. The fight seemed to drain out of her, leaving her shoulders slumped and her gaze cast downward. "Fine," she whispered, barely audible. "I'll do it.

"Good," the man said, his voice smooth with satisfaction. He stepped out the far side of the alley without being seen, his footsteps echoing against the brick as he walked in the opposite direction.

Olivia's heart thudded in her chest as she watched Liz stand there, frozen, before wiping a tear from her cheek and hurrying off down the path. Who was this shadow man that Liz kept meeting with and what did he know about Emily's death that others didn't?

The realization hit Olivia like a punch: Someone had known about Emily's death all along and was using it to his advantage. This wasn't just about conservation or town politics. It was deeper, more sinister, and it involved Emily's work—and possibly, the very secrets she had been trying to protect.

Later that evening, as the streets of Emerald Ridge quieted under the soft glow of the streetlights, Olivia's phone buzzed in her pocket. Frowning, she pulled it out as she reached her Jeep parked at the edge of the town square. Three missed texts from Edward Barnes.

Her pulse quickened as she opened the first: *Alicia's missing. Her car is here, but she's gone.*

The second: *I've looked everywhere.*

And the third—a photo of a note, pinned to Alicia's lab coat with a shard of glass. The message read: *Is it worth it?*

A chill ran down Olivia's spine. Whoever had taken Alicia wasn't playing games anymore.

Without a moment's hesitation, she texted back: *On my way.*

The noise of the town square, the distant hum of cars, and the warm summer breeze faded from her awareness. The events of the day—Liz's cryptic defensiveness, Samuel's ominous hold over her—rushed back in a flood of urgency. Olivia started the Jeep, her hands gripping the wheel tightly as she navigated the darkened streets.

Alicia's disappearance changed everything. What had begun as an investigation into Emily's death now felt like it had spiraled into something far more insidious. Olivia's mind raced as she connected the threads—Liz's ambition, the threats the man in the shadows made. She had a sinking feeling that Liz's drive to reclaim her family's name came at a cost much greater than she had imagined. And that cost was now putting more lives at risk.

CHAPTER 25

Olivia swung by her house to pick up Elmer before heading to Edward's. She figured his nose might come in handy for sniffing out clues, especially with nightfall approaching, though from the way he lazily hopped into the Jeep, it was clear Elmer wasn't thrilled about having his evening interrupted. He shook himself off, sending bits of dirt and garden soil flying across the dashboard. His displeasure was unmistakable.

"I'm sorry, boy, but something important came up," Olivia said, glancing over at him. His response came through loud and clear: *How important?*

"Alicia is missing," she replied. That got his attention. His ears shot up, and he straightened in his scat as if preparing for a mission. His attitude shifted, and he stared out the window with renewed focus as they sped toward Edward Barnes's house.

When the Jeep screeched to a halt in front of Edward's, kicking up a cloud of gravel, Elmer was ready. He didn't wait for Olivia to open the door, instead clambering over the console and squeezing out behind her. With a determined trot, he headed for the house. The door was slightly ajar, immediately setting off alarm bells in Olivia's mind. She called out for Edward as they made their way inside, moving quickly toward the outdoor lab.

Before they could reach the door, Edward stumbled into the hallway, his face pale and frantic.

"Olivia! Thank goodness you're here!" Edward's voice shook.

"I got your messages and came as fast as I could. What happened?" Olivia asked, trying to keep her voice calm despite the tension in the air.

Edward took a shaky breath, glancing around nervously as if expecting someone to appear. "Alicia was here, working in the lab, a little later than usual. I stepped out to pick up some dinner for us both, and when I came back, she was gone. I searched everywhere—the greenhouses, the entire property—and found nothing. Then, I saw her coat...and this."

He handed Olivia a crumpled note, the same one from his message: *Is it worth it?*

A chill ran down Olivia's spine. Elmer, standing by her side, gave her a knowing look, waiting for his cue. Olivia crouched down, holding up Alicia's jacket for him to sniff.

"Think you can track her scent, boy?" she asked.

Elmer cocked his head, clearly thinking, *I'm no bloodhound, but I'll try.*

With a deep snort, he sniffed the jacket before setting off toward the greenhouses, nose low to the ground. Olivia followed closely, casting a glance back at Edward, who looked both confused and hopeful.

"He's smarter than he looks," Olivia assured him with a shrug. Edward didn't seem entirely convinced but he handed her a flashlight and followed them anyway.

They trailed Elmer as he zigzagged through the rows of plants and the darkened property, occasionally stopping to investigate a suspicious scent or object. The path led them to the far end of the property, where Elmer abruptly stopped in front of a small, rusty shed. He pawed at the door and whined, pressing his nose against the lock.

"I haven't used this shed in years," Edward muttered. "I don't even remember what's in here."

Edward and Olivia noticed the rusted padlock, lying on the ground next to the shed. A sure sign someone else had been there. Archibald, Edward's parrot, swooped down and landed on his shoulder. With surprising precision, the bird pecked at the lock, and within seconds, the rusty latch popped open.

"Well, that explains where all the treats have been disappearing to," Edward said, blinking in disbelief.

They pried open the creaky door, and Olivia shown the flashlight around the interior of the shed. Inside, slumped against a pile of old gardening supplies, was Alicia. Her hands were bound, and a gag covered her mouth. A small starling berry plant rested awkwardly in her lap.

Olivia rushed over, checking for a pulse. "She's alive!" she called out to Edward, relief flooding her voice. "Help me get her out of here."

They carefully lifted Alicia and carried her outside, laying her on the grass. Her eyes fluttered open as she groaned, struggling to regain her bearings.

"What...happened?" Alicia croaked, her voice weak.

"That's what we need to figure out," Olivia said, brushing dirt from Alicia's cheek. Elmer sat protectively by her side, as if sensing her unease.

Alicia blinked, trying to piece together what had happened. "There was a woman," she whispered, her voice barely audible.

Olivia leaned in closer, exchanging a glance with Edward. "A woman? Do you remember what she looked like? Anything she said?"

Alicia pressed a hand to her forehead, her brow furrowed as she struggled to piece together the memory. Her eyes darted back and forth, as if searching for the elusive details hidden in the night. "She wore a hood...moved quickly...I couldn't see her face clearly. But she was strong. Stronger than I expected."

Elmer, ever watchful, gave a low growl, his fur bristling as he picked up on Alicia's distress. Olivia reached down to pat his head, feeling the tension in his muscles. "It's okay, boy," she whispered, trying to soothe both him and Alicia.

Alicia's fingers trembled slightly as she continued. "She grabbed me from behind in the lab," she said, her voice dropping to a whisper. The words seemed to sap the strength from her, and she swayed slightly before catching herself. "I tried to fight, but she put something over my mouth. It smelled like chemicals—sharp, acrid. I couldn't breathe. Everything started to blur, and then...nothing. Just darkness."

Olivia's pulse quickened, each heartbeat thundering in her ears. She leaned forward, her gaze steady but full of urgency. "Did she say anything? Anything at all, even just a word?"

Alicia's face contorted as she searched her fragmented memory, her eyes squinting in the effort. "There was something," she said, her voice cracking. "She mentioned Emily. I think she said Emily was too close. That she had something the woman wanted. Something important."

The air suddenly felt colder, heavier, as the implications sank in. Olivia's mind raced, connecting dots that had been scattered up to this point. Whoever had attacked Alicia wasn't just after Emily's research—there was a personal vendetta at play. A shadow of danger had crept closer, and it was no longer just hovering at the edges.

Edward's face turned pale as he exchanged glances with Olivia, his usual composed demeanor shaken. He had already called the paramedics, and the wail of sirens in the distance signaled their approach. Alicia's breathing steadied as the shock wore off, and a blanket was draped around her shoulders by Edward.

The paramedics arrived, their presence swift and efficient. Alicia's gaze met Olivia's as she was helped into the ambulance, a silent plea for answers reflected in her eyes. Olivia clenched her fists at her sides, a surge of protectiveness rising in her chest. She wanted to promise Alicia that it would all be okay, but she couldn't. Not yet.

With Alicia safely on her way and the police updated on the latest developments, a strange, thick silence enveloped the front lawn. The air carried the faint scent of damp leaves and freshly cut grass, a jarring contrast to the grim reality they were now facing.

"It was a woman," Edward muttered, rubbing a hand over his stubbled jaw. He stared at the ground, as if trying to process the idea. "Does that match what you've been investigating, Olivia?"

"Yes," Olivia said, her voice steady but low. She looked out over the darkening horizon, the weight of the unfolding mystery pressing down on her shoulders. "From what I've been finding out a woman is definitely involved, but I think there might be someone else too. I just can't quite put my finger on why the other person would be involved, I don't have enough to go after anyone yet. She, or they, have been careful—meticulously careful."

Edward let out a long breath, one that spoke to the exhaustion and worry etched across his face. "I need a drink," he muttered, turning on his heel and heading back inside, leaving Olivia and Elmer standing alone under the deepening twilight.

Olivia turned and climbed into the driver's seat of the Jeep, Elmer hopping up beside her with a soft whine. For a moment, she sat motionless, her hands clutching the steering wheel until her knuckles turned white. The realization of how deeply personal this was becoming hit her like a punch to the gut. The stakes were no longer just about uncovering the truth—they were about protecting what remained of Emily's legacy and the people she cared about. And the threat felt closer, more immediate.

Elmer, sensitive as always, shifted in his seat to nuzzle Olivia's arm, his eyes full of quiet concern. He could feel the tension vibrating off her, like a wire pulled too tight. She turned to him, forcing a half-smile that didn't quite reach her eyes. "Don't worry, boy. We're okay," she said, her voice wavering just enough to betray her own doubt. "We just need a break."

She took a deep breath, filling her lungs with the cool evening air, trying to steady the tremor in her hands. The murmur of the paramedics packing up, the chatter of curious neighbors gathering on their porches, and the distant hum of the crickets all blurred into a low, persistent noise. But Olivia knew there was no real pause to be had. The clock was ticking, and the answers were somewhere out there—hidden, waiting to be found.

Elmer rested his head on her lap, a silent promise that whatever came next, he was with her. And for now, that would have to be enough. With a turn of the key, the Jeep roared to life, and Olivia pulled out of Edward's driveway. Her mind racing about the road that stretched ahead.

Olivia allowed herself to sleep in the next morning. She knew this wasn't the time to be slowing down, but she was exhausted and she just needed some time to piece it all together. Coffee wasn't going to be enough today; she needed something more comforting. Then she remembered a place she'd heard about—a small, cozy deli that tourists loved, the Rustic Roll. She had never been, but the idea of a quiet spot to gather her thoughts was too tempting to resist.

"Hey, Elmer, how do you feel about a sandwich?" Olivia called. The large dog came bounding in front the backyard, skidding to a stop at the bottom of the stairs. *Did you say sandwich?* was all Olivia heard as she made her way down the stairs and out to the Jeep.

As she drove, Olivia spotted the wooden sign hanging from a post, half-hidden by the surrounding pine trees. "Rustic Roll Deli," it read, with an arrow pointing down a narrow gravel road. She turned onto the path, but the road was barely wide enough for two cars. Just as she rounded a curve, a gray SUV came barreling down toward her, nearly clipping her side mirror.

"Jeez, in a rush much?" she muttered, glancing at Elmer, who yelped from the sudden jolt. She reached out to pat his head. "You okay, buddy? We'll be out of this madness soon."

The gravel crunched under her tires as they pulled into the deli's small parking lot. The place was adorable, with a rustic charm that made it look like it belonged in the middle of a postcard. The smell of fresh bread and smoked meats wafted through the air, making her stomach growl in response. A sign near the entrance caught her eye: *Dogs Welcome on the Patio*.

Elmer's ears perked up as he sniffed the air, clearly interested in this new development. "Guess that's our sign," Olivia said, smiling as she led him toward the outdoor seating area.

Opting to order from the window, Olivia scanned the chalkboard menu. "Summit Sub for me, plain turkey sandwich for him, and two waters," she said to the woman behind the counter. In minutes, they were seated at a sunny spot on the patio, away from the bustling crowd of tourists.

As Olivia settled into the wooden chair, she let out a long, deep breath. She had too much on her mind, but for now, she just needed a few moments of peace. Elmer, ever the food enthusiast, quickly devoured his turkey sandwich while Olivia picked at her sub, lost in thought. Then, her foot nudged something under the table.

She glanced down and spotted a small, leather-bound notebook lying in the dirt. "Huh," she muttered, bending down to pick it up. Probably someone's misplaced journal. She figured she would drop it off at the counter on the way out. A sudden gust of wind flipped the pages open, revealing something that made her freeze. Neat, scientific-looking drawings filled the margins. Her heart skipped a beat as she realized it looked just like Emily's research.

Her pulse quickened as she flipped through the pages. Scribbled notes, familiar phrases like "Emily," "tincture," and references to the starling berry stared back at her. Tucked inside were folded pages in what looked unmistakably like Emily's handwriting. Then she saw it—angry, erratic rants scribbled in the margins: *"She doesn't deserve the legacy"* and *"It's mine by blood!"*

A cold chill ran through Olivia. This wasn't just any notebook. This was Liz's. Quickly, Olivia shoved the notebook into her bag, her heart hammering in her chest. She glanced at Elmer, who had already sensed her urgency and stood ready to leave. "Come on, Elmer," she whispered. "We need to go. Now."

Elmer, always quick to adapt, trotted by her side as they headed for the Jeep. Just as Olivia was about to back out of the parking lot, that same gray SUV from earlier screeched to a stop at the far end of the lot. Olivia's breath caught in her throat. Through the windshield, she saw a flash of brown hair as someone stepped out of the driver's seat and hurried toward the deli.

Her gut told her exactly who it was—*Liz*.

With a calm but urgent breath, Olivia pulled out of the parking lot, trying not to draw attention. She couldn't afford to look suspicious, not now. Elmer glanced at her, confused but alert, his instincts picking up on her tension.

"I think we just found the missing piece of the puzzle," Olivia muttered, pressing down on the gas pedal a little harder. It was time to get out of there—fast.

CHAPTER 26

Olivia paced the length of the loft like a restless cat, her mind racing with a thousand tangled thoughts. Her gaze kept darting toward the leather notebook sprawled open on the bed, its pages filled with Liz's neat, yet sometimes cryptic, handwriting. It felt as though the notebook itself was a puzzle box, one that refused to open no matter how many times she tried to solve it. Every inch of her body hummed with anxiety. There were answers in there, she could feel it, but she wasn't sure how to piece them together.

Elmer, her ever-loyal companion, stretched out on the floor with an exaggerated sigh, casting a sideways glance at her. He tracked her every move with half-lidded eyes, clearly not impressed by her pacing. His expression shifted from mild amusement to genuine concern. Elmer was a creature of habit—he'd much rather be curled up on the couch or out for a walk, not waiting for Olivia to crack some secret code that only seemed to lead to more questions.

"I know, Elmer," Olivia muttered, her words more for herself than for him. "That notebook is the key, but how do I make it fit?" Her fingers twitched with the impulse to grab it, but something held her back, an instinctual hesitation. It was as if the very act of touching it again might trigger a series of events she wasn't ready to face. The notebook carried the weight of the questions Olivia couldn't yet answer, and she wasn't sure if she was strong enough to confront them all.

Elmer let out a long theatrical sigh and flopped onto his back, looking at her with a mixture of impatience and exasperation. His eyes met hers with a silent plea: *Just read the damn thing already.*

Olivia shook her head, oblivious to his silent plea. "I can't hand this over to the police without making sure it's airtight," she muttered to herself. She had combed through Emily's notes a dozen times already, hoping for a breakthrough, something that screamed *Here's your answer!* But nothing had jumped out at her. It was maddening, like trying to find a needle in a haystack that didn't even seem to exist.

She stopped mid-pace, her eyes catching on something new. A smaller, sapphire-blue notebook partially hidden beneath a pile of paperwork and old receipts she had taken from Emily's office. Had she missed this one? Kneeling down, she pulled it out and flipped it open. The pages were filled with neat, methodical handwriting—Emily's appointment book. A soft, bittersweet smile tugged at Olivia's lips. "Of course," she whispered. Emily had always been a stickler for old-school scheduling, despite Olivia's teasing. While everyone else had long moved on to digital apps, Emily had kept her color-coded planner like it was sacred. The act of crossing off a task with a physical pen, of seeing the day's plans laid out before her, had always given Emily a sense of order and control, something she had clung to in a world that was increasingly chaotic.

Olivia flipped through the pages casually, scanning the usual meetings, canceled appointments, and random client notes. But as she neared the date of Emily's death, her hand froze. One entry stood out like a beacon.

6:30 PM – Liz Stevens.

And beneath it, in Emily's careful script: *Called in. Asked to meet at the Ridge? Seems urgent. Mentioned needing clarity on something related to family matters and past disputes. Sounded more anxious than usual. Possible connection to research discussions? Has asked before about the starling berry properties but with more insistence this time.*

A secondary, hastily scribbled line appeared beneath: *Tension palpable—didn't want anyone else to know about this meeting. Why the Ridge, of all places?*

Olivia's eyes narrowed as she scanned the words. The urgency in Emily's notes seeped into her, the unease becoming her own. Emily had been thorough, but these cryptic details felt different—darker somehow. It wasn't like her to leave an entry so incomplete. Olivia knew Emily—if she'd written it down, there had to be a follow-up. A conclusion. But there wasn't one, just this disturbing snapshot of something that seemed off. The mention of family disputes caught her attention, aligning with what Mabel had said about Liz's personal vendetta tied to the starling berry and their family's reputation.

Beneath the hurried notes, another line stood out, underlined twice: *Is someone pressuring her? Seemed conflicted but determined. Must revisit this conversation soon.*

Olivia's heart pounded as she read that last line. The urgency, the shakiness in Emily's handwriting, spoke volumes. The Ridge, usually known for its peaceful vistas, had become the backdrop for something more sinister than just a casual meeting.

"The Ridge?" Olivia murmured, a chill creeping down her spine. Emily had clearly noted the oddity of Liz requesting to meet there. Olivia knew Emily—she would have shrugged it off, convincing herself it wasn't a big deal. She always went above and beyond for her clients, even if it meant meeting them at strange, isolated locations. But this—this was no ordinary appointment. Liz had been the last person to see Emily alive.

Elmer, sensing the shift in Olivia's mood, rolled back onto his belly, his eyes alert now, locked on hers with the intensity of a seasoned detective. He was done lying down.

"We need a plan," Olivia muttered, sitting down on the floor next to Elmer, her thoughts racing. She stared into his soulful eyes, seeking some kind of reassurance, some clarity. He tilted his head, as if considering her words. *Plan?* he asked, a flicker of confusion in his eyes. *Like the one where we sneak off to the deli?*

"No, not that kind of plan," Olivia said, rubbing his ears. "A real plan. We need a confession."

Elmer blinked, his tail giving a small, unimpressed thump against the floor. He nudged her gently, as if to say, *Then stop talking and do something.*

Olivia chuckled softly, her resolve solidifying just a little. "You're right," she sighed. "But we can't just rush in. Liz is dangerous, she might have killed Emily, and if we don't play this right, she'll slip away. I can't let that happen. Not after everything Emily went through."

Elmer yawned, stretched, and then rolled over, clearly signaling his impatience. *Well, whatever it is, figure it out soon. I'm not waiting all day.*

Olivia smiled, the tension in her chest easing a bit. "Okay, boy," she said, pushing herself to her feet. Her determination was hardening again. "We'll get her. But we need to be smart about this. If we can get her to slip up, to admit what she's done, there's no way she can escape."

As she resumed her pacing, an idea began to take shape in her mind, the pieces falling into place like a jigsaw puzzle. She glanced down at Elmer, who was watching her intently, his tail wagging in lazy anticipation. "I've got it," she said, a mischievous glint lighting up her eyes. "But it's going to take some work...and maybe a bribe or two. You in?"

Elmer's tail thumped harder against the floor. *Always.*

With that, Olivia knew—Liz Stevens wouldn't know what hit her.

***

Olivia spent the entire night scribbling notes and half-formed ideas into her notebook, tossing and turning like a fish out of water. Elmer, lay sprawled at the foot of the bed, periodically sighing dramatically, as if to say, *Really? Can we just sleep already?* Each time she shifted, his ears flopped, and he let out another long, groaning protest, his patience wearing thin.

"I know, Elmer," Olivia whispered, staring blankly at the ceiling. "This plan has to work." The plan itself, though, was still a tangled mess in her head. She was trying to set Liz up, to get her talking about Emily in a way that might lead to a confession, but it wasn't going to be easy. Liz wasn't just going to casually admit, *Oh, by the way, I'm guilty.*

By the time morning arrived, Olivia was bleary-eyed, with dark circles under her eyes, and a very unimpressed Elmer pacing behind her. Despite the fatigue, she was ready to start setting her plan into motion. The first step: call Edward Barnes. The plan was too elaborate to explain over text, and Edward needed to hear the conviction in her voice.

She grabbed her phone, found Edward's number, and took a deep breath before pressing *Call.*

"Edward?" she said when he picked up. His cautious tone told her he wasn't sure if he was about to hear another one of her wild theories.

"Olivia," Edward replied slowly. "What's this about? You've got that tone in your voice again..."

Despite her nerves, Olivia couldn't help but smile. "Well, I need your help to trick Liz Stevens into confessing. No big deal."

There was a pause, then a faint sigh. "I'm sorry, *what*?"

Olivia dove into her plan, explaining how Edward could present a fake piece of Emily's research, claiming it was something newly discovered. "We'll say Alicia suggested you call Liz for help interpreting it, since she's, you know, the next best 'scientific mind' in town," Olivia added with a hint of sarcasm.

Edward let out a long sigh, and for a moment, Olivia thought he might back out. But then, to her surprise, he spoke with a hint of determination. "I can pull something together that looks convincing—something subtle but confusing enough to make Liz take the bait. This is...risky, Olivia."

"I know," she admitted. "But we don't have much time, and we need Liz to slip up."

Edward agreed, albeit cautiously. One step down.

Next call: Alicia. Olivia hesitated. After the attack, asking her to get involved again felt wrong. But she needed

Alicia's name to lend credibility to the setup. Bracing herself for potential resistance, Olivia dialed, but to her surprise, Alicia sounded enthusiastic.

"I want to help," Alicia said, her voice steady. "If Liz is behind this, I need to know. Emily deserves justice."

Relief washed over Olivia. "Thank you. I really appreciate it." Two key players were on board.

But there was one more call to make—a person she wasn't sure she *needed* but *wanted* to be there. Noah. She hesitated, her thumb hovering over his contact. Could she handle it if things went south between them? Worse, what if the plan spiraled out of control with him involved?

Get it together, she scolded herself, and pressed the call button.

"Hey, Liv," Noah's familiar voice came through, warm but cautious, as though he already sensed something big was coming.

Without preamble, Olivia launched into an explanation of the progress she'd made in her investigation, Liz's possible involvement, and her new plan to get a confession. Noah listened quietly, occasionally offering an *uh-huh* to let her know he was following along.

"Would you maybe want to be on standby?" Olivia asked, suddenly feeling silly. "I can keep an open line so you can hear the conversation. If anything goes wrong, or if Liz tries something—"

"I'll be there," Noah interrupted firmly. "You won't be on your own, Liv. If things get ugly, I've got your back."

She exhaled, not realizing she'd been holding her breath. "Thanks, Noah. It means a lot."

After hanging up, Olivia sat at the edge of her bed, staring at her phone. Elmer came over, his heavy head dropping into her lap with a low huff, as if to say, *Finally, you've got your act together.*

"I know," Olivia muttered, ruffling his ears. "But this plan still feels like it could go either way."

Elmer gave her a reassuring *hmph*—*Don't worry, we've got this.*

With everyone on board, Olivia felt a strange mixture of confidence and dread. The pieces were in place. Now, all they had to do was spring the trap.

CHAPTER 27

Saturday morning arrived with a moody, overcast sky that perfectly mirrored Olivia's frazzled nerves. The rain tapped lightly on the window as she sat on the edge of her bed, staring at the leather notebook.

Her plan to set up Liz was in motion, they had been able to pull it together quickly, but with hours to go before anything happened, all she could do was wait. And Olivia hated waiting.

She drummed her fingers on the windowsill, her mind racing through the million ways the night could go wrong. Elmer groaned, letting out a low, dramatic sigh saying, *Will you relax already?*

The rain suddenly stopped, leaving behind the fresh, earthy scent of wet grass and leaves. Olivia glanced at Elmer, who had perked up at the change in weather. "Come on, boy. Let's take a walk. I need to clear my head," she said, grabbing his leash.

Elmer gave her a look that clearly read, *Really? In this weather?* But he rose to his feet with a resigned huff. Olivia wasn't asking—she was telling.

They climbed into the Jeep and headed toward downtown Emerald Ridge. Her thoughts were spinning too fast to walk the entire way, and besides, Elmer looked like he had the energy of a lazy Sunday morning. She stopped near the local park on the east end of downtown, a place filled with memories of town gatherings and school events.

As they stepped out onto the damp grass, Olivia breathed in deeply, the cool air filling her lungs. The tension in her chest began to ease, just a little. They started along the winding path that cut through the park, every corner stirring something inside her as familiar sights brought back pieces of the past.

There was the pond where she and Emily would sit for hours during their high school days, talking about everything and nothing. Emily always had this way of seeing the world that made Olivia feel like they were part of something bigger. They would make wishes on the stars that reflected on the water, whispering dreams they only shared with each other. Emily's laughter, bright and unguarded, would echo across the pond, filling the air with a sound Olivia now desperately missed.

A smile tugged at Olivia's lips as she recalled how they would take their ice cream from Mr. Cobb's shop and race to the pond before it melted in the summer heat. Emily always chose cherry, her lips stained red as she grinned through brain freezes. "Live a little, Liv!" she would say, teasingly nudging Olivia whenever she hesitated. Olivia had always been the more cautious one, but around Emily, she felt braver—lighter.

As they continued along the path, her eyes landed on the playground in the distance, now replaced with shiny new equipment where the old wooden swings and monkey bars used to be. That's where it all began, she thought, remembering the countless afternoons spent there with Emily. They'd race each other across the monkey bars, daring each other to jump off at the highest point, screaming with a mix of joy and fear as they landed on the soft grass below. It had been their place, their secret kingdom where they made grand plans and shared whispered secrets.

A sharp pang hit her chest, the familiar ache of missing Emily almost too much to bear. She felt the sting of tears but blinked them back, swallowing hard as the memories flooded her.

"We're almost there, Em. I promise," she whispered to the breeze, hoping her words would somehow reach wherever Emily's spirit now resided.

Sensing the shift in her mood, Elmer gave a gentle tug on the leash, pulling her forward as if urging her not to dwell too long on what couldn't be changed. Olivia took a deep breath, following his lead as they rounded a corner, the path opening up to Main Street where the shops stood in their familiar lineup. The town was quiet, the dreary weather keeping most people indoors—a blessing, considering she wasn't in the mood for small talk.

They passed by the bookstore, its window displaying the familiar sight of an orange cat curled up in the sun. Olivia paused, smiling as she recalled spending afternoons in there with Emily, thumbing through novels and dreaming of their future adventures. "One day, Liv, we're going to see all the places we read about," Emily had promised, her eyes shining with excitement. The memory warmed Olivia's heart, but it was bittersweet. She exhaled, her breath fogging up the glass for a moment before she turned away.

Next, they passed the Doozie, the hair salon that had been around for as long as she could remember. Generations of mothers and daughters had kept that place alive. She could almost hear the chatter and laughter from prom day, when she and Emily, along with their friends, had crowded inside to get their hair done. They'd talked about dresses and dates, and Emily had joked about being the most glamorous one there, winking at Olivia in the mirror. Olivia chuckled softly at the memory, the warmth of it mingling with the bittersweet ache in her heart.

As they neared the Jeep, Olivia spotted Ashley through the window of Perks and Peaks and gave her a small wave. *Not today*, she thought. As tempting as the coffee shop was, the last thing she needed was to accidentally spill her entire plan to the friendly barista, no matter how close of a friend she was.

Elmer let out a low whine, the kind that said, *Okay, enough with the nostalgia trip—let's go home.* He looked at her with those soulful eyes, clearly ready to return to his napping schedule.

"All right, all right," Olivia laughed, letting him guide her back to the Jeep. Her mind continued to swirl with memories as they strolled past the last of the shops, making her question why she had been so eager to leave Emerald Ridge in the first place.

When they reached the car, Elmer flopped into the passenger seat with all the grace of a sack of flour, clearly done with the day's adventure. Olivia smiled, feeling the exhaustion settle into her bones. *Maybe I should follow his lead and try to get some rest before tonight*, she thought as her mind raced through the events ahead.

They drove back home, the weight of what was coming hanging in the air like a storm waiting to break.

CHAPTER 28

Olivia watched the clock anxiously as the minutes ticked down to six p.m. The trap was set, but her nerves were on edge, her mind spinning with possibilities. Elmer, sensing her tension, paced the floor, his nails clicking against the hardwood as he followed her movements like a silent shadow.

When the clock finally struck six, Olivia shot to her feet, grabbing her bag. "It's time, Elmer," she said, her voice steady, though her heart pounded relentlessly in her chest. Elmer, ever attuned to her mood, stopped pacing and trotted after her, his ears pricked and eyes alert.

The drive to Edward's house was quiet, the mountain air thick with the weight of what was about to happen. The trees loomed over the dirt road, casting long shadows as dusk settled in. As Olivia turned down the hidden road just before Edward's driveway, she spotted Noah waiting in his truck. She pulled in beside him, giving a brief nod before grabbing her phone.

Noah rolled down his window. "You sure about this?" he asked, his voice steady but laced with concern.

"We're close, Noah. I can feel it," Olivia replied, though her palms were slick with sweat. She dialed Edward's number, listening to each ring as it amplified the tension in the air. When Edward answered, his voice was shaky.

"I'm ready, Olivia. She should be here any minute," he said.

"Remember, our code word is 'indecision.' Use it when you're ready for me to come in. We'll be listening," Olivia reminded him. She heard the rustle of Edward setting his phone down on his desk.

As soon as their conversation ended, the familiar growl of a car engine echoed through the woods. Olivia and Noah exchanged a glance as a gray SUV came into view—the same one she'd seen at theRustic Roll. It was Liz Stevens. Olivia's pulse quickened.

She quickly muted her phone and eased the Jeep deeper into the trees. "Stay quiet, Elmer," she whispered. His ears perked up, and he sat perfectly still, sensing the gravity of the moment.

Inside the lab, Edward did his best to remain calm as Liz approached, her face a mask of cold detachment. "Good evening, Liz," he greeted, his voice strained as he forced a smile. "Thank you for coming."

Liz nodded curtly, her gaze sharp. "I assume this is about Emily's work?" she asked, her tone tight and controlled.

Edward gestured to the table strewn with papers, the fake research notes he had crafted to resemble Emily's work. "There's something I couldn't make sense of," he said, his voice careful. "I thought you could help me interpret it."

Liz's eyes flickered with interest as she picked up the papers, though her expression remained hard. "Emily's research?" she muttered, scanning the pages. "I'm surprised you're still working on this, considering...everything."

"It's what Emily would have wanted," Edward replied, his voice steady. He glanced at Alicia, who stood quietly to the side, playing her role perfectly. "Alicia suggested I contact you, said you have the next best mind for this stuff, after Emily."

Outside, Olivia's knuckles tightened around the steering wheel as she listened. Liz's voice, cold and calculating, sent a shiver down her spine.

In the lab, Liz's fingers trembled slightly as she held the papers, though she masked it well. "You've done the right thing by calling me," she said, her eyes narrowing as she scanned the fake notes. "It's obvious Emily was onto something, but she didn't have the experience to handle it. She would have made a mess of it."

Edward glanced at Alicia again, then spoke. "It looked like she was facing some...indecision...about what step she should take next. We could really use your help figuring it out."

That was the cue. Olivia met Noah's eyes, nodding before slipping out of the Jeep with Elmer at her side. They moved quietly up the driveway, the weight of the moment pressing down as they neared the lab.

Inside, Liz's expression darkened as she muttered, "Emily always left a mess for someone else to clean up. That's just like her. I'm sure she would have gotten stuck at this point and brought me in for help anyway."

Olivia paused just outside the lab door, her heart hammering in her chest. She could hear the tension in Liz's voice, a dangerous edge creeping in. Without hesitation, Olivia pushed the door open and strode inside, pretending not to notice the cold tension in the air. "Edward, there you are! I knew I'd find you here," she said, dropping the notebooks onto the desk with a thud. Then, feigning surprise, she turned to Liz. "Oh, Liz! I didn't see you there. Are you helping with Emily's research too?"

Liz's eyes narrowed, flicking between Olivia and Edward. "Something like that," she muttered, clearly unsettled by Olivia's unexpected presence.

Ignoring Olivia, Liz turned back to Edward, returning to the topic of Emily leaving messes for others to clean up. Olivia didn't miss the way Liz's jaw clenched as she tried to maintain control of the situation. "Emily was reckless," Liz snapped, breaking the silence. "I warned her, but she didn't listen. And look where that got her."

"Reckless?" Edward asked, keeping his tone even. "What do you mean?"

Liz's eyes gleamed with a dangerous intensity. "She was meeting people at the Ridge, alone, in the dark. Stupid, really. She should've known better. You can't trust everyone in this town."

Olivia's breath caught in her throat. None of the reports about Emily's death had ever mentioned her meeting anyone. Liz had just revealed something only the person responsible for Emily's death would know.

Edward stiffened, realizing the same thing. "Wait...how did you know Emily was meeting someone at the Ridge?" he asked slowly, the tension in his voice unmistakable. "There was never anything about that mentioned in the reports."

Liz's face paled. Her mouth opened, then closed, as if she were scrambling for an excuse. "I...I heard about it. It was common knowledge," she said, trying to casually brush off her slip, but her voice trembled, the lie hanging heavy in the air.

Olivia stepped forward, her gaze locked on Liz. "Funny, I don't remember anyone else knowing about that detail. I didn't even know about those details until recently, and I'm sure I didn't mention it to you," she said, her voice sharp. "Sounds like you had some personal knowledge of the situation. Maybe because you were the one who called her out there?"

Liz's eyes darted around the room, looking for an escape, but Olivia pressed on.

"You were at the Ridge, Liz," Olivia said, her voice low and accusing. "You were the last person to see Emily alive."

Liz's composure shattered. "She deserved it!" she spat, her face twisting with anger. "She stole everything from me—my research, my reputation, even my relationship! I had to stop her!"

The confession hit the room like a bomb, the weight of it suffocating.

Olivia took a step closer, her voice steady. "So you killed her."

Liz's breath hitched, her face contorting with a mix of rage and regret. "I didn't mean to!" she cried, her voice cracking. "It was an accident! I just wanted her to understand...but she fell!"

Her hands shook as she spoke, recalling how she slipped into Emily's house and added some of Emily's tincture into the tea she was drinking before their meeting. Liz had hoped the tincture, would make her more vulnerable, more open to her arguments. She hadn't expected it to have such an effect. Instead of making Emily more agreeable, the tincture had caused her to lose her balance, confusion clouding her thoughts as she struggled to stay steady. Liz had watched, horrified, as Emily faltered, the reality of the situation crashing down on her too late.

"I put some of the tincture in Emily's tea before we met up. I was hoping it would make her more open to my...arguments, about her research. Instead, the only effect it seemed to have on her was cloudy thoughts and lack of balance. I stepped close to her while I was talking and that's when she lost her balance...and fell." Liz dropped her head into her hands.

Elmer growled low in his throat, sensing the tension. Olivia nodded, her voice firm but calm. "It's over, Liz. The police are on their way."

Liz's eyes darted wildly around the room, but there was no escape. She collapsed into a chair, her hands trembling as the realization of her actions settled in.

Liz's shoulders shook as she buried her face in her hands. A long, shuddering breath filled the silence before she looked up, her eyes red-rimmed and desperate. "If I'm going down, then Samuel Carter is going with me."

Olivia's pulse spiked at the mention of Samuel's name. She exchanged a quick glance with Elmer, who quieted but remained tense, ears flicking forward as if listening intently.

"What do you mean?" Olivia demanded, stepping closer.

Liz's voice dropped, tinged with bitterness. "Samuel's been blackmailing me ever since he found out about Emily's research. He knew I needed it—needed it to restore my family's legacy. He said if I didn't secure the findings and cut him in on the profits, he'd make sure everyone knew what I'd done." Her eyes brimmed with tears, a mix of fury and defeat. "I never wanted things to go this far. But he pushed me, threatened me...and I was too far in to stop." Liz took a deep breath to steady her nerves for the next things she was going to reveal. "He was there. Samuel was. The night Emily fell. He'd been walking nearby and head our voices. He saw what happened and has been holding it over my head ever since. He said he would tell the police that I pushed her off the Ridge if I didn't go along with his plan."

A heavy silence settled over the room, broken only by the distant wail of approaching sirens. Olivia's heart pounded as the pieces began to fall into place. Samuel had known more than he let on, and his involvement in this twisted web was deeper than she had feared. Samuel was the shadowy man Liz had been meeting with. That's why the voice sounded familiar.

Elmer's low whine seemed to echo Olivia's thoughts. This was more than just a desperate act by Liz—it was a conspiracy that had ensnared them all.

Olivia took a steadying breath, eyes fixed on Liz. "It's time the whole truth came out, Liz. No more secrets."

Liz's gaze hardened, the fight leaving her eyes. She slumped back in the chair, defeated. "Then tell them everything," she whispered. "Because I won't let him walk away from this."

As the distant sound of sirens drew closer, Olivia finally exhaled, her heart still racing. The plan had worked, but the confession left a bitter taste. Justice was coming, but it had come at a cost.

Elmer leaned against Olivia's leg, and she gave him a soft pat. "Good boy," she whispered, her voice shaky with relief. "We did it."

And as the sirens wailed, bringing the inevitable consequences with them, Olivia knew the truth had finally come to light.

***

As the police arrived at Edward Barnes's house, the flashing blue and red lights illuminated the tense faces of everyone present. Officers moved efficiently, securing the area and ushering Liz to a waiting car. But before they could take her away, Liz turned to Olivia, desperation and resolve mixed in her gaze.

"Wait," Liz said, her voice cracking. "I have something to offer."

The lead officer, a tall man with a stern expression and salt-and-pepper hair, paused, his brows knitting together. "What could you possibly offer that would change anything now?"

Liz glanced at Olivia, a silent plea passing between them before she looked back at the officer. "Samuel Carter. He's the one who blackmailed me and pushed this entire situation into motion. I can get him to confess—if you let me help."

The officer crossed his arms, weighing her words. The tension was palpable, each second stretching like an eternity. Finally, he exchanged a glance with a colleague and sighed. "We'll need more than your word, Ms. Stevens. This isn't a simple situation."

Olivia stepped forward, determination etched on her face. "I'll help. Samuel trusts Liz, or at least thinks he has control over her. We can use that. If we set up a meeting where she confronts him, I can be there, hidden, to corroborate the conversation and make sure it's recorded."

The officer's eyes narrowed, considering the proposal. "We'd need complete control over the situation. Liz would be on house arrest, and we'd coordinate the entire setup. Any deviation, and this whole thing falls apart."

Liz nodded, her shoulders slumping with the weight of the moment. "I'll do whatever it takes. He can't get away with this. Not after everything he's done."

The officer took a deep breath and gestured for one of his colleagues to step forward. "All right. We'll make the arrangements. But understand this: if this goes sideways, there's no second chance."

Olivia nodded. "We'll do it right. For Emily."

Liz met her gaze, a flicker of hope breaking through the storm of guilt in her eyes.

As the police began to coordinate the sting operation, Olivia felt the adrenaline coursing through her veins. This was their chance to bring the whole truth to light—and she wasn't going to let it slip away.

The tension had barely begun to dissipate after Liz's confession when Officer Bennet stepped over to Olivia.

His presence was commanding, a mix of authority and concern etched into his features.

"Olivia," he said, his tone serious. "We asked you not to get involved in this situation. Do you have any idea how much trouble you could have gotten into? You put yourself in harm's way."

Olivia opened her mouth to respond but hesitated, meeting his stern gaze. "I know."

Bennet rubbed the back of his neck, a sigh escaping his lips. "I get your loyalty to your friend. I really do. But you have to understand, this isn't just about you. There are protocols for a reason. You could have jeopardized the entire investigation."

"I understand the risks," she replied, a hint of defiance in her voice. "But I also found details you weren't looking at. I helped connect the dots."

"Right," he conceded, a hint of sheepishness creeping into his demeanor. "And for that, I have to thank you. It's a bit of a backward compliment, but you did bring our attention to things we overlooked. We appreciate your efforts, even if it wasn't exactly by the book."

Olivia felt a mix of pride and frustration at his words. "I just want to make sure justice is served.

"I understand that," Officer Bennet replied, his tone softening slightly. "But please, in the future, let us handle the investigations. You don't need to put yourself in danger for someone else. You're important to this community too, Olivia."

She nodded, the weight of his concern settling in. "I appreciate that, Officer. I really do."

"Good," he said, giving her a nod of acknowledgment. "Just promise me you'll be careful. We need more people like you in this town, not fewer."

With a final look of understanding, Officer Bennet turned back to the rest of the other officers, leaving Olivia with a renewed sense of purpose. She had faced the darkness to bring light to the truth, and while the risks had been high, she knew that standing up for what was right was worth it.

CHAPTER 29

The evening sun cast a warm, golden glow over Emerald Ridge, bathing Liz's house in hues of orange and pink. The house, a tidy, brick cottage with ivy creeping along the walls, looked deceptively serene. Inside, however, the air crackled with tension. Liz paced nervously in the living room, wringing her hands and casting anxious glances at the clock on the wall. The seconds seemed to tick louder, each one marking the approach of Samuel Carter's arrival.

Outside, the scene was anything but calm. Two unmarked police cars were parked discreetly around the corner, their occupants carefully observing the street for any sign of movement. Officers in plain clothes mingled on the nearby sidewalk, blending in as pedestrians taking evening strolls or dog walkers pausing for a chat. The air was thick with anticipation, each officer's radio buzzing intermittently with hushed updates.

"Remember, stay calm," Olivia said from her spot inside the coat closet. It smelled faintly of cedar and mothballs, and coats brushed against her arms as she shifted, trying to find a more comfortable position. Her phone in her hand felt slick with sweat, but she held it tightly, refusing to let nerves get the better of her. Olivia had a narrow view of the living room where Liz paced nervously, through the doorframe of the closet door. She could see Liz, her face pale and tight, running through her script one last time.

Elmer, ever Olivia's shadow, had been reluctantly left at home this time. The stakes were too high for even a well-trained dog to be a distraction. She could almost imagine his worried eyes as she'd closed the door behind her, and she silently promised him she'd be home soon.

Liz nodded, her eyes darting toward the closet as if to reassure herself that Olivia was still there. "Easy for you to say. You're not the one facing him."

Olivia smirked, though Liz couldn't see her. "True, but I am the one crammed in here like a sardine with your collection of trench coats. Trust me, this isn't exactly a spa day."

Liz let out a small, shaky laugh, and the tension in the room lightened for a moment. The humor didn't last long, though. The officers had set up a signal system, just in case. Liz would tap her glass twice if things got out of control or if she needed to stall for time. A wire discreetly nestled under her blouse would transmit the conversation to the officers listening outside. Everything had to go perfectly.

Liz glanced at the clock one more time, the old brass pendulum swinging in an agonizingly slow arc. She took a deep breath, smoothing her skirt with trembling fingers, and whispered to herself, "It's just one more performance, Liz. You've done this before."

Suddenly, the sound of gravel crunching outside sent a bolt of adrenaline through the room. Olivia's pulse quickened at the sound. Samuel Carter's silhouette appeared in the driveway, illuminated by the last rays of the sun. His stride purposeful as he approached the front door.

The sound of heavy footsteps echoed up the walkway, and Liz's posture stiffened. She forced herself to take a deep breath before opening the door.

Knock. Knock.

The sound reverberated through the quiet room, sharp and authoritative. Liz swallowed, casting a brief glance toward the closet where Olivia hid before turning toward the door. She reached for the doorknob, hesitating for only a moment before pulling it open.

"Liz," Samuel greeted, his voice smooth but laced with impatience. His eyes darted around the room, scanning it as if trying to catch a glimpse of hidden truths.

"Samuel," Liz replied, forcing a smile as she stepped back to let him in. "Thanks for coming. I just thought we should go over everything again, to make sure we're on the same page."

Samuel Carter stepped into the room, his presence imposing despite the years that had added lines to his weathered face. He wore a neatly pressed hat, tilted just enough to cast a shadow over his sharp, scrutinizing eyes. The thin smile that tugged at the corner of his lips failed to reach those eyes, giving him an unsettling air.

He paused in the entryway, his broad-shouldered frame filling the space and casting a long shadow across the room. His gaze swept methodically over Liz's cozy living room, taking in every detail with the vigilance of someone who always anticipated an ambush.

Olivia, tucked away in the narrow confines of the hall closet, held her breath as his eyes grazed past her hiding spot. The tension thickened, the silence stretching out between Samuel and Liz, who stood motionless, eyes wide and posture stiff.

Samuel's voice finally broke the silence, low and edged with suspicion. "So, you wanted to talk through the plan again, did you?"

Liz's throat bobbed as she swallowed, trying to mask her nerves. "Yes. There are some details I think we need to revisit."

The room seemed to shrink as Samuel stepped further inside, the weight of what was about to unfold pressing down on them all.

Samuel arched an eyebrow as he took off his hat and set it on the side table. "I hope this isn't another stalling tactic."

Liz managed a tight smile and motioned for him to sit. "No stalling," she said, her voice wavering slightly. "I just need to make sure we're on the same page."

Samuel's eyes narrowed, but he sat, leaning back with an air of confidence that set Olivia's teeth on edge. "We've been through this, Liz. I deliver on my promises, and you deliver on yours."

He paused, letting his words hang in the air like a threat. "My promise is simple: I keep your little secret safe—the one about Emily and your involvement. No one will ever know what really happened that night, as long as you hold up your end of the deal." His gaze intensified, boring into her. "You understand what that means, right? It means no talking, no slipping up. You need to stay under the radar."

Samuel leaned forward, a sly smile creeping onto his face. "And your promise? You cut me in on the money from that research when you sell it. I know it's bound to be a tidy sum, and I want my share. It's a fair trade, don't you think? You get to keep your freedom and reputation intact, and I get a little something for my silence."

He straightened, crossing his arms, the confidence radiating from him almost palpable. "It's a win-win, but if you fail to deliver, I won't hesitate to make your secrets known. You've got a lot to lose, Liz."

Liz hesitated, wringing her hands together again. "And if I don't?"

Samuel's jaw clenched, the easy demeanor slipping for just a second. "Then I let the whole town know of your little involvement with Emily's fall. It's quite the story, really—one that could ruin everything you're trying to build."

The air in the closet felt stifling, and Olivia's fingers tightened around the phone in her hand. This was it—the proof they needed.

Liz's chin lifted, defiance flickering in her eyes. "I can't do this anymore, Samuel. It's gone too far."

Samuel leaned forward, his voice dropping to a low, dangerous growl. "It's too late to back out now. You're in this as deep as I am. And if I go down, I'll make sure you do, too."

The tension in the room thickened as he shifted closer, invading her personal space. His hand slammed down on the table, causing the glasses to rattle and sending a jolt of fear through Liz. She could feel his breath, hot and heavy, brushing against her skin, and the intensity of his gaze felt like a vise tightening around her throat.

From her hidden spot in the closet, Olivia pressed her ear against the cool wood, straining to catch every word. The atmosphere was thick with tension, and she could almost feel the heat radiating from Samuel as he shifted closer to Liz. Her heart raced, a mix of fear and adrenaline surging through her as she tried to steady her breathing, the phone in her hand capturing every threatening syllable.

Through a crack in the door, Olivia caught a glimpse of Liz's expression. The determination in her eyes clashed with the fear etched on her face. She could see Samuel's menacing posture as he slammed his hand on the table, rattling the glasses, and she instinctively clenched her fists, wishing she could intervene.

"I'm not the kind of man you want to cross, Liz," he continued, his voice barely above a whisper but laced with menace. "You don't know what I'm capable of."

Her heart raced, and instinct kicked in. She discreetly lifted her glass and tapped it twice against the table—her signal for help, a signal that meant things were spiraling out of control and she needed time to think.

Samuel narrowed his eyes at the sound, momentarily distracted. "What are you doing?" he snapped, his tone sharp as he leaned even closer, the threat in his demeanor intensifying.

Olivia's stomach churned. She wanted to burst through the door and confront Samuel, to protect Liz from his threats, but she knew the best chance they had was to gather evidence and wait for the right moment. She focused on the sounds—Liz's soft tap against her glass, her signal for help.

"Just...trying to figure out how to negotiate this to work out best for both of us," Liz replied, forcing a steadiness into her voice. She knew she had to stall him, to buy herself a moment. "We can work this out, Samuel. Let's not get hasty."

He hesitated, his grip on the table tightening, but the glimmer of doubt in his eyes gave her hope. She needed to keep him talking, to keep him from realizing just how desperate she felt. The clinking of her glass against the table echoed in her mind, a reminder that help was on the way.

"I won't be your pawn," she said, her resolve hardening as she met his gaze. "You think you can control me, but you're wrong."

As he leaned back slightly, his expression shifting from aggression to contemplation, Liz silently prayed that her signal would reach someone who could help before things escalated further.

When Samuel leaned in even closer, Olivia's pulse quickened. She shifted slightly, trying to keep her eyes locked on the scene without being noticed. Each word exchanged felt like a knife's edge, and she couldn't help but mentally calculate her next move. She needed to get Liz out of there safely, and she needed the evidence Samuel was about to reveal.

"Liz, don't let him intimidate you," Olivia whispered under her breath, though she knew Liz couldn't hear her. She wished she could convey her support, to reassure her that she was not alone in this fight.

As the confrontation unfolded, Olivia's grip tightened around the phone. If things escalated, she would be ready to act—she just hoped it wouldn't be too late.

***

Outside, the faint hum of engines signaled the arrival of the police, their cars hidden just around the corner. Olivia's heart raced at the sound, a wave of hope washing over her. They were so close to having help, but would they arrive in time? She felt a mix of anticipation and dread, knowing that the situation inside was teetering on the edge.

Samuel didn't seem to notice, his focus laser-locked on Liz. "Is that so?" Liz whispered, her voice trembling but determined. Olivia could see her hands clench into fists, a defiant posture that masked the fear evident in her wide eyes. Liz was standing her ground, even as Samuel leaned closer, his presence looming like a shadow.

Inside the closet, Olivia felt a surge of solidarity with Liz. She wanted to scream for her to hold on, to keep fighting. The knowledge that help was just a few steps away intensified her desire to act. Olivia instinctively pressed the phone closer to the door, hoping it would capture everything—every threat, every moment of tension. If the wire Liz was wearing missed anything, Olivia wanted to be sure she caught it.

Liz swallowed hard, her throat dry as she faced Samuel's hostility. "You think you can control me?" she shot back, her voice steadier now, though Olivia could sense the quiver beneath it. "*You* obviously don't know what *I'm* capable of."

Olivia's chest tightened at Liz's words. She admired her courage, even as she worried about the consequences of such defiance. She was acutely aware that the police were waiting for the right moment to intervene, but she feared that a sudden move could escalate the confrontation.

Then, just as Liz held Samuel's gaze, Olivia heard the crunch of gravel underfoot—a clear indication that the officers were approaching the door. Her breath caught in her throat. Would they burst in before Samuel had a chance to react?

"Stay strong, Liz," Olivia whispered to herself, willing her to sense her support from behind the door. She was ready to spring into action the moment the police made their move, praying that they would arrive just in time to prevent any more threats from Samuel.

Samuel's eyes narrowed, but before he could respond, the sudden pounding of footsteps up the porch broke the tension. The door burst open, and officers flooded the room like a storm, their shouts and commands echoing through the space. The abruptness of their arrival punctuated the end of Samuel's reign, a dramatic shift that sent a ripple of relief through Olivia.

The look of shock and betrayal on Samuel's face was almost satisfying as he turned back to Liz, his mouth opening and closing like a fish out of water, scrambling for words he would never find. The air crackled with anticipation, and Olivia could hardly contain her excitement as she watched the officers move with precision, surrounding him. They were a force of authority, and the weight of their presence felt like a long-awaited victory.

"Hands behind your back!" one officer barked, stepping forward with a firm grip on Samuel's shoulder. Olivia could see the struggle in his eyes, the realization dawning that he was trapped, his plans unraveling in an instant.

Before he could muster a protest, the officers had him in handcuffs, the metallic click resonating like a gavel striking down. They began reading him his rights, their voices a steady mantra of justice, and the sheer finality of it sent a thrill down Olivia's spine. She stepped out of the closet, her heart racing as adrenaline coursed through her veins, ready to face the aftermath of this moment.

"It's over, Samuel," she declared, her voice steady and unwavering as she met his stunned gaze. The fire in her eyes reflected the triumph she felt, and she savored the moment as he turned to her, his shock morphing into desperate anger.

"Olivia," he spat, a mixture of disbelief and venom in his tone. "You set me up?"

"Not quite," she replied, a slight smile playing on her lips. "I just made sure you couldn't hurt anyone else."

The officers pulled Samuel back, leading him toward the door as he struggled against their grip, but the tide had turned. The weight of his threats was lifted, and Olivia could finally breathe freely, knowing she had stood up for what was right.

As the officers ushered Samuel outside, Liz watched with a mixture of relief and dread. The tension gripping her chest began to loosen, yet a heavy cloud of reality loomed over her. This victory was bittersweet; while she felt a sense of liberation from Samuel's threats, she couldn't shake the impending dread of her own fate.

"Olivia," Liz murmured, her voice shaky as she caught her eye. "It's over for him, but for me..." Her words trailed off, the weight of potential jail time hanging in the air like a thick fog.

Olivia's heart sank as she grasped the gravity of Liz's situation. They had faced this together, but Liz still had to contend with the consequences of her choices. They had emerged victorious over Samuel, but the battle for Liz's future had only just begun.

Before Olivia could respond, the officers returned, their expressions serious. "Liz, we need you to come with us," one of them said, motioning for her to step forward.

Liz's heart sank, and she nodded, her shoulders slumping as the reality of the situation set in. "Okay," she whispered, trying to keep her composure. She turned to Olivia, her eyes filled with a mix of gratitude and sorrow. "Could you do me a favor?"

"Anything," Olivia replied.

"Could you check in on Newton, while I'm...away?" Liz asked, a slight tremor in her voice. "I know he'll be confused without me."

Olivia felt a strange twist in her gut at the request. The irony was not lost on her; her original return to Emerald Ridge had been for a pet-sitting job for Emily, and now here she was, agreeing to look after the cat of the woman involved in Emily's murder. Life had a twisted sense of humor.

"Of course, I'll take care of him," Olivia assured her, forcing a smile despite the heaviness in her heart. "He'll be in good hands."

Liz managed a faint smile, though it didn't quite reach her eyes. "Thank you."

As the officers gently guided Liz toward the door, Olivia felt a swell of determination. She would keep her promise to Liz, no matter how she felt about her. Newton wouldn't suffer for his owner's choices. And as the door closed behind them, she stood alone in the room, the weight of the moment settling heavily on her shoulders.

With a deep breath, she glanced around, her mind racing with thoughts of Newton and the responsibilities she now held. This was just another chapter in her unexpected journey, and she was ready to face whatever came next.

Chapter 30

Olivia stepped into Perks and Peaks, the familiar scent of fresh coffee mingling with the sweet aroma of pastries. The cozy café buzzed with chatter, and a wave of comfort washed over her, a stark contrast to the chaos of the previous day. She found a small table near the window, hoping to gather her thoughts over her usual latte.

As she settled in, the locals' conversations swirled around her, drawing her attention. Millie Partridge, the town's notorious gossip, was perched at the counter, her silver hair framing her face like a halo as she leaned in to share her latest scoop with an eager audience.

"Can you believe that scoundrel Samuel Carter?" Millie exclaimed, her voice a mix of shock and disdain. "I always knew he was trouble, but this? I never would have thought he'd stoop so low!"

A chorus of agreement rippled through the café.

"Right? I saw him acting all high and mighty just last week," said Betty, a regular who often shared her opinions on town matters. "I never trusted him. Always had that shifty look in his eyes, if you ask me."

"Honestly, I'm surprised it took this long for someone to do something about him," chimed in Frank, an older gentleman nursing his coffee. "You mess with the wrong people, and you're bound to get what's coming to you."

Olivia felt a pang of frustration; while Samuel had indeed caused trouble, the townsfolk's collective scorn felt like a hollow victory. She listened intently, the discussions swirling around her like a whirlwind.

"And poor Liz," Millie continued, shaking her head. "She got caught up in his web. I just can't understand what she was thinking."

"She's made some terrible choices," Betty countered, her brow furrowing. "I mean, look where it got her! I hope she finds a way out of this mess."

"She better be careful," Frank added. "With her name in the mix, she might be in more trouble than she realizes."

Olivia took a sip of her coffee, the warmth spreading through her. Despite not being close to Liz, she felt an unexpected sympathy for her. The weight of potential jail time loomed over Liz, and hearing the townsfolk talk about her mistakes stung more than she had anticipated.

As Millie prattled on, recounting stories from the past, Olivia couldn't help but feel a sense of determination rise within her. She would keep an eye on the situation, if only to ensure that the town didn't lose sight of its humanity in the face of scandal.

After all, beneath the judgments and assumptions, there was still a person navigating a complicated life, and Olivia wasn't about to let the town's gossip dictate the narrative.

***

As the morning crowd died down Ashley made her way over to Olivia and settled into the booth across from her, the aroma of freshly brewed coffee wafting around them, they couldn't help but notice a couple at a nearby table. The pair exuded an air of sophistication that set them apart from the usual tourists who frequented the shop.

"Look at them," Ashley whispered, nodding subtly toward the couple. The woman wore a tailored dress that shimmered in the light, while the man, with his perfectly styled hair and a designer watch peeking from beneath his cuff, held a conversation with an ease that suggested he was used to being in charge.

"Definitely not from around here," Olivia remarked, raising an eyebrow. "They look like they stepped off the set of a movie."

Ashley giggled softly, leaning in closer. "I wonder what brought them to Emerald Ridge. Probably looking for a quaint escape from their high-flying lives. Or maybe they're here to scout for a vacation home."

"Right? I can hear them now: 'Darling, let's buy a charming little cottage here among the peasants,'" Olivia teased, rolling her eyes playfully.

Ashley stifled a laugh. "Or maybe they're trying to find out what real coffee tastes like. You know how the elite can be."

Olivia watched the couple for a moment longer, her curiosity piqued. "Whatever their story is, they definitely stand out. I'd love to know who they are."

"Me too," Ashley replied, glancing back at them. "But something tells me they're not your average weekenders. I mean, look at that purse!" She gestured discreetly to the designer handbag perched on the woman's lap.

"Yeah, that's probably worth more than my Jeep," Olivia said with a laugh.

As they sipped their coffee, both women exchanged knowing glances, intrigued by the couple and unaware of the ripple effect their presence would soon have on Emerald Ridge.

***

After finishing her coffee at Perks and Peaks, Olivia stood up, her mind still swirling with the gossip about Liz and Samuel. She needed to clear her head, and the fresh air outside would do her good. As she walked down the street, she decided to stop by the pharmacy to see Derek. He had been one of her initial suspects in Emily's murder, but now she wanted to apologize for the accusation.

The bell above the pharmacy door jingled softly as she entered, and she was greeted by the familiar smell of antiseptic mixed with faint floral notes from a nearby display of scented candles. Derek was behind the counter, sorting through a stack of prescriptions. When he saw Olivia, he smiled.

"Olivia! What a surprise!" he exclaimed, putting down the paperwork. "To what do I owe this visit?"

She approached the counter, her heart racing slightly as she gathered her thoughts. "Hey, Derek. I just wanted to stop by and talk to you for a minute."

His smile faded a bit, replaced by a look of concern. "Is everything okay?"

"Yeah, everything's fine," she assured him, taking a deep breath. "I wanted to apologize for suspecting you earlier. I know I jumped to conclusions, and I really shouldn't have."

Derek's shoulders relaxed, and he chuckled lightly, visibly relieved. "Well, considering the circumstances, I can't blame you for thinking that way. But it's good to know you're not convinced I'm hiding a body in the backroom or something." He winked playfully.

Olivia laughed, the tension easing between them. "I promise I'll avoid the crazy theories in the future. You seem like the kind of guy who would help if someone was in trouble."

"Definitely," he said, leaning against the counter with a relaxed demeanor. "I appreciate you coming by to clear the air."

"I just want to make sure I'm seeking the truth," Olivia replied sincerely. "Thanks for being understanding, Derek. It means a lot."

Derek simply nodded.

As she turned to leave, she felt a sense of closure. The weight of suspicion had been lifted, and she was grateful for the opportunity to clear the air. With her spirits lifted, Olivia stepped back out into the fresh air, ready to face whatever came next.

***

As Olivia left the pharmacy, the sun was beginning to dip below the horizon, casting a warm glow over Emerald Ridge. She took a deep breath, the air tinged with the scent of pine and earth, a familiar comfort that had been missing for far too long. The weight of the day hung heavily on her shoulders, but there was a sense of lightness now, a clarity that came from resolving the tension between her and Derek.

With each step toward the Ridge, she found her mind wandering back through the twists and turns of the investigation. It had been a dark journey, one filled with shadows of doubt and fear, but she had persevered. She could still hear the whispers in the wind that had followed her from the very beginning—"Find out." The phrase echoed in her mind like a haunting melody, guiding her through the uncertainty.

Arriving at the overlook, Olivia paused to take in the breathtaking view of the valley below. The vibrant colors painted the landscape, and a renewed sense of purpose washed over her. It was here, standing on the edge of the world, that she had often confided in Emily, sharing her dreams and fears. It was here she could imagine her friend's spirit lingering, urging her to keep fighting for the beauty they both cherished.

"I found out, Emily," she whispered into the breeze, feeling a connection to her friend in that moment. "I found out what happened to you. I won't let your story end in darkness."

She closed her eyes, letting the wind tousle her hair as she envisioned Emily's smile, the way it would light up a room. Olivia resolved to honor Emily's legacy—not only by seeking justice, but by protecting the natural beauty and heritage of Emerald Ridge that they had both loved so dearly.

With a deep breath, she opened her eyes and gazed out at the sprawling landscape, feeling a sense of closure settling in her heart. "I'll do everything I can to keep this place safe," she vowed softly. "For you, and for everyone who loves it."

The sun dipped lower, and as the first stars began to twinkle in the evening sky, Olivia felt a wave of determination surge within her. The journey had been arduous, but she was ready to embrace the future, guided by the whispers of the past and the memory of a friend she would always carry with her.

CHAPTER 31

The sun dipped low in the sky, casting a warm glow over Edward Barnes's house as Olivia arrived with Elmer trotting happily by her side. The atmosphere was intimate, the soft sounds of laughter and light conversation spilling out onto the porch. Inside, the modest living room was adorned with a few colorful decorations—a simple acknowledgment of the occasion.

"Olivia! You made it!" Edward exclaimed, his face lighting up as he opened the door wide. He stepped aside to let her in, his smile genuine and welcoming.

"Of course! Wouldn't miss it," Olivia replied, feeling a wave of warmth wash over her as she stepped inside. The cozy space felt safe and inviting, a stark contrast to the chaos of recent days.

Noah was already there, leaning against the kitchen counter, a plate of cookies in hand. His eyes brightened when he saw her.

Olivia glanced around. "I thought it would be nice to gather everyone for a quiet moment together."

Alicia, sitting on the couch with her feet tucked beneath her, looked up with a smile. "I'm glad you're here, too! It's nice to have a moment to breathe after everything that's happened."

Elmer padded over to Alicia, nudging her hand for attention. "Well, aren't you a friendly one?" she cooed, scratching behind his ears as he leaned into her touch.

Just then, Archibald the parrot flapped his wings from his perch, squawking, "Polly wants a cracker!" The bird's antics brought a laugh from everyone, lightening the mood even further.

"Archibald thinks he's the star of the show," Edward chuckled, pouring himself a cup of tea. "But he might have to share the spotlight with Elmer today."

As they settled into casual conversation, Olivia felt the tension of the past weeks begin to melt away. The camaraderie of this small gathering reminded her of the strength found in friendship and support.

"Here's to new beginnings," Edward said, lifting his cup. "To honoring Emily and cherishing the beauty of this place."

"To new beginnings!" the others echoed, raising their drinks in unison.

Olivia smiled as she watched Elmer happily sniff at Archibald, the parrot offering playful squawks in response. This moment felt significant—a small but meaningful celebration of resilience, friendship, and the promise of brighter days ahead.

As laughter filled the room, Olivia couldn't help but feel grateful. Surrounded by her friends and the warmth of the gathering, she knew they would continue to protect the beauty of Emerald Ridge, together.

For the first time in a while, there was no more mystery to unravel, no unanswered questions. The air felt strangely light—almost too light—as though none of them quite knew what to do now that the chase was over.

Edward was the first to break the quiet. He turned to Olivia with a half-smile, shaking his head. "I've got to hand it to you, Olivia. You're relentless. There were moments I thought you might get one of us killed, but I'm glad you didn't." His expression softened, his eyes sincere. "And I'm glad the truth about Emily finally came to light."

Olivia grinned back. "Thanks, Ed."

Edward blinked in mock surprise, the corners of his mouth twitching upward. "Did you just call me 'Ed'? Well, mark this day down in history." He chuckled softly, "If you need me again, you know where to find me. Just...maybe give me a bit of time before you do." He glanced toward a plush recliner in the corner. "For now, I'd like to get reacquainted with my bourbon and my recliner."

As the gathering wound down, Olivia and Noah drifted outside.

Noah turned to Olivia with a burst of energy, sweeping her up in a hug that lifted her off her feet. "You did it!" he exclaimed, spinning her slightly before setting her down gently. They stared at each other for a moment, the adrenaline of the night still buzzing between them.

Noah cleared his throat, dragging the toe of his boot in the dirt as he searched for the right words. "I know I didn't play a huge role in all of this," he said, gesturing vaguely, "but I was worried about you the whole time." His voice softened. "I'm proud of you, Liv. Emily would be too."

Olivia noticed a faint blush creeping up Noah's neck, even in the fading light. He gave her a smaller, more restrained hug this time and placed a gentle kiss on her forehead. Before either of them could dwell on the moment, Noah quickly stepped back, putting a little space between them.

Elmer, having observed the whole scene with narrowed eyes, firmly positioned himself between them, clearly declaring his place as Olivia's protector. His stance made it obvious—Noah, or anyone else for that matter, wasn't getting too cozy with *his* human.

"So, what now?" Noah asked, rubbing the back of his neck awkwardly.

Olivia let out a long sigh. "Good question. I don't have school or a job waiting for me...and honestly, I don't really have a reason to leave."

Noah's smirk widened as he kicked the dirt playfully. "Well, if it helps you decide, I wouldn't mind if you stuck around a little longer."

Her heart skipped a beat, but Olivia kept her response light. "Duly noted."

Noah's grin grew. "How about celebrating with a pizza? You've more than earned it."

At the mention of pizza, Elmer's ears shot up like satellite dishes. Olivia burst out laughing, shaking her head. "As tempting as that sounds, I think I need to raincheck the pizza. I feel like I haven't slept in a month, and my bed is sounding way better than pepperoni right now."

"Fair enough," Noah said with a chuckle. "But I'm holding you to that raincheck."

Elmer gave a confirming huff. *Me too.*

Noah waved one last time before heading back to his truck. Olivia and Elmer climbed into the Jeep, and she noticed the forlorn look on Elmer's face—clearly disappointed at the lack of immediate pizza gratification.

"I'll get you a snack when we get home, promise," Olivia said, ruffling his ears.

That seemed to placate him, and he settled into the passenger seat, his earlier disappointment temporarily forgotten.

***

When they finally pulled into the driveway, the sky had deepened into a velvety blue, and the cool night air carried the soft scent of rain. Olivia let Elmer out of the Jeep, watching as he trotted into the kitchen, his eyes fixed on the cupboard with a single-minded determination.

"All right, all right. A promise is a promise," Olivia muttered as she pulled out his favorite treat. Elmer accepted it with a satisfied look that seemed to say, *You're lucky you keep your word.*

With a tired smile, she gave him a quick pat on the head and made her way to the bathroom. Stripping off her jacket, she stepped into the shower, letting the hot water cascade over her, washing away the stress and grime of the day—and the weeks before. It was really over. Emily had her justice.

Dressing herself in her most comfortable pajamas, she padded softly into the bedroom, her body deliciously heavy with exhaustion. Elmer was already sprawled out on the bed, his large form taking up most of the available space.

Olivia chuckled, nudging him over gently. "Scoot over, you big lump."

Elmer grumbled but complied, curling up at the foot of the bed as she slid under the covers. As soon as her head hit the pillow, an overwhelming sense of peace settled over her. It was done. Really, truly done.

Her eyelids grew heavy, and just before sleep claimed her, her thoughts drifted to Emily. Though the case was closed, the ache of her absence lingered. A part of her would always miss Emily, but at least now—finally—there was some closure.

Elmer let out a contented sigh, and within minutes, they were both fast asleep, the weight of their journey finally lifted.

EPILOGUE

T he sun hung low in the sky, casting a golden glow over the jagged peaks that cradled Emerald Ridge. Olivia rocked gently on the porch swing, her feet barely touching the wooden boards below as a soft breeze rustled the trees. Elmer lay sprawled beside her, twitching in his sleep like he was dreaming of chasing squirrels or digging up a garden—probably both. It had been a peaceful few days since Liz's arrest, and for the first time in what felt like forever, Olivia could finally exhale. The weight of Emily's murder had lifted, leaving her with a quiet sense of relief.

She looked down at Elmer, a fond smile tugging at her lips. "Well, boy, it looks like we're staying."

Without opening his eyes, Elmer let out a low rumble, the sound of contentment she now knew as his way of saying, *You bet we are.*

Staying in Emerald Ridge hadn't been part of the plan when she first returned. Solving a murder wasn't either, come to think of it. What had once felt like a temporary stopover before figuring out her next move was beginning to feel...permanent. Maybe it was the mountains, maybe it was the people, or maybe it was just this strange sense of peace that had settled over her like a blanket. For the first time in years, she felt grounded—like she belonged.

"I guess I'm going to have to figure out how to make a living here," Olivia mused, more to herself than to Elmer. "Working at the local shops isn't exactly my thing. Pet sitting, though...now that I could do. People around here seem to love their pets as much as their kids. Plus, I could set my own hours. What do you think?" She glanced down at Elmer, whose tail gave a single wag of approval.

The sound of tires crunching on gravel broke the peaceful moment. Olivia turned to see a small car pulling up the drive. Lucas, the painter, stepped out, giving an awkward wave as if he wasn't sure he should be there. Elmer raised his head, interested but not alarmed.

"Hey, Olivia," Lucas said, his voice soft, almost hesitant. "Ashley at the coffee shop told me where you lived. Hope you don't mind me dropping by like this."

Olivia smiled and waved him onto the porch. "Of course not! We never turn away a friendly face. Come on up."

Lucas climbed the steps, glancing around nervously as if he were still trying to figure out how to act in social situations. But something about him seemed lighter—less burdened than the last time she'd seen him.

"I just...wanted to say thank you," he began, rubbing the back of his neck. "Since everything with Liz...since she got arrested...the nightmares stopped."

Olivia raised an eyebrow. "Really?"

He nodded, his expression softening. "Yeah. It's like now that it's over, my mind's cleared up. I'm not seeing faces anymore, not dreaming about the Ridge." He hesitated, his eyes dropping to the ground. "I didn't know what to think before, but I guess...maybe sometimes your mind knows things before you do."

Olivia chuckled gently. "Maybe. I'm just glad you're sleeping again."

Lucas let out a relieved laugh. "Yeah, me too."

For a moment, they stood in comfortable silence, the weight of everything that had happened lingering between them, but not as heavy as before.

"I'm going to keep painting," Lucas said, sounding more confident. "But I think I'm going to try something brighter. Lighter. No more dark landscapes. Maybe something with color this time."

"That sounds perfect," Olivia said, grinning. "You've got the right setting for it."

He glanced down at Elmer, who was watching him with a skeptical eye. "And if you ever need a painting of Elmer, let me know. I kind of owe him after, you know, calling him a mutt."

Elmer gave Lucas a slow blink, clearly unimpressed but willing to forgive. *Just this once.*

Olivia smirked. "I'll hold you to that. Elmer has a reputation to uphold, you know."

With a final nod, Lucas headed back to his car, pulling away as the last rays of sunlight painted the sky in warm oranges and pinks. Olivia watched him go, a sense of closure settling over her. The town had been through enough. It was time for all of them to move forward.

"I guess we're all getting a fresh start," she said softly, stretching her arms above her head. Elmer was already dozing again, content to stay curled up at her feet.

As the evening air cooled and the sky darkened, Olivia gave Elmer a gentle nudge. "All right, buddy, let's get you a snack before I hit the shower."

Elmer perked up at the word *snack* and bounded inside, as lively as ever after a day of lounging. Olivia followed, shaking her head with a chuckle as she set out a treat for him.

After a long, hot shower, Olivia finally climbed into bed, the exhaustion of the last few weeks catching up to her. But for once, it wasn't the kind of exhaustion that weighed her down—it was the kind that came with knowing things were right where they should be.

As she settled under the covers, she thought of Emily. Justice had been served, and now, it was time for a new beginning. Emerald Ridge wasn't perfect, but it was home. And, she thought with a smile as Elmer curled up at the foot of her bed, it wasn't a bad place to build a new life.

With a contented sigh, she closed her eyes, ready to embrace whatever came next.

Find out what comes next for Olivia and Elmer in Tails of Trouble Book 2, Danger in the Dogwoods.

ALSO BY JENNA MAESON

Tails of Trouble: The Emerald Ridge Mysteries
Shadows on the Ridge
Secrets Underground

ACKNOWLEDGEMENTS

Writing a book is never a solitary journey, and I am immensely grateful to the many people who have supported me along the way.

First and foremost, my husband, for always encouraging my dreams. He has always known that writing a book was a goal of mine and didn't let me talk myself out of it, though I tried many, many times. To my son, whose love and encouragement have always been invaluable. To my larger family and friends. for their unwavering encouragement and love. Your belief in me kept the spark alive that I needed to finish this project.

I owe a special thanks to my editor, Caryn, for polishing my words and bringing clarity to my story, my social media, and marking gurus, Shari and Jill, and my cover artist. Your expertise made all the difference.

To anyone and everyone who got a glimpse of the story as it came together, your feedback, encouragement, and shared experiences have been a cornerstone of this process. I couldn't have done it without your honest critiques and enthusiastic support.

Finally, to the readers, for giving this story a chance. For Indie authors, reader support is everything. You make us beleive that we can actually do this writing thing and it's beyond encouraging to know that someone, somewhere wants to read your book. You make all the hard work worthwhile.

www.ingramcontent.com/pod-product-compliance
Lightning Source LLC
Chambersburg PA
CBHW070315310726
48976CB00005B/1728